Alexandra

A Ukrainian psychologist's exploration of women's sensual fantasies

Copyright © Brovary Ltd 2014
Published by Brovary Limited
All rights reserved.

ISBN 978-0-9927213-7-4

Brovary

Dedication

This book is dedicated to my Mum and Dad who have been the best and supported me in everything I have done. They know everything and I tell them everything. To them, a huge thank you.

Acknowledgements

I wrote this first in Ukrainian, my mother tongue, and then it was translated into English. Through all this, I was given some help, but I take the blame for all failings in the translation. I hope my English is up to scratch.

This is my first book, and before now I never understood all the work required to move from my thoughts to a finished product. It is an immense task, and I would like to thank everyone at Brovary Ltd, my publishers, for all their support and help. I have to thank Viktorija Neimantaite and Anna Black. Literally, it never would have happened without such a committed and enthusiastic team.

Cover design by Dragan Bilic

Alexandra

I. INTRODUCTION

I expect and hope that by now you have already dipped in and read many of the fantasies, and only now you are coming back to the beginning. If you haven't, why not go and do just that, as I want you to understand what this is all about? Off you go and have a skim, and only later if you want an answer to the question, 'why expose yourself so openly?' should you come back here!

Okay, welcome back. Now you know what this is all about and I hope you enjoyed yourself in my fantasy world. I want you to be at peace with the content and know that you are not alone because we are all fascinated by fantasies. Even as I write, I can see thousands of women lost in their own world of eroticism. Isn't that a wonderful thought?

My original plan was just to set out the fantasies and do nothing more. I didn't really want to write and tell you anything about myself, I thought the fantasies told you all that you would want to know or maybe even all I wanted to tell. But my friends said that there should be more, so you can see that really, I am just a normal woman and not some nymphomaniac or over-sexed girl. In so many ways I am just like you.

There are more than fifty of my naughty, erotic, sexual fantasies which pretty much describe me. However, and whatever you may think, let me again stress that the only difference between us is, firstly, that my imagination is possibly just a little broader than yours; and, secondly, I am happy to share it with you all. But in my life, I am not a sexually promiscuous slut (sorry to any men who have strayed in here – I know that is not what you really wanted to hear).

Everything you read in these stories is true! That doesn't mean I have done everything I write about, only that I have thought or dreamt about all of these stories; sometimes many times. Of course, when I say, "I haven't done everything" it doesn't mean that I haven't lived out many of my fantasies in the real world! Okay, yes, I have done a striptease; I have had a man take his cock out in a restaurant for me to look at, touch and photograph, and many other naughty things; but the question of which-is-which? Well, you will have to decide that for yourself; you will get no more clues from me!

If you consider yourself a little bit prudish then there are many good reasons why you are exactly the type of woman who should read my book. It will help you understand that many sane and intelligent women are enjoying erotic fantasies.

But this book is not for those with a closed mind. I want you, my readers, to read with the expectation that you will form an opinion all of your own when you have finished.

For all of us, there are two reasons to read this book. The first and most important is to enjoy what you read. If it makes you excited, horny, wet, or sexy, then I will take that as a result. That will make me very happy and is a total justification for my efforts. This is meant to be an enjoyable experience.

However, it would be even better if this book changes your perception of yourself, or improves your relationship with a partner or the world at large. I am not offering any advice in this book other than to say that for me, with all my background and experience, having and enjoying personal fantasies is both important and satisfying.

If there is one aspect of my personality that differentiates me from others is that I am extremely confident in my self-image. I have a consistent view of how I look which may or may not be the real reflection of what is in the mirror.

It is not for me to say what is a good relationship. You can be a submissive mouse, a strident Brunhilde or a woman who shares every emotion and experience with your partner, there is nothing more important than holding a clear image of yourself as a beautiful woman.

You are beautiful. Whatever your shape you are beautiful. Never forget; you are beautiful.

My name is Alexandra. I am Ukrainian. I am sometimes called Alexa and sometimes his Queen.

I have always known how to control men, to make them mine. I knew this very early in my life. It is not about sex. Men can have sex any time they need or want it, so control of a man is in the mind. It is about stimulating his imagination and desire. Feed the imagination and desire will come. You may call it 'teasing' but that would be wrong.

Imagination is a powerful force. It takes us to places we normally can't go, but make that image real and we all follow.

You may want to know more about me. Where was I born, who are my family and what of my life? You don't need to. You will learn all you need to know about me from my stories. I will describe myself, but only in practical terms.

I am tall. I am thin with beautiful long legs. My hands and fingers are those of a pianist: thin and slender. I wear little makeup or jewellery. My hair is fair, like many Ukrainians. It is long and fine and often pulled away from my face. My face is striking. I would be beautiful on the cover of any magazine. I am a model and an academic and I hate when I see my face on the magazine cover at the bookstall or on the billboard as I drive; it means that your imagination is outside my control. You can do what you want with me. My eyes are deep and green, large, and sensual. They see you and see through you, deep into your mind. They can see what you need and what you want. They see all your strengths and your weaknesses.

My clothes are from the best shops in Kyiv and I always dress in puritan colours. My lingerie excites both men and women. It is black, brief, and sheer. When I stand, naked except for my lingerie, I know that my breasts are outlined. I know the tiny triangle of my panties is small but it is a transparent veil. I wear it only to excite, it has no practical purpose.

You know me now, for in your imagination you already have my picture. I am whatever you want me to be. That is the power of imagination.

Alexandra

1. MIKHAIL'S QUEEN

This is my story about him, and if I want him now, he is mine. It is not slavery for he can leave whenever he wants, but he knows he won't. I lead him through a story that slowly unfolds and he always wants more.

He is not Ukrainian. He is a powerful man and he believes that he has power over all things. He believes that he can shape his world. He has visions which encourage others to follow but he doesn't see that he is just like all those who follow. He is one in a chain, each following another. Who leads that chain? Who can break that chain?

Alexandra is always meticulous in the way she prepares herself. She will never leave her apartment unless everything is completed, ready and perfect. Tonight, was no different. If you were there you would have seen her, with very little hesitation, lay out her clothes for the evening on the large bed.

There was the black blouse which, when held up to the light, dimmed little more than summer clouds. Her skirt, also black, of course, was full and flowing. When she danced, it followed half a turn behind, unable to keep up with her energy and enjoyment. She wore the finest, sheerest black stockings. Her shoes were elegant: handmade in Milan.

You would have noticed that there was no bra. What is the point of wearing a bra, she would have thought? There is a raw excitement knowing that those who see her are drawn by a glimpse – just a fleeting glimpse – of her breasts through her blouse.

With her clothes laid out, Alexandra went to the bathroom. First, she lay still in the warm water of her bath and closed her eyes as the water swirled and eddied around her, before sinking deeper so that the water washed over her elegant body.

Then her hands, at first by her side, slowly moved to feel and caress each breast in turn. Later you would have seen her hands reach down under the water, and move along to stroke each thigh as she thought about the night ahead. As her hands moved in towards her pussy her excitement grew, but then she stopped. Later, she thought. There's plenty of time for that.

With a large white bath towel wrapped around her, she moved back to her bedroom. Making no effort to dry herself she just lay on the bed.

When the time came, she had already dressed and her car had arrived. It was late spring and tonight there was no need for a coat. As she crossed the pavement she didn't notice who else was on the street. It didn't matter, but those that were there both saw and noticed her. Every head turned. Some thought she must be someone famous. Men and women alike wondered what she would be like in bed. All the men were excited and some of the girls were just jealous.

Whatever Alexandra wanted, it seemed she could have.

Whatever she might tell you now, I will tell you that she wasn't the most beautiful of all women; her beauty lay in the fact that she was the most wanted of all. She excited men. They wanted her but Alexandra wanted just one man and she hadn't seen him yet. When she saw him she would know what to do. That man would be her man, with whom she could do whatever she wanted.

I left my apartment that night just as I have left it many times. My car was waiting and we drove to the newly opened Nogi Club. You won't know Kyiv well, but these days there are many exciting and expensive nightclubs. Kyiv isn't like it was when we were repressed. This is the new Kyiv. There are life and enterprise. Now the rich and poor are defined by work and effort. Nogi is a club where the rich and powerful go. This is the new home of Kyiv's nightlife crowd.

Kyiv is now a bright and lively city and the journey was illuminated by flashing neon in a way it had never been before. It is exciting. It is the place to be. I have read about Berlin early in the last century and wondered if this was what it was like.

Entry to Nogi is through a heavy, safe-like door guarded by two large bouncers. The door opens and before you unfold a booming disco. The club is narrow and festooned with classic paraphernalia, each piece fighting for attention among the swirling lights. Upstairs, through a labyrinth of catwalks and views onto the floor below, is a bar busy with the usual mixture of one-off and regular visitors.

There are dancers in cages and occasionally flying dyevs who swoop down from the top dance cage onto the dance floor below. Nogi is a large club. There are bars all around, all raised above a dance floor. Columns are reaching up to the edges of a high-domed ceiling. Tonight, many were sitting at the bars, and some were drinking. Some were dancing and others were at tables. Many were talking. Some were already in an early evening lovers' embrace. Did they know each other before tonight? It doesn't matter. As I walked I felt the sideways glances of each man hoping to see the lines of my breasts beneath the chiffon blouse. I threw my head back and my hair pulled back and tied, traced the curves in the flashing lights. My breasts were firm and strained to break free from their cover.

I saw him first in a crowd. He didn't look Ukrainian. Leaning against a bar, he was talking and drinking. All my senses told me that this was my man; I could almost feel his power. He looked up and saw me.

I moved, I was gone. He looked around, searching for another glimpse. I moved and still, he searched. I watched him carefully. There could be no mistake. Occasionally there was fleeting eye contact but it betrayed nothing of my intentions. Some believe that every moment is an opportunity, a point of destiny and that in every move and every decision there is an opportunity to shape the rest of your life.

I know that destiny comes only a few times in life and when it is there it must be seized and taken quickly. It comes for a moment and then, like a flashing bird taking its prey from the skies, disappears again. We are only offered a few decisive chances in life. This was one of those moments.

I went to the bathroom and there I took off my panties. They were small panties – a G-string, high at the sides with a tiny triangle of modesty. I was now naked beneath my skirt.

There is an excitement all of its own in the feel of covered nakedness. It is about freedom, constraint and control. It is not unbridled freedom, but a feeling of what you know that others don't. I was excited and hot. I could start to smell that beautiful sweet odour of sex.

Around the floor, I moved with purpose and the conviction of certainty. He was standing with some others, occasionally leaning, and craning forward to hear the conversations drowned out against the throb of the music. I moved towards him, pushing others aside. I stood in front of him, my breasts pressed into his chest. I cupped a hand to his ear and whispered,

'I want you, I feel hot. Take care of these.'

With that, my left hand reached deep into his jacket pocket where I placed that tiny piece of exotic material.

'Find me later.'

I kept on walking. Our encounter had been just a few seconds but I knew it was the start of a lifetime. I moved to a bar and sat on a tall wooden stool.

'Vodka!' I said.

I took the shot. I had pulled my dress out so that it covered both my legs and the stool. The seat tingled and excited my naked bottom.

'I think it's time to go home,' he said. One hand was on my shoulder, moving to stroke my neck, the other around my waist, encouraging me to stand up.

'Yes, I think it's time to go home.'

To a casual onlooker, it would look like a mutual attraction; a pretty girl and a handsome man, a natural coming together of likes.

Alexandra saw him and wanted him. She didn't know why. Maybe it was physical at first but she knew he would suit her. There were other handsome men, but none who would give her the satisfaction of control. He was a powerful man. Not just athletically powerful but a man who controlled others, and now she had tamed him and she was in control.

He might think that she wanted him for his looks and that he was the seducer. But he would be wrong. She seduced him with a purpose and he was seduced by the power of her imagination. She made him imagine a world with Alexandra.

Later, Alexandra was sitting in her chair in the corner of the bedroom. A comfortable, deep chair with a high back so that she was able to curl her legs under herself to sit on her heels. Like everything in Alexandra's life, her room was a set of black and white. The large antique bed, dominating the middle of the large room, was the focus – the purpose of the room. The room was free of unnecessary furniture, other than her full-length mirror and the chair on which Alexandra was curled, half asleep. Early spring light was forcing its way through flimsy white voile curtains, which rustled gently in the breeze from the open windows.

Alexandra was naked except for the cover of a white bathrobe. She was looking at the bed where his shape was barely visible through the black silk sheets.

That night, they were hardly through the door before he had started to kiss her and grab at her clothes. But she had stopped him, slowed him down. She took his hand and led him to the bedroom where she carefully took off his clothes while making him stand, still as a statue, before her. When he was naked she had walked around him, admiring every line of his body as if he was a naked Greek statue in an exhibition. Her fingers had etched the contours of the well-formed muscles of his chest. She ran her hands down his belly to feel the muscular tightness while avoiding doing anything that might make him more excited.

She made him stand while she undressed. She sat in her chair to remove each stocking, holding out each leg in turn to admire the fineness of its shape. She moved towards him and, standing close as her blouse slowly dropped to the floor, exposed the breasts once so beautifully silhouetted by the sheer material. Standing back, she undid her skirt, and with one last swirl, it danced to the floor. Now she, too, was naked.

She led him to the bed and made him lie down. She sat astride his belly and leaned forward to kiss him. Then, pushing further forward, she allowed him to caress and suck each nipple until it was hard. She slid down his body until his cock was nestled between her breasts and he moaned with pleasure.

Later she would describe the sex that night as 'athletic'. He was rushed and wanted her and he took her. He wanted to demonstrate his prowess, his experience and his skills. But he had a lot to learn and that was for the time ahead.

I had left the bed to see the daybreak over Kyiv and was curled up in my chair. I looked towards the bed and saw him slowly rise.

'Krasivaya, beautiful,' I whispered.

He turned slowly, eyes still half-closed from sleep. 'Beautiful'.

'It's time for you to go home,' I said, and slowly he moved to sit up.

'Come here and lie with me and—' he started to say.

'No. It's time to go home,' I said. 'There will be another day, another night. I will tell you when.'

As he reached the door he felt inside his jacket. 'These are yours,' he said, through a confident, slightly arrogant smile.

'Mikhail. No, they are yours now. I will tell you when you can return them.

So that is the context. Now I want to answer one or two of the questions that I am often asked and I know you will be thinking. First, I want to answer why I feel the need to share my life with you. Well, I think it is an important message and it is not just my life that I want to share with you. In writing this book I might be just a little too arrogant for my own good, but I do believe I have a message. When you have finished reading you will be able to judge for yourself.

The core message is best explained with an example. In Ukraine, my country, the men still seem to believe that sex is for their personal gratification and that a woman's feelings don't count. I know through experience that western men are a little bit more enlightened – but not by much. It is against this backdrop that I know women are slowly coming out of their shells and enjoying their own sexuality, but that is not good enough for me. I want to take that further and say to women: we do have sexual and erotic fantasies and it is allowed. In fact, more than being allowed, it is to be encouraged. Through this openness, I am sure it will help all women to move closer to a position of full equality in all aspects of life.

My justification for letting you share my innermost thoughts is that you, like me, can grow. More importantly, we, as women, should take from men the exclusive domain of sexual fantasies; then maybe our other aspirations can finally be fulfilled.

Another question often asked is why do I sometimes write in the third person, or even from my partner's perspective? Well, in my fantasies I am often outside myself watching the interaction. I can see myself, and even though it is my fantasy, often I don't think of myself being in control of the imagery so I just have to watch and let events unfold. These stories are then written in the third person. In the same way, I like to think about what effect my beauty and actions are having on my partner. I know I am a tease and I like to fantasise over the effect and turmoil my teasing is having!

Finally, these are erotic and sexual fantasies and so I must describe sexual acts, but these stories are not graphic in their explanation, and like most people, I can become embarrassed trying to describe sexual organs and the sex act. Anyway, I am far more interested in people's thoughts, because often the brain, at least for women, is still the most erogenous organ in the body.

Enjoying sexual fantasies is normal and not a problem, but if you have felt guilt while you fantasise then please dismiss it; there is no reason for any feelings of guilt. We all like the idea of looking inside someone else's mind. It's a great sanity check, and as you read more you will discover that you are normal. You will have your fantasies, which may be outrageous, but whatever happens, they will be wildly different to mine; for you, they will be just as exciting.

Although many of my friends have said that while I am still so young it is either very arrogant or stupid to write an autobiography. I fully understand what they are saying but, in my defence, I'm sure that I have something worthy to share. When you have finished, I hope you will judge that this effort is neither arrogant nor stupid.

So before we get into the stories maybe now is the time to introduce a little understanding of the simple taxonomy of the fantasies. To save you from researching all the dull academic discussions and papers, I have pulled together a list of the most common female fantasies. It is not an exclusive list, but they are the most frequent. Ok, I know this is the normal erotic tittle-tattle, but it is based on user surveys, and although not academically accurate, the top female fantasies do tend to group into the following:

- **SUBMISSIVE FANTASIES.** These are where I give up control to either a man or another woman. We have to be very careful to differentiate between submissive fantasies and abusive relationships, which are very different and to be abhorred.
- **DOMINANT FANTASIES.** These (which I think are my favourite) are where I take control of the sexual relationship. But this does not mean that he walks two paces behind me in the street – domination does not cross over into normal, everyday behaviour.
- **EXHIBITIONISM AND VOYEURISM.** These cover those moments when I either watch or am being watched in a range of provocative or sexual positions. This has clearly become a very popular pastime, noted by the big increase in 'dogging', but as you have seen, I tend to like those moments in public places such as restaurants.
- **GROUP SEX.** It seems that most of the group sex fantasies among women are lesbian, although there are also lots of group sex fantasies with either mixed couples or just men. At this level, there is no clear differentiation between all these categories. Swinging parties are sometimes categorised as group sex and sometimes as 'three or more-somes; they also sometimes include various submissive fantasies.
- **TEACHER / STUDENT.** Don't we all have a fascination with teacher/student relationships? It's something to do with the trust relationship, with overtones of submissiveness and dominance. In the common fantasies, I can either be the seduced or the seducer, and we have also noticed many times that the fantasy involves a younger and inexperienced male. The rise of the cougar!
- **SEX WITH A STRANGER.** This is a fantasy that satisfies my

lustful desires, while also allowing me to take the normally male role as the seducer and dominant person. There is also less guilt involved for women who are in a committed relationship, as the object of the fantasy is not a known person.

- **THREESOME WITH TWO MEN.** We say threesome, but the fantasy is often sex with many more than three men. Again, the differentiation is not easy, as sometimes these are loving and romantic moments where the men are transformed into 'handmaidens', fulfilling the woman's every sexual wish, and sometimes a more aggressive form of sex, with the woman being the centre of a gang-bang scenario.

- **FORCED SEX FANTASIES.** No woman wants to be, or should ever be, raped. But forms of rape fantasies are common, although perversely they often feature a known male, where the woman wants her man to be aggressive and dominant in their lovemaking.

- **STRIPTEASE AND PRIVATE DANCER.** We all love this, and it is probably the most common form of seduction we all practice in the privacy of our own homes. We sit our man in a chair, we dance and we strip for him. Don't tell me you have never done this! Of course, the exhibitionists among us want to take this further and imagine themselves in a theatre with a predominately large male audience, slowly teasing and turning them on. There's usually no threat of actual sex in this fantasy, although in my experience, and in the cases I have recorded, the fantasy often finishes with one attractive man being taken from the audience for sex, although by then the audience has mysteriously disappeared.

So there we are. I have held you back long enough. Now is the time to let you lose on the stories.

Finally, my research shows that women who are open about what they really want have better sex lives and are also happier and far

more content. Consequently, you might even live longer!
Your new friend,
Alexa

Alexandra

II. ALEXANDRA: STUDENT

My name is Alexandra and I was born in October 1981, in Lviv – a cultural centre in the far west of Ukraine, near the Polish border. I was born into an old, traditional and well-established Ukrainian family. I am the first of my parents' two daughters and older than my brother. I lived very uneventful early years, showing nothing of what was to follow.

Now I am a social psychologist and my specialisation is the use and impact on social behaviours of erotic and sexual fantasies among women. I have spent much of my adult life, apart from a couple of awful years working in an office, thinking about how women think about sex! I am one of those lucky people who really enjoy their work.

With a selection of my own fantasies, this is my story.

I worked hard at school and studied diligently for my university examinations, but, even as a young teenager, I could quickly and easily become immersed in a world of my own. As a child, I would play in my nursery with my dolls and other toys and I would live in a wonderful world of innocent adventures. Later, I was a daydreamer, and during lessons I would often find myself with my head propped on my hand, staring out of the window. Of course, these weren't erotic fantasies; that all came later.

As I grew up, like all my friends I had a few boyfriends, but these were typical teenage romantic relationships – the only dreams I had were of a prince saving his princess in a moment of gallantry. If I had any frustrations, they were not sexual but more prosaic, like waiting impatiently for a phone call that never came. I dreamt of a white wedding; I kissed my fair share of frogs who never became princes; but I never worried or fretted about the day when I would first have sex, for I was in no particular hurry. In short, I was just like every one of my friends, and far more concerned about studying and working for entrance to university in Kyiv than anything else.

I was nearly eighteen and it was just before I went to university that I lost my virginity to a then long-term boyfriend. On reflection, it was a sort of present for him before I left for Kyiv.

It was a fumbling event. We had kissed and groped before and on this day he was round at my house, my parents were out working, and I decided that today was going to be the day for both him and me. We kissed and his hands were all over me and wandering south. Previously, it was at this moment when I would slap him away, but today I let them go.

'Tell me,' I said, 'will we still be together when I am at university? Tell me that you will be faithful to me while I am away. Tell me you love me.'

'Yes, of course,' he said, as his hands explored inside my knickers.

From that day the die was cast and I felt for the first time the rough exploration of a man. It was a mechanical biology lesson which lasted a very short time. It was also his first time and neither of us knew exactly what to do. I couldn't say if his cock was large – I had no experience – but it was a painful and thankfully short-lasting event. The earth didn't move and I vowed that the next time would be with an experienced man who could teach me and, more importantly, make the experience enjoyable.

We had been dating for over a year and before that moment I always assumed that I would be in love with him forever and nothing much would change. I thought I would come home at weekends during term time to feel his love but that was one dream that, thankfully, never came to pass.

Once in Kyiv, I hardly ever saw him again.

It was 1999 and I was eighteen when I moved to Kyiv to start my new university life, after deciding to take a degree in psychology. It was not a choice based on anything in particular other than I liked the idea of the content; but more than this, I had dreamed about what it would be like when I was qualified. I liked the idea of my mum telling her friends that her daughter, Alexandra, was a psychologist with an office suite in the middle of town. I think, actually, in those early days I confused psychiatrist and psychologist!

So, I arrived with a clean sheet, leaving my parents tearful and a boyfriend crestfallen. Although I was not a virgin I was hardly experienced in matters of sex and affairs of the heart, so this move to a new and much larger city was both intimidating and exciting.

In those early days as an undergraduate in psychology, my real interest in erotic fantasies started to take hold, driven by my rapidly increasing self-awareness of both my own sexuality and sensuality. So, it wasn't just an arcane or academic interest, but one built around my own experiences. I was still an extreme dreamer and I would often disappear into my own world. I know now that many women daydream, but back then I thought I was alone in that so many of my day (and night) dreams were erotic and very sexual.

The liberal education from my parents had already taught me not to feel guilty, so I enjoyed each one of them, but I was still not sure that every woman was as lucky as me; so I started on the path that was to become my career.

On the psychology course, we always worked hard and there was a normal mixture of lectures, tutorials and essays. By the time summer came in my first year, I was way ahead with my reading and had been to every lecture. I knew my subject well, which may have made me just a little complacent, so when a warm summer's day and a stuffy lecture theatre were thrown into the pot with a drink or two at lunchtime, it led to me slipping into another daydream.

One day with this heady mix, my thoughts drifted away during a lecture and I lost concentration; with disastrous results.

Alexandra

2. A HOT LECTURE ROOM

It was a very warm summer's day, just after lunch in the early afternoon, and not for the first time in the year the lecturer was boring; he had droned on and then droned on some more. I was sitting at the back of the steeply sloped, dimly lit, far too warm auditorium with most of my fellow students ahead of me, and I knew that my eyelids were very heavy – probably just like most of the other students sitting there. The lazy lunch sitting outside, plus the heat, were taking its toll, and I was drifting slowly off to sleep.

I wasn't quite asleep, but neither was I awake when I looked up and watched intently as a young male student stood up from the front row and turned to face the class. In jeans and a T-shirt, he was as handsome and beautifully built as any athlete I had seen (although I should add that my experience was not that great). He stood there and looked around, capturing everyone in a stare from his deep blue eyes.

I looked around, expecting everyone to wake up and sit up, but no one else seemed to take any notice of him. The professor didn't stop talking and the other students were still taking notes when very slowly and provocatively he started to take off his T-shirt. Then, with a flourish, he threw it to a female student (who didn't seem surprised) sitting in the front row, before turning and leaning forward to show her a tight but jean-covered bum.

Now the auditorium had woken up. The female students were all sitting forward; the guys had sunk deep into their seats while the handsome young student, still without his shirt, pranced and pouted as he flicked back his ragged blond hair. I couldn't believe what happened next!

He faced the class, undid his belt and teased us all with the zip on his jeans; he pulled it up and then pulled it down. Up and down the zip went until finally, it stayed down, and as I blinked, his jeans were gone and all he was wearing was a pair of tight white underpants.

Of course, I was transfixed, but it wasn't just the rippling six-pack that held my focus; it was the huge bulge in the pants. I couldn't take my eyes off him and that bulge and I was sure that he was returning my stare. He was looking straight at me and no one else, and with my gaze fixed on him, he hooked a thumb into each side of his pants, leant forward and took them to the floor, releasing an erect cock.

I could see in his tender eyes that he would make a great lover. I had always been told that size isn't everything and I was sure that at any size he would give me great sex; but he was large, and even as I looked at his cock, it grew some more. Was it twenty centimetres or was it even bigger? I was fascinated and transfixed with a large, hard, upright cock, with its eye now seemingly pointing straight at me.

The professor and the rest of the class had become a blur and all I could see was the naked man with his beautiful cock, surely meant just for me. At that moment I wanted him; I wanted him there and then in the lecture room and I could feel myself becoming wet as my pussy started to throb with desire. I knew that it had to be relieved and almost involuntarily my hand went between my legs and I started to rub myself.

He was still standing there, totally erect, and as if to emphasise his size, he took a ruler and started to place it next to his cock, which I was sure was still growing; by now it must be at least twenty-five centimetres long – and its girth was also wide. He winked at me, and with a waving hand, he was beckoning me down to join him. I wanted him and stood up.

'Alexandra, is there something wrong?' It was the professor. I looked around and realised that in my daydream and fantasy I was now standing. There was no naked student, no growing cock waiting just for me, just my own embarrassment. By now I had taken two steps towards the front of the auditorium. I daren't look down because I was sure that there would be a dark stain on my jeans.

'No, nothing. It was just a little cramp. I'm sorry,' I said.

I sat back down and felt my face go red, hoping that I had neither said nor muttered anything in the middle of what was now clearly my first real, public erotic fantasy. I hoped I wasn't moaning or anything like that.

When I arrived at university I was very shy and initially, I made very few friends, but this at least allowed me to concentrate on my studies. I had a natural empathy with the subject which meant I had a fantastic grounding; although this was not what I had hoped for from University.

My days were marked by the routine of rising early, eating healthily and attending lectures, followed by hundreds of hours of study in the library. In the early days, this is where I worked and studied.

The library could be a lonely place as we sat quietly with heads bowed in silence over our books and, even without my natural predisposition to fantasies, this quiet world could easily have induced them. It was there that I used to look at many of the male students and think about making out with them.

I watched the librarians push their trolleys of books around and I wondered if they were more successful in their pursuit of love, and – of course – sex. They always looked so quiet and timid, I could never imagine them in the throes of passion, with discarded clothes spread hastily around a bedroom.

At night at home in my room, as I prepared for sleep, I would often relax with one of my fantasies. My favourite was the one about an encounter in the library with a sexually inexperienced librarian, which was, at times, just how I felt.

Alexandra

3. THE LIBRARIAN

You may have a mental picture of librarians: shy little mice, timid and stay-at-home girls, hair pulled back tight from their faces, heavy glasses, woollen jumpers and long skirts. Well, not all are like that, but Alexandra was.

She had been shy at school, puberty was late and she much preferred to spend her time with her cat Sheba, rather than with her very few friends. But now that she was older, she was no longer at school and she had become a woman.

Once, she had looked at boys and thought them running around, shouting and fascination with sport faintly ridiculous, but now she was older, she desperately wanted to be with one. She wanted to feel one touch her, undress her and then… Well, that was the problem; she didn't quite know what happened next. Her parents had never talked to her about sex, nor could she find the courage to be open with her friends to ask the obvious questions; and she was far too shy to even think of picking up a book about the subject.

It was only in her late teens that she started to understand her body. It was only in her mid-twenties that she had first seen a picture of a penis in a magazine. She had cut out the picture and kept it in a drawer in her bedroom. At first, it disgusted her, but still, she kept the picture. Then, over the days and weeks, she looked again. She had even started to imagine it inside her, but as she looked, its size frightened her, and with those thoughts, she supposed that couldn't be what happened. The thoughts gnawed at her, and day by day (or, in fact, night by night) she sat alone at home, more frequently than not feeling deep urges between her legs.

Late one night she had no choice but to explore the 'itch', as she called it. She had been lying on her bed and the itch was there. She had started touching it. Slowly at first, and soon faster and faster, and it felt better and better, but she felt so guilty. Was it right and was she different from everyone else? Did other girls do the same?

Then one night the itch was worse and deeper than she had ever experienced before and she didn't know what to do. Her fingers and hands were not enough and couldn't or wouldn't satisfy what she felt. She needed something inside her, something deep inside her.

She looked around her home. What could she use to scratch the itch? Something like a penis, she thought, something like the picture in her drawer. She hunted around to find something appropriate. There was one thing that was possible, but the thought appalled her and she rejected that idea, but then the itch was so bad she had no choice. She decided that the only thing she could use was a cucumber from the fridge.

That night she lay on her bed and slowly and very tentatively pushed the cucumber into her pussy; and then there was a new experience, she felt her pussy getting wet and a white creamy liquid oozed onto her leg. She panicked and stopped. She felt the cream on her finger and tasted it. This must be normal, she thought, but it didn't matter because the itch was still strong and this was making it better. She had stopped just for a moment; the hiatus was short before she started again. The feeling was so good. But did that happen to every girl? Was she normal?

She frightened herself when suddenly the heat spread through her thighs and pussy, she trembled and shook, she could hardly breathe and finally, she screamed. Surely everyone in the apartment block had heard and wondered what she was doing?

Despite now being racked by guilt, she had started, and couldn't now stop and go back. When she went shopping she bought cucumbers. Even if she was going to eat them in a salad (which was normal), she assumed everyone knew what she also used them for. She blushed at the checkout. Why, she wondered, wasn't everyone else who was buying cucumbers blushing at the same shame?

She was innocent in the extreme, but now with time, her thoughts were becoming naughtier. Soon the cucumber no longer scratched the itch. She needed more and she found it there on her bed. At each corner of her bed was a decorative wooden bed knob; a ball of wood just smaller than her fist. The first time, as with the cucumber, was frightening, and she feared that she was going to hurt herself, but the itch was so strong. She was wet with the thought of what she was about to do as she slowly lowered herself onto the bed knob. She moved up and down as it filled her in a way that nothing had ever filled her. It was better than she had ever experienced.

She had become so addicted to her evenings of pleasure that while at work, in the library, she could think of nothing else but getting home for a 'scratch'. Is this what sex with a man was like? Indeed, was this how sex happened? She worked out that sex must be something to do with her pussy, but in detail – how and what it was – she was very unsure. For now, she could think of nothing more than her itch.

At weekends she thought about sex but knew that she could not spend all her time in her room. However, the temptations were far too strong and days spent out shopping and denying her urges made satisfaction when they arrived, much stronger. She liked shops and shopping and found herself attracted to the displays of sexy lingerie; the more provocative it was, the more she liked it. She wanted the sexy, flimsy bras and the teeny, tiny panties, the basques that pushed and held her breasts and the stockings with their dark black seams. She satisfied the need by buying so much that soon she almost needed a whole new wardrobe to store it.

After shopping or after work, she would come home and prepare herself with a deep bubble bath, before sitting in front of her mirror and carefully applying her sexy makeup. She would look into the wardrobe and drawers and decide which of her sexiest lingerie to wear, transforming herself from mouse to purring tiger. Before heading to her bed she would look at herself in the mirror and admire the sexy siren, with wild hair and deep red lipstick.

Eventually, she started wearing her special lingerie to work. It added to her excitement and made her think about what was going to be her reward later, back at home. She would wake up early and spend an hour getting dressed. She would choose her lingerie for the day, admire herself in the mirror and then, to hide her shame, put on her shapeless, baggy jumper and calf-length skirt. She would pull her hair up high on her head and set off to work.

As she took the bus to the library there was no indication that this day would be different from any other day. For her, ordinary days were just normal days, and special days were just normal days with a twist. The twist today was a twist she had never, ever thought about, or, in fact, even dreamt about.

She was doing what librarians do all the time – filing. She was returning books to their proper places on the shelves. She never saw the titles, just the reference, as she returned them to their places. Nor did she see who was watching her. It was either fate or coincidence that she happened, at that moment, to be returning Richards & Younis: 'Sex: Practices and Taboo' to its rightful place when he spoke.

'Have you read that?' he said. 'It's a very interesting selection of thoughts about bondage and sadism.'

Alexandra turned, looked at him and blushed. Library visitors didn't normally talk to her, and never did they flirt with her. She took a reference to bondage and sadism as flirting.

She stood still while holding the remaining books. Quite suddenly, her itch became stronger and more demanding than ever before, and definitely in need of scratching. She wanted to be home and on her bed with her thoughts. She didn't say anything but just looked into his eyes.

She had never done that before – that is, never looked so closely into a man's eyes. She didn't know if she thought him handsome or not because all she could feel was the desperate need to scratch her itch. Her itch was as strong as it had ever been and the source of the heat in her thighs.

She looked to her left and then to her right. No one was there, the library was empty, and on impulse, she took his hand and led him through the aisles to somewhere between psychology and physiology. If there was a look on his face, she didn't see it – now she was possessed. Around a corner – nearly out of sight – she ripped off her jumper and skirt and pulled his hand onto her pussy. He will scratch my itch she thought. This is the way it's done.

But to her surprise, no, horror – he pulled back. She was about to say *sorry* and apologise and say it would never happen again. She was thinking that he would report her and she would have to explain to a tribunal and then resign, but then, to her surprise (or horror), he dropped to his knees, pulled her panties aside and pulled her pussy onto his mouth. She felt his tongue lick her clit and go as deep as it could into her. It was the most wonderful feeling. It was so soft and so exciting and nothing like the hard cucumber or the bedpost, but even better was that it scratched the itch like nothing else.

Alexandra leant back against the book racks and closed her eyes, allowing herself to feel and enjoy the waves of excitement and pleasure overwhelming her. Her stranger stopped, stood and again she was looking deep into his smiling eyes. He put his hands on her shoulders and pushed her down so she was on her knees. She didn't know why or what to do; she had never had this experience. Slowly he undid his belt and then his trousers, and as they dropped over his hips to the floor, there in front of her – for the very first time in her life – was a penis.

She looked at it. She saw the lines of the blue veins with blood coursing through them. So large, so magnificent, she stroked it and saw how it twitched and jumped on its own. She had this sudden strong desire to take it in her mouth. Was that normal? She kissed it and slowly she sucked on it and then took it deep into her mouth. A penis was no longer something to frighten her. She looked at him and saw the absolute delight in his eyes. She liked it and he loved it but her itch was getting worse. What happened next? She still didn't know.

As good as this was, it wasn't what she needed. She stopped and stood up, still gripping his cock. He looked at her and pushed her back against the wall; suddenly and surprisingly, she felt the most wonderful of feelings – he had pushed his cock into her pussy.

So this was sex! Bigger, but still softer than anything she had experienced, and so much better. She revelled in every moment and felt every itch being scratched as he pushed deeper and deeper and faster and faster. She was reaching that moment when she knew she would scream out loud – could she hold it in? She tried and pulled him in deeper and suddenly the thrust became long, hard and deep and she felt a new warmness in her pussy. Well, now you can imagine the end. She was left in a crumpled heap on the floor. He headed home and Alexandra started a brand new life, and many, many more men saw her very sexy lingerie.

4. FOUND

Despite my first faltering steps, I soon reconciled myself to my sexuality, while the increasingly wild fantasies had started to develop.

I had had a few long-term boyfriends (at this age a month seemed like a long time to be dating anyone) and a few, but not many, even shorter-term romances (not quite one-night stands, but just long enough to be classed as a relationship).

On many nights I would be alone, lying naked on my bed with my favourite dildo, wondering what it would be like if I did have a new man every week; and then my imagination would take over.

I would think about exploring new, firm male bodies.

Maybe one week it would be a rich man, with his fancy cars and extravagant presents in exchange for my body and sexual favours.

Then, the next week, it could be a soldier returning from battle who had been away from sex and lust for months, alone with only his naughty thoughts. With him, I would be in bed for days on end without a break from sex.

Then, the next week, it could be a shy but handsome academic professor; maybe he could be a virgin and I introduce him to the joys of sex?

And then… I am sure, by now, you get the picture.

Some nights I wondered: what if, instead of a new man every week for a year, those fifty-two men were not spread over the year, but were all together with me in my room? All lusting over me. All those men on just one night! As I lay on my bed I could almost feel their touch all over my body. I could smell and taste the scent of testosterone as they fought to get to me; I could smell sex, and one after the other I could feel them penetrating me; fifty-two times. Then I could decide who has sex with me and who I suck, but because this is my fantasy, I decide when I am going to orgasm; I would have orgasm after orgasm. Now, tell me you have never had any similar thoughts.

But back to my early university days. Initially, I was a little timid – the proverbial working mouse – and I have to admit to being a little socially inept. I was, however, envious of the fun that I assumed others were having. I saw the cliques with all their little 'in-jokes', and as an outsider, I wanted to hang out with these 'cool' people, but I couldn't find a way in. I was a newcomer, so instead, I concentrated on my work and set out to master my subject.

But life was about to get a lot better.

Because I am tall and beautiful, I started modelling when I was just seventeen. Over the years I have become a little less enamoured and more cynical about the profession, but in those early days, I absolutely loved it. Being on a shoot really is very hard work, but being so young I didn't see that. I saw only the glamour and excitement of travel, and being at the centre of everyone's attention.

I carried on modelling right through my university days (and for many years after that), which gave me not just money (which I spent unwisely in shoe shops and nightclubs), but, more importantly, status at university.

It was a fellow student who spotted me in a magazine and I remember the way he timidly approached me with the pages spread open.

'Is this you?' he asked.

I looked at the open page. It was from a shoot taken just before I come to Kyiv and it was a series of lingerie shots for a major supplier. There were shots of me wearing only very small panties. In some I was photographed with my back turned to the camera, the very clear line of my breasts and just a hint of nipple. And there was another, sitting in a chair with my legs spread wide, covering my breasts with my hands. And then there was the one where I just stood there brazenly in tiny, almost transparent panties, a bandolier across my naked chest and large, dark sunglasses; my stance was aggressive and provocative. Pictures like that normally only appear in men's magazines, and for the time they were very sexy and very naughty.

I nodded.

From then on, I was a celebrity and quickly brought into the university and Kyiv social scene. No one can resist the thought of meeting a beautiful nude model.

Through my diligent first year, I had cemented a great

background in my subject, and with this mixture of a solid subject foundation with the cash from my modelling work, it meant that for the last two years I could relax and coast in my studies. Also, without compromising anything, I could spend weekends and many evenings in clubs and bars enjoying a good social life.

From social mouse, I had become a socialite and the queen of the club scene. My modelling was a passport to a much different and greatly enhanced life.

5. SUN AND SEX ON THE BEACH

At university I loved my subject; I had found my niche and now I was well on my way. In my second and third years, we could start to specialise, and my very open-minded tutors helped me set up the electives for my final undergraduate year.

I remember that the first discussions on my new subjects were in my professor's office. Due to the sensitive nature of the topics, these could have been very uncomfortable conversations, but they were conversations that had to be had and I wasn't used to holding back.

'So, Alexandra, what do you want to specialise in? I assume you have read the list of options?'

'Thank you, professor. Yes, I have read the list, but none of them is really what I want to do. But I do have something else in mind. It is something that really interests me.'

'Tell me about but you understand it is not common to find and define new electives, but it is good that there are areas that are of real interest to you.'

And this is when I started to embarrass myself when I know now that I really should have stuck to the script.

'You see, professor, I have these magical and very special fantasies. Can I give you an example, Professor?'

'Of course,' he said.

'I have this dream that I am on holiday with my boyfriend and we are relaxing on the beach. It's not crowded, but still, there are lots of people sunbathing around us; all of us are enjoying the holiday sun in our own way.

We have had a good day. It has been relaxing; we sunbathed in the morning, and after breakfast, we had a sensuous session of lovemaking.

Maybe I don't need to tell you all about that, but let's just say I love strawberries; we had a light lunch and now here we are in the late afternoon, lying in the sun again.

Can you imagine what I'm wearing? It is one of my small, sexy bikinis. Just like the ones in the photoshoot that everyone is showing around. Anyway, I'm reading, but I'm bored.

'Stroke my hair please, darling,' I say, 'I like having my hair stroked and you don't have to stop reading.'

Maybe you are also bored as you put down your book, or maybe it is just that you are horny; but when aren't you? I was right because your hands do more than stroke my hair, they wander all over me, outlining the top of my bikini and then circling around a nipple. You're probably wondering if you can make it hard under the cloth. You are always such a naughty boy, with all your naughty thoughts, and you smile as you see how successful you are and how I am losing my concentration; there is no chance, now, that I can carry on reading!

'Of course, professor, when I say 'you' I mean my boyfriend and not actually you. I'm getting a little carried away here.'

I looked at the professor and I suddenly realised just how uncomfortable he had become. I suppose he was uncomfortable with the subject matter, but I had started on this line and so I felt I had to finish it.

'And so, like him, I give in and put the book down, prop myself up on an elbow and we look into each other's eyes. I see love, passion and a naughty glint. We kiss, and you – I mean he – puts his hand into my bikini top and plays with my nipple, so I put my hand down his swim shorts and play with your— I'm sorry, I did it again – *his* beautiful, growing cock. He pushes the material away so that my breasts are bare and he leans forward and furtively sucks at my nipples. We both want sex, but how?

We won't let the location or all the other people around us stop us. Without losing eye contact I sit on his lap and pull down the front of his swim shorts while he pulls my bikini bottoms to one side so that I can take hold of his cock and guide it into my wet and expectant pussy. Okay, maybe at first we're a little self-conscious and scared that someone will see us, but they are really not that close; soon we are oblivious to them anyway because we are so into each other that no one else matters.'

'So, what do you think, professor?' I say. 'That is what I want to work on for my electives.'

Well, he just looked at me, slightly flushed, and said, 'Alexandra, I have to be honest and say that I don't understand one word of your request, but thank you for the story. It was rather exciting and very imaginative. Now, would you like to start again?'

And so I did, and thus started on the journey of what is now my passion and my work.

III. MIKHAIL – MY STORY

In these early days, my academic work at the university was mainly around reading and understanding, and I was the subject of any research. Well, to be honest, I used my degree as an excuse to have some normal student fun as I started to live out my new life.

As well as fun I thought of it as research, and it gave me an excuse to be more outgoing and gregarious, although I didn't really need too much encouragement. If I had been in my shell when I arrived at university, I was now well out of it – so far, in fact, that had I been asked to find my old self I wouldn't know where to start looking.

I was now into my stride and felt in control of both my life and, of course, my relationships; but my time as an undergraduate at university was coming to an end. I enjoyed everything about my life and I didn't want it to end, so I explored the idea of staying another two years and signing up for a master's degree, again in Kyiv. It just seemed the easiest option.

As I researched the subject and worked on my studies, I wanted and needed to know so much more about fantasies, and I wanted to know what fantasies other women have. Do they have these same thoughts? Do they look at their work colleagues or men at bus stops and have sexy thoughts and erotic fantasies? In fact, are women just as lustful as men?

I wanted to know more, and so by the time I started my master's there was no doubt about the subject of my research: female sexual fantasies; this merged my personal and academic interests. My work was also my pleasure. Everybody was fine with that. I passed my undergraduate degree with first-class honours, so the professors were happy; I had money from modelling, so my parents, who didn't need to support me, were happy, and the clubs and discos were happy!

6. MAKE HIM WAIT

Alexandra had waited nearly five weeks before contacting Mikhail again. She knew how this would have affected him – too much pride to call, but a churning mixture of deep longing and yearning, confused by hope and expectancy.

Each day he would have looked at her panties, wondering what to do next. He would have picked them up, held them, and remembered the moment she gave them to him. Every night as he drifted off to sleep he would have thought about that night in her apartment, wishing he was there again.

He would have gone out and probably met and screwed other girls, but each time there wouldn't be the excitement and raw tension of Alexandra. No doubt they would have been pretty and accommodating girls, each trying to please so that they could call him theirs. Each would have wanted more than he wished to give and he would have left them where he found them.

But she knew he wanted her.

As always, she had planned and prepared. She had left a message telling him where and when to send his driver to collect her. Her message was brief and told him what he needed to pack and how long they would be away. She hadn't waited for, or wanted, a reply.

Everything had been organised at the dacha. Fifty miles outside Kyiv, it was set on the edge of woodland. It was small, more of a cabin. But inside was the luxury that Alexandra always expected.

Outside, beyond the small walled garden slowly coming to life as spring brightened into summer, was the woodland where Alexandra had played as a child. She knew this land well and always felt a deep sense of comfort and relaxation when she was there. She had walked in these woods with her mother and grandmother. Running along to keep pace between them, she had held their hands and been pulled up, twisted and turned before again being let down to run on. 'Fly like a butterfly,' her mother would say.

His car arrived on time. He was sitting in the back. He started to get out and open the door but the chauffeur was there first. Alexandra stepped in, leaving him in an embarrassing no man's land. Alexandra told the driver where to go, closed her eyes and relaxed. In the back, he – of course – was lost; not sure when to talk, if he should hold her, what to do. He did nothing. The impotence of control.

I had made the arrangements and we were on our way to the dacha. Across the summers of my youth, I was brought up in these woods after we moved from Lugansk to Lviv when I was still young. It brought back distant and happy memories of the past. It also bore memories of a time with my mother and grandmother. They were happy times.

We arrived just as the sun was setting: a fiery orange ball of hope for another day. We ate food like many Ukrainian peasants were eating that night. He was nervy and fitful and I wouldn't let him touch me. At first, he was gentle. I was standing at the window and he came behind me and tried to put his hands around my waist.

'Not now, later,' I said, but later never came.

Then he was angry. 'Why have you brought me all this way? I need you. I want you.' Anger and resentment were swelling up in his voice. I raised a single finger and gently touched his lips.

'Not now, later.'

'Tomorrow, you can have me. Tomorrow, but not tonight. Tomorrow I will do wonderful things for you. I will make you so happy; tomorrow, but not tonight. Tonight you will sleep by yourself and think about tomorrow.'

I turned to walk away when a despairing hand came to grab me and pull me back; I turned and looked deep and unblinking into his eyes. He saw that I would leave right then, I would walk out if he carried on like this, and slowly the grip relaxed and I went to my room.

Alexandra had her plan. It wasn't thought out like the strategy and tactics of a general might be. It wasn't written down. She was intuitive and knew at every moment what she had to do. He would not sleep. He would lie alone thinking about her, alone in a bed just a few metres away. He would think of coming into her room, but then he knew that if he did, he might never see her again.

He had hoped that in the middle of the night, with hardly a sound, she would miss him so much that she would slip quietly into his bed. He would be half-awake as she pushed herself closer to him with a hand around his body, slowly reaching down. But he knew that wouldn't happen. He would think of relieving the growing pain in his loins to alleviate the continual erection, but he knew that if he was heard or caught he might never see her again.

She would sleep, she would sleep well; she wouldn't think of him next door, awake and restless. He was right. Alexandra was asleep, naked beneath the loose sheets. Her dreams were not of him but of those days as a child when she had the comfort and love of her mother.

The morning was bright, and as ever I was up early. He was still asleep. I showered and dressed and had breakfast ready as he came to the table. He wasn't Ukrainian so we didn't eat as Ukrainians but as Europeans. The croissants were hot, the jams homemade, the coffee strong. I flirted and teased him. My skirt was just too short and my blouse had just enough buttons undone so that he had the certainty that I was not wearing a bra, but not so much that he could think of me as naked. As I leaned across the table he would see a breast, maybe a nipple and think that maybe it was hard in thoughts of him.

I made him walk with me, first in the garden and then out into the woods. I danced along, picking flowers, and told him about how my mother and I had walked here. I held his hand and he tried to draw me close to steal a kiss.

'No, not here. In the dacha. I have wonderful things in store for you,' and with that, he quickened the pace. He wanted home and was always ahead of me as I stopped and conjured up the last of all the memories I could from all of my previous times here.

'Wait here,' I said, as we arrived back. 'I need to get ready.'

'Close your eyes, turn around, look away from me,' I said to him. So he stood like a naughty schoolboy, in the middle of the room. Just like before, I walked around him at a slow and deliberate pace and from behind his back, I slowly reached round to stroke his chest.

'Stay still.'

I leaned my head on his shoulder and pulled him back towards me. As I loosened my grip he moved to turn.

'No, stay still.'

I slowly wrapped a long white linen cloth around his eyes. It went around twice and I tied a simple knot to keep it in place. I turned him round to face me and looked at his face. He moved to hear better but there was not a sound. I ran a finger down his unshaven chin. I swayed from side to side and he could not see.

'You see, it's your imagination which drives you on,' I said after a moment. 'By now I might be naked or I might just leave you standing here. I could walk out the door and be gone. How long would you stand there, unable to see? Would you risk my wrath after five minutes? I may be sitting quietly in the chair just looking at you. What do you want?'

'I want you here. I don't want you to go.'

'Good,' I said as I walked again behind him. I reached forward and slowly brought each arm behind him. I wrapped a rope around one wrist first and then the other until he was tied.

Again I turned him to face me. 'I will tell you what I am doing. Do you want to know?'

He nodded but there was no hint of a smile or the satisfaction he would have had if he could see. There was frustration and concern.

'I have undone the last buttons on my shirt and it is hanging loose. If you could see you would see my breasts rising slowly with each deep breath. My nipples are hard as I rub them. Can you imagine? Do you want to see?'

'Yes, I want to see. Please let me see.' There was breathless anticipation in his words.

'Please? Surely you can do better than that?' I asked.

Hesitantly, he started to try and form the words. 'Yes, Mistress?' I laughed and he turned red.

'I am not your mistress. You are free to do whatever you want. But maybe you have found your own princess. Will you do whatever your princess wants? Now I have taken off my shoes.'

He started to take a step forward but I pushed him back.

'Now I have undone my skirt and it has dropped to the floor. I had no panties on. Did you know?'

'I had hoped, but can I see?'

'No, and I am standing here naked ready for you. How does it feel?'

Again he started to take a step toward me, but again I pushed him back, with a gentle palm pressed into his chest.

'Imagine me standing here naked before you,' I said, as I reached out to unbutton his shirt. It was undone to his belly and I put my hands on his chest and slowly massaged him. As each button was undone he straightened and started to arch back towards the wall. He tested the rope on his wrists and turned his head to try and see. Each was to no avail.

His shirt was hanging loose and I pulled it back over his shoulders so that it hung limp on the rope on his wrists. I pushed myself against him and he strained forward now, to try and kiss me with the feeling of my nakedness on him. My breasts were pressed tight against him, slowly rubbing deep into his chest. I dropped to my knees, and as I knelt down in front of him I reached down to remove his shoes. He bent forward in the forlorn hope that he could see me under his blindfold.

I knelt upright and pulled the belt out through his trouser loops, finishing with a swish that made him momentarily wince. My hands were deep inside his trousers and, undone, they fell to the floor. He kicked out ridiculously with each leg, in turn, to make sure they were gone.

With my hands around his buttocks, I pulled him towards me and felt him growing larger through the material of his pants. I circled his cock with a single finger, watching the outline shudder and twitch.

I pulled down his pants and took his cock in my mouth. He pushed forward and I took more. With my tongue I explored, I cupped my hands around him; I took him deeper and faster and felt him swelling inside my mouth. He arched his back, muffled a cry, a mixture of delight and anguish, and I swallowed spurt upon spurt of warm, salty cum. I licked him dry as his body, like his cock, sank down and relaxed.

I stood up and looked at him, the blindfold hiding any expression in his eyes and his arms now relaxed behind his back. I admired his body and the faint hint of a smile. Quietly I dressed, then undid first his blindfold, then freed his arms.

As he turned he was suddenly embarrassed by his nakedness. Scooping up clothes, he was soon dressed. 'Why?' he asked. 'Why did you get dressed?'

'Because our car will be here soon.'

It was a quiet journey back to Kyiv.

Sitting in the car, Alexandra was pleased with herself. He was now captivated. He had had her in a way that he hadn't expected. He had revelled in the moment but in the end, had been left frustrated as all power and control had been taken away from him.

7. A WEEK WITH MIKHAIL

Saturday

I was at the bar with friends when he came in. Maybe he was not the most handsome of men, but I could feel that sexual chemistry between us. While others talked, we kept throwing glances, always just catching each other's eye. He smiled and I couldn't help smiling back. He bought champagne for us all and as I raised my glass to him, he raised his glass in return. We were like two magnets drawn together. We detached from the group and it was as if all around us were caught in a moment of stillness. We were in focus and the rest was a blur. We whispered sweet nothings, and with hardly a word being said, we left, hand in hand.

As we drove through town I moved across the seat closer to him. First, my hand was on his knee and then his thigh. I undid three buttons on my blouse and as we stopped at lights, had he glanced at me he would have seen my naked breasts and, deep inside, my beating heart. He did more than glance; he looked and smiled.

Heading out into the countryside he drove quickly but precisely, soon leaving houses and shops far behind us, while all the time the electricity between us was increasing. My hand moved and I could feel his excitement. I undid more buttons, and in a sudden burst of freedom, I removed my blouse. Without a word, he stopped the car, reached towards the front panel, hit a button and the roof slowly and quietly slipped back. Now we were in the warm summer evening with stars above.

Each moment we were together the sexual tension was building; it had never before been like this. I was fully aware of my body in so many new ways and I had this deep urge to be naked with him. It was an urge I could hardly control. He drove on. I didn't know our destination, but the journey was everything.

The cool wind was in my hair and the heat in my body was irresistible; still, I wanted to be naked. I wriggled and slipped my dress and panties down. There! As we drove through the lanes I was happy and free, and I was naked.

I reached across and slowly undid his belt and then his zip, and felt a large cock through his pants. He glanced across at me, taking his eyes briefly off the road as I bent down, reached for his cock and took him deep in my mouth. He held my hair, I did not resist, and slowly and rhythmically he pushed me more and more onto him, and then he stopped.

I felt the car come to a halt as he pulled onto a rough track in the forest now surrounding us. I stopped and he opened the door before leading me by the hand to the front of the car. I felt the soft grass on my feet and allowed him to lift me into his arms as he placed me gently on my back on the bonnet.

I felt the engine's warmth as he held my ankles and spread my legs, and I felt his tongue go deep inside my pussy. The release!

Tuesday

I had been at work and would be back late. I arrived home tense and grumpy. I said I was going to have a bath. He said. 'put on one of my shirts after you're finished. You will be more comfortable'. I lay in the bath relaxing and heard music from the lounge.

I bathed, dried, grabbed a shirt from his wardrobe and went into the lounge. The lights were turned down low, candles burned everywhere and the music was rhythmic, quiet and soothing. Cushions were spread across the floor.

I could smell the sweet, relaxing aroma of the candles and turned to look at him, just as he said, 'come here'. All my senses were excited. In the near darkness, I felt his hand stroke my hair. Like a blind man, he was seeing me with his hands alone. I did the same. Our movements were slow. We did not rush. With hands and lips, we explored each other anew. We saw each other again. When and how we became naked I don't know. When and how we made love I can't remember.

Time passed and we were as one, asleep on the cushions.

Sex and 'making love' are both important. Sex is an animal instinct of lust while 'making love' is more and is the wonderful joining of both bodies and souls; both are important in a relationship. That night I came to know the difference.

Sunday morning

We lay in bed. It was a late morning after a late night. I moved closer to him, pulling the duvet over us both. Neither asleep nor awake we lay there. I loved the comfort of his body as I pressed against his back, arching my body to fit his shape. He pushed back towards me. We were as one.

Neither asleep nor awake we made slow and gentle love.

Neither asleep nor awake we lay in bed, ready for the new day to begin.

Weekend

At first, it started by accident as we both headed to the shower at the same time, but now it has become a regular occurrence. We love to shower together. Sometimes we have sex but often we just talk as we wash each other. It's like an animal ritual of cleaning. Now we shower together at least twice a week, but he is still awful at washing my hair!

Saturday night

Food is to be eaten? Of course! But I love it when he takes the chocolate sauce or the whipped cream and covers my body – especially my pussy – and licks me clean.

We have many favourite foods!

Last night

Every night we go to bed together at the same time – never one before the other. It's a ritual only broken when one of us is ill.

We always cuddle close and sometimes just go to sleep in each other's arms. Sometimes I sense that moment when half asleep, we move apart, to drift into a deep sleep. I say to myself: 'my love, I will see you on the other side'. Even as we roll apart we still hold hands; very silly maybe, but romantic.

Sometimes we do not go straight to sleep but move closer and make love. When we have both reached that erotic climax, we just lie there and fall asleep, our bodies never separating. We are as one.

I was learning very quickly, and not just on my course at university; I was learning very quickly about men. I learnt what I wanted and exactly what they needed. My modelling was giving me celebrity status and I enjoyed my freedom. I didn't want to be owned by anyone and I didn't want anyone dependent on me, and that was what boyfriends and lovers meant to me. Men like to own. That is what they mean by the 'trophy wife'. I had a very strong independent streak which was soon to be further honed and tuned.

I had everything and I didn't want to be tied down, so there was no room for any single man with all the baggage of a complicated relationship.

That is what always happens with men – it gets complicated. I broke a few hearts, although it was never my intention. I took no great pride in what was happening, it was just that I had to concentrate on my studies and exploration. I couldn't let a single man get in my way. But however much I told them and no matter how often I told them, they always wanted to own me, or at least make me promise them, undying love. I never could and I never would, as I had no intention of being owned.

From the little girl that left Lviv for university wanting love and attention, now I wanted to be in control; I wanted men but I wanted men on my terms. Later, as I built my relationship with Mikhail, I would fully explore control and all its many aspects, but for now, my aim was to stay liberated and be successful by finishing my degree.

Of course, I knew the more I resisted, the more I teased, the more attractive I became. I was even more desirable. As a psychologist I knew what was happening and what I was doing; I was perfectly able to rationalise it, but I wanted to feel it. It is a recurring trend in my life that I need to touch and feel something before I really believe or I understand it.

8. IN A SHOP CHANGING ROOM

I know men are useless at shopping and hate being dragged around from shop to shop, but when I am out shopping for lingerie I want you there with me. I choose my clothes first for me and then for you. I want to know what excites you.

First, we would go around the shop trying to decide what we like. We would be just like furtive teenagers, holding up flimsy, see-through panties to the light. Maybe we would choose four or five items and then I would have to leave you to go to the changing rooms to try them on. You would just sit down outside, twiddling your thumbs and waiting for me to come back. Of course, you wouldn't look at any of the other pretty women there – you are too well behaved for that and you know the punishment if I catch you!

I know it can be really embarrassing for a man sitting around in a lingerie shop, trying to tell other shoppers with his eyes that he is waiting for someone, and that he's not just a pervert with a fetish for lingerie. But then I peek my head around the curtain and whisper, 'come here!', beckoning you in with my finger. It makes me smile to see how you react. You try so hard to look casual, while I am sure you must also be getting just a little excited at the thought of what I am going to ask you or show you. As you get very close, I grab your jacket and pull you quickly into the cubicle with me to make sure you don't change your mind.

'Help me choose,' I say, knowing I must be a beautiful sight for you, wearing just a tiny bra and panties. 'I'm not sure which ones I like best,' I say. 'What do you think?' This must be one of your fantasies becoming reality.

'I'm not sure,' you say, 'I've only seen one set.'

'That's true,' I say, with a naughty look in my eye, holding another set of lingerie. 'Well, what do you think of these?'

You fidget in your seat, watching as I change from one set of sexy lingerie to the other. You are mesmerised as I strip and then get redressed. I know what is happening as I see your hand move to your cock, which I can see is getting very hard. Well, it would, wouldn't it?

I know what I am doing and I love teasing you. Naked, I stand in front of you holding up a tiny pair of panties.

'Do you think the rest of the shop would like to see me like this?' I ask, pulling slightly at the curtain that separates us from the other shoppers. 'Do you think I should go out there now, like this, to choose some other lingerie? Look at that man waiting like you were a moment ago. Do you think his wife will be jealous if he watches me?'

For a moment we see another couple rustling through sexy underwear; I can see at least three women and two assistants from here.

'What do you think? Should I go like this? Maybe I should send you out and then come and collect you? My darling, are you getting excited?' I ask innocently. I know the answer. I can see. 'Show me, darling,' I say, leaning forward to slowly unzip your trousers to release a now very large cock.

'Pull the curtain closed, Alexandra. Please.' There is a plaintive tone to your voice. I love your cock so much and I love it, even more, when I see it in illicit places, so I reach down to touch it and stroke it, and then pull the curtain closed.

I've been winding you up, but now it's me who's getting excited. I turn, and with my back to you I slowly sit down on you, feeling your cock enter and go deep inside me. You hold my breasts as I rock backwards and forwards, up and down, and then the pace increases, faster and faster, before I come – just managing to stifle all my screams and groans.

But enough is never enough. 'I want to come again,' I say, 'I feel so hot. My pussy is wet and needs cleaning. Your Queen wants you to clean her pussy.' So I take your place on the seat and make you kneel before me, and with your tongue you bring me to another soaring orgasm, sucking out all the pussy juices that flow so freely.

Finally, we do manage to choose some lingerie and we go to the counter to pay. The assistant looks at us. Does she know? Maybe, but to be honest we don't really care!

9. TIED UP FOR LUNCH

It was just mid-morning and today the office seemed drab and cold. Of course, people were running around doing their jobs and phones were ringing, but Alexandra was alone in her world of work. She looked at the words of women from all around the world telling her about their dreams and fantasies, but she took nothing in.

She reached for the phone.

'Hi Mikhail, do you fancy lunch today? I feel so lonely at work and it's so boring not having you here as well.' She listened for a moment as Mikhail answered.

'Oh, that's good, darling. Did you manage to work this morning? Sorry, I left a mess when I went to work but it was your fault. You should have made me tea and not given me all those kisses in bed. Okay. Bye, darling. See you at one o'clock at the restaurant. Yes, the one on the main street next to the clothes shop. Now I have to get back to work. I miss you and want to see you soon.'

Mikhail was also at work, and, finishing the sentence but not the paragraph, he saved the document. Alexandra marked the model portfolio she was reviewing, showing where she had reached; both momentarily hunted for their car keys; both put on coats and headed out of the door and into their cars, then drove to meet each other.

It was Alexandra who arrived first, with the traffic being kinder; she chose a table hidden away in a corner. She liked the privacy and intimacy it offered. He arrived just a few minutes later and saw her sucking on a straw dipped into a glass of orange juice. As he looked, he marvelled how, even though they had now been together for nearly a year, he still found her the most beautiful of all women.

Each time they met it was like seeing her again for the first time and it always rejuvenated his love. It wasn't just the feeling of eternal love that swelled in his heart (that was certainly true), it also spurred on a primaeval passion that excited him in a way that was verging on lustful. Every time he saw her, every word she said, had just one effect on him: it caused him to fall even more in love with her.

He had spent many hours considering this juxtaposition of emotions. He had had lustful relationships and he had been in romantic relationships, but never both at the same time. He had previously wondered if that was even feasible, but here, now, was the proof, and his conclusion to anyone who would listen was that this was a definition of the most intense and therefore sustainable love.

Alexandra saw him and rose from the table to meet and greet him. She, too, liked the physical aspects of love and neither of them was embarrassed to show the world their feelings for each other. That is why Alexandra had stood up; it had allowed her to throw her arms around his neck while he put his arms around her waist and they kissed like the lovers they still were. A few of the more conservative diners looked and tut-tutted, others showed casual indifference, but all wished they had a relationship like theirs.

'Sit down, darling,' Alexandra said, 'I have already ordered our lunch.' He sat close, next to her with his back to the wall.

'Now, tell me about your day. What did you do today?' Alexandra asked as the surly waitress served their food.

'It was naughty stuff this morning,' he said. 'I had to write a sex scene between Jake and his girlfriend. Want me to tell you what happened?' and over lunch, Mikhail told Alexandra about the film script, including all the torrid sexy adventures. He left out none of the details, knowing that Alexandra loved these parts of his stories.

'Now, tell me, Kitten: what did you do today?'

'Oh, nothing special, just work. But I did go to the shops on the way back from a meeting. Want to see what I bought?' He nodded.

'Well, I can show you some but I can't show you everything here,' she said. 'I will have to keep some back for later,' and she reached into her handbag and pulled out a pair of shiny silver handcuffs. These weren't soft and fluffy handcuffs, they were heavy-duty and sturdy.

'Problems at work, or is one of your clients annoying you?' he tried to joke at the sight of the handcuffs, but he was concerned with what he saw. He knew her intentions and he knew that one day he would be wearing them and that the consequences may be painful. She laughed.

'No, darling. Let me show you how they work. Put your hands

behind your back.'

'No, Kitten. We can't do that here,' he said.

'Oh yes, we can. Now be a good boy and do as I say.' Reluctantly he turned his back on her and she clamped his wrists, locking his arms around the back of the chair.

'See how good they are? You will never get out of them,' she said. 'I want you to be my little boy,' and she teased him by taking a piece of cake on a fork and feeding him. He tried the best he could to look as though they were just lovers being playful with each other while hiding that he couldn't move. However, Alexandra was amused and that encouraged her to try even more exaggerated feeding rituals. She even undid a button on her blouse and nibbled at his ear.

'My good boy,' she said, 'I wonder if you are getting excited by this? Let's see,' and she ran her hand over the growing bulge in his trousers. His cock never needed much encouragement and quickly it started to press against his jeans. He wanted to move to ease the pressure but the handcuffs prevented this. Alexandra saw his discomfort but did nothing to ease it. As she fed him she talked while running a hand across her breasts, which reminded him of the last time they made love. All the while he saw that her nipples were getting harder and he saw that they protruded and pressed against her blouse. She undid one more button, which allowed him to see the line of her breasts.

'Oh, are you hurting, darling?' she said, knowing full well the answer. 'Maybe we should do something about that.'

'I am and I agree. Let me go and I'm sure we can find somewhere less public,' he said. 'What can we do here? '

'Oh, lots,' she said, and with that, she reached down and with one hand slowly undid the zip of his trousers, grasped inside his pants and withdrew his engorged cock. He looked around, trying to look disinterested, wondering if anyone could see what was going on.

Alexandra pulled him gently. 'Mmmm. That is nice,' she said. 'Would you like to come, right here and now?' He just looked at her as she stroked and pulled at his cock and there was nothing he could do. Of course, he wanted to come, but he didn't want to come here in public, in a restaurant, but he knew that the decision had literally been taken out of his hands. He was getting larger and both he and Alexandra knew a finish was imminent. Then Alexandra turned (without letting go or stopping as she slid her hand up and down) and looked across the restaurant; she waved her spare hand and beckoned over the waitress. The slightly disinterested girl acknowledged the signal and sauntered over.

Keeping hold and still moving his cock, which seemed to him only partially hidden by a tablecloth, she negotiated the bill and even chatted to the waitress. All the while he just smiled, trying to hold himself back. Then it happened. Alexandra was still chatting to the waitress when he exploded but still, Alexandra didn't stop; if anything, she pulled on him even faster. He tried hard to retain the emotion and not say or show anything but there was enough for the waitress to ask him if everything was alright. He nodded and just managed to say, 'yes, everything is fine,' as he felt the cum drip down her hand and his cock. The waitress left and, smiling, Alexandra undid the handcuffs, put them back in her bag and left him to put his cock away.

'Now, don't you want to know what else I bought this morning?' Alexandra said, licking her fingers, but after this, he wasn't so sure.

That afternoon, neither of them managed to concentrate or do any meaningful work. Although he had meetings in the afternoon he was still home first and was thinking about dinner when the text message came. 'I will be home slightly late. At 7:30.' That caused him a little disappointment. He hated being apart. A minute later another message arrived. 'But be ready: naked, blindfolded and in a proper position.'

Mikhail knew what that meant and he started to prepare. Even if he didn't want it he knew that at moments like this it was not good to complain. He went to the cupboard in the bedroom and looked in the box. There were many sex toys, but which would she want? There were things there he didn't like because they hurt or were humiliating, but to exclude them would be noticed, interest Alexandra more and guarantee that they were used on him. He got them all out and laid them neatly a few feet from the door of their apartment. He checked his watch.

Six-thirty. He had to be ready early in case she was home early. He showered and shaved (she hated his stubble when they kissed) and thought about getting dressed, but that was unnecessary.

Seven fifteen and he was in place: naked, blindfolded and kneeling on the floor in front of the main door. God forbid, he thought, what would happen if he ever misinterpreted the message and she came back with a friend? He put that thought aside.

He was there for no more than ten minutes when he heard the door open and heard her shoes click on the marble floor. 'My good boy,' she said, running a finger down his back. 'Stand up,' and he did as he was told. 'I have been thinking about you all afternoon and how good you were in the restaurant. Such a good boy. Now, put your hands out in front of you. You need to try the handcuffs again.'

Normally he was tied with his hands behind his back. This was a change, he thought. He put his hands out and felt the cuffs clasp his wrists tight. What was happening? He could only guess. He couldn't see but he was lead into the lounge, stumbling in his blindness, and his hands were jerked up over his head. With his back to the wall, she had found a way to secure him with his hands high above his head. It was pointless to ask or expect to be told. He had only to wait.

He started to count. One, two, three ..... could he estimate how long he was being left? It was not worth it. He had no control.

Alexandra was now in the bathroom having a shower. For her the thought of what was going to happen made her excited. It was all about anticipation. The water brushed across her body and she felt the smoothness of her skin drenched in soap. She didn't think about him and what he felt and concentrated on herself. This was special of him, she thought. In these moments he didn't think about what he wanted. He didn't want a reward for these moments. Maybe he enjoyed it, maybe he didn't, but that didn't matter. He was doing this so that she, Alexandra, could do exactly what she wanted. He was giving himself completely, for her enjoyment. What more could she ever ask from the man she loved so much? Her makeup done, she looked at the clothes laid out on her bed. She dressed, put on her high-heeled red shoes, and the seven inches of stiletto heel propelled her towards the stars. She checked herself in the mirror and headed back to him.

Mikhail was still suspended, as she expected, exactly where she had left him. He knew better than to try and escape. She looked at him with love; vulnerable yet determined and more a man than any other man could ever be. Alexandra reached to the floor and took a long piece of red cord and placed it loosely around his neck.

'What should we tie tight, my darling? This?' she said, tightening the noose slightly, 'or this?' reaching down and grabbing his cock.

She took the rope and it slipped off his neck, then carefully she looped it around his cock, separating it from his testicles, and tied him uptight. She watched as his cock grew; every spurt of blood was retained, making his cock harder and harder. She looked in awe as the blood vessels pumped and pumped.

'Do you want to see what I bought today? Especially for you.' He nodded and carefully she took the blindfold off him and his eyes opened wide with excitement.

He looked at her from head to toe and back again from foot to hair. He was desperate to reach out and touch her but the shackles stopped him. Her hair was pulled back tight off her face; she wore a thin bandana stretched thinly across her large and beautiful breasts; a small leather skirt, just short enough that he could see the top of the dark hold-up stockings, and then the very high-heeled red stiletto shoes that made her much taller than him. She was a picture of divine beauty. She moved closer to him, pressing her body against him; this was as much for her benefit as his, as she was also feeling horny. Standing close, she whispered in his ear.

'My darling, I have a real treat for you tonight. I have bought you a wonderful present. I phoned a special agency and there will be someone else joining us. Would you like that?' I am sure you would,' she added before he could say anything. 'Later there will be three of us. Mmmm. But maybe you won't like it. I don't know. Have you ever been fucked by a man before? Have you ever sucked cock?'

His face turned pale.

"Don't say anything, darling. You can say thank you later,' she added with a laugh. 'I know you want to thank me, but in fact, I don't want you to say anything,' and she took a ball gag and tied the leather strap behind his head. Now he really couldn't say anything.

'Let's get you down from there and ready for him. Kneel on the coffee table'.

She tied his still-handcuffed wrists and opened his legs, exposing his arse, then tied each of his legs to a table leg. She could see him quiver. Was it fear or excited anticipation? She knew that this was all new to him.

He had once said that it would be exciting to see her with another woman, although it was not high on his list of fantasies; however, the thought had remained with her. But her watching him with another man was one of the very few things they had never discussed. He looked up at her, still unable to speak through the gag, and saw that she was stepping into a strap-on with the most enormous dildo.

'Should we get that arse ready? I think we should.' He wanted to see what she was doing but could only feel as she spread lube on his arse.

'I think first I will use my strap-on while you suck his cock and then we will switch. You can feel him come in your arse and you will then know what it is like for me. You will do this for me, won't you? He'll be here soon.'

He could do no more than wait, and then her phone rang.

'Hello,' said Alexandra, 'you're downstairs. That's good. It's Flat Seventeen. Come on up. He is ready.'

He could hear Alexandra walking around the room and then the door opened. 'Come in,' she said, and he heard the click of her shoes as she walked back.

'I have booked him for an hour,' she said. 'I hope you can last that long? I want you to see what is happening,'

She was still standing behind him. He felt the tip of the dildo starting to explore his arse. He tensed and then Alexandra laughed.

'I am sorry darling,' she said, undoing the ropes. 'There is no one here. I couldn't do that to you unless, of course, you upset me very badly. Are you okay? It was cruel of me but you know that pain, like all sensations, is really in the mind; also, I learnt something very important. You really do love me so much. You really would do anything for me to make me happy, wouldn't you? I love you too. Now, come here.'

He was standing, the gag removed, but his cock was still standing proud. 'If you ever do that to me again I will have to smack your bottom,' he said.

'Is that a promise? But not too hard, my darling. I know you couldn't hurt me.'

'We could test it now?' he said. 'Are you wearing anything under that little skirt?

'What do you think?' said Alexandra, bending over to touch her toes and let him see.

I learned quickly that I especially liked not just outwardly powerful, but also creative men. In their creativity I found the strongest emotional response, but when we parted (and it was always me that ended relationships), their emotional responses were so much stronger. It was never easy, but I always believe that I left them far stronger. I never knew for sure what it meant to them but I could imagine the pain I caused, but I had no choice. It had to be done. I had my own plans and aspirations.

I'm sure that my interest may have started as a defence mechanism to keep them where they had to be, but soon I learnt that I actually enjoyed my role. The stronger they were then the greater the challenge, and the greater their satisfaction.

Mikhail was both powerful and also a creative writer. It was destiny that brought us together.

Alexandra

10. WRAP, TAPE AND SUBMISSION

The idea came to Alexandra as she was in the hardware store at lunchtime, just buying some ordinary household goods. She had been feeling naughty all day and tonight she wanted something different; suddenly, here was the solution. She made the purchases, and sent a text message to him, who was working from home that day. Everything was ready.

At work that afternoon she couldn't concentrate as the thought of what was going to happen that night took hold.

The plan needed further consideration. Would she wait until they had had dinner or would she have her fun as soon as she arrived home? She sat at her desk and tried to work, but found that her hand kept moving to her pussy, which she started to stroke gently. It took all her self-control not to have an orgasm right there and then at her desk.

Although her initial thought was to wait until after dinner, as the afternoon dragged to a finish she knew that she couldn't contemplate any delay. The hands of the clock moved very slowly around the face, to six o'clock. It was time to go home and she knew she wanted him so badly that she sent him a text that she knew would both excite and worry him: 'be ready for me in 30 minutes'.

She gathered up her purchases and started to drive. Her pussy was almost a fountain of excitement at the thought of what waited for her at home. She drove slowly, afraid that she might crash as she couldn't concentrate properly, but also both to intensify and prolong the anticipation. She wanted to feel the excitement increase slowly. She parked, collected her shopping, locked the car, walked to the door of their apartment, put the key in the lock and turned it. She took a deep breath as she pushed it open.

Mikhail had done all that he had been told to. He was standing naked, facing the front door, blindfolded and with his hands behind his back. It was now her turn to get ready, but to add to the excitement she didn't close the door; in fact, she opened it wide so that anyone passing by would be able to see him standing there, silhouetted by the light of the room, erect and awaiting instructions.

Alexandra went to the bedroom to prepare herself. At these

moments she also liked to dress in the role of his queen, his mistress and his dominatrix. She laid out her clothes on the bed: first her stockings, black and silky; the red, high-heeled stilettoes; and a black basque that pushed her breasts high and together, but didn't even cover her nipples. She thought for a moment about which panties to wear, then rejected them all. She wanted to feel the sexual excitement of nakedness – not that he would see anything anyway!

She dressed slowly, knowing that he would still be standing there in front of the open door. Even that thought made her wet. Finally, she was ready and she walked back to the lounge. On the way, she slammed the front door, which made him jump. He hadn't even realised that he had been exposed in front of an open door with the prospect that all his neighbours could have seen him, and with that realisation, his trepidation increased, as he knew that tonight she had another of her more devious plans.

She grabbed him by his cock and balls and led him to the bedroom. He was stumbling and falling in his blindness as he held back the cries of the pain of the walk. She stood him with his back close to the bed and she opened the first of her purchases.

Alexandra pulled out a large roll of cling film. Kneeling at his feet she started with his ankles, slowly wrapping it around him. She worked the plastic up his legs as she wrapped it tightly. By the time it reached his knees he was already unable to walk or move. She told him to put his hands by his side as she continued wrapping; covering him and immobilising him. She took great care as she moved up his legs. He had to be totally wrapped but she wanted his cock free and ready to be played with. She worked up his belly, past his chest, around his neck, over his face and round his head. He said nothing, but she knew that there would be fear, as by now he couldn't breathe, but she quickly relented by sticking a finger through the plastic into his mouth; he relaxed straight away.

She stood back to check her work. He was covered head to toe in cling film, except for his cock which stood out proud, twitching slightly; but she hadn't finished yet as there was still the main purchase to be applied. She took the first of the rolls of wide, black, heavy tape. She had really wanted to apply it directly, but she was concerned enough for him not to subject him to the pain of the tape being pulled off his skin when she had finished. Again starting at his ankles, she wrapped the black tape around his legs and up and up and over his head.

He was tottering, finding balance difficult, so with a gentle push on his chest he fell onto the bed. She could imagine his fear, not knowing if there was going to be a soft landing. She moved him to the middle of the bed and finished wrapping his feet with cling film and tape.

She stood back to look again at her handiwork. Apart from his cock and balls, you could see nothing of him. He was immobile, blindfolded, probably couldn't hear, could hardly talk and reduced to precisely what she wanted right then: a hard cock.

She now had what she wanted, and first, she gently stroked his cock, making sure it was hard, which is just how she wanted it. It would be a long time before she would let him come, however much he wanted it. She played with and teased his cock with her hand, her mouth and then her pussy when she sat on him with his cock deep inside her; it was in this position that she played with her clit, coming quickly to a large orgasm. This was the orgasm she had been waiting for all afternoon. She felt him get larger but still, she didn't want him to come just yet; she still had one more idea of how she would use him.

Now was the time to leave him alone for a moment. She wanted him to go soft for her next moment of enjoyment. She went to pour herself a glass of wine before returning. She was not away long; she would never leave him restrained without being watched, and so she sat in the chair at the end of the bed, watching him surely trying to understand what was happening and wondering what she would do next. He would want to know if she was there or not. He would want to know if he was going to be left for long. He knew she would be taking photographs, and in that, he was right.

He thought he was failing her because he knew his erection was leaving him, but that was exactly what she wanted.

She finished her wine and went back to the bed. She placed on his cock the 'five gates of hell'. These were five rings of steel joined by a leather strap, in total about twenty centimetres long. As he felt the cold steel and leather he knew what was happening, and she knew that he would now be desperately trying to avoid another erection. But as she placed it on his cock, she stroked it, and again he grew. Each ring was smaller than the previous one, but more importantly, all were smaller than the circumference of his fully expanded cock. Now they just fitted snuggly, but Alexandra kept stroking his cock to make it grow. As it grew, each ring started to dig deeper into his flesh, constraining his growing cock. She knew that he was in great pain, she could hear his muffled screams and that made her smile as she enjoyed the power she had over him. At this moment he would surely have given anything to have the rings taken off; but that was a forlorn hope because as his cock got larger and the rings dug in, they were constraining the blood coursing through it, keeping it huge – they could not have been taken off.

Alexandra looked at his beautiful large cock, straining under its constraints, and started to massage the tip; she knew that he was feeling both pain and pleasure: the pain of the rings and the pleasure of imminent orgasm. As he got larger and started to move and squirm, she took him in her mouth and drank deeply of the squirts of cum that exploded down her throat.

Alexandra was satisfied and knew that he would also be content that he had given himself for her enjoyment. She took the scissors and cut him free of his tapes and wrap. As his cock subsided she also took off the rings, wondering if she had gone too far as she saw the dark bruising forming on his cock where the rings of steel had been.

They showered together and held each other reflecting on their shared experience. They talked about dinner, they had dinner and all the while Alexandra was wondering what it would be like to tie him up so that he couldn't move, and then go to sleep next to him like that. That would require some more thought as she also deeply loved being held at night. But maybe…

11. IN A CITY CENTRE CAR

We are in our large 4x4 with tinted windows. I have been in a frisky mood all day and when I said that we should go for a drive into town, I had already decided that we were going to have some fun.

As soon as we are in the car I tell you to strip – totally, everything, the Full Monty! I love that plaintive and pathetic look you have when I make these suggestions. It's not that you don't want to do it; it's not that it doesn't turn you on; it's just that it's always me that has the idea first!

You sit next to me as I prepare to drive, and obediently you take off all your clothes, which I put into a bag and then put into the boot. I'm not going to let you get dressed again until I say so.

Then I have another surprise for you, my darling Mikhail: handcuffs and rope. It's not easy, but I manage to tie your hands behind your seat. I make sure you can't move and then drive to the centre of town.

Can anyone see through the darkened windows? Possibly. As we drive I take the opportunity to play with you, feeling your cock get harder and harder. In the middle of town, I park the car right on the side of the road where people are walking to work or just doing some shopping and stretch across to take you deep in my throat.

Maybe at first, I will just play with you, then slowly I will get naked too and we can have sex while people are walking past us, not six feet away. I will decide on that later.

12. CUCKOLD

The evening was falling late in Kyiv and Alexandra was thinking of him. He had become complacent and was starting to take her for granted. He had started to think that he was in control. Tonight he would learn his lesson.

Alexandra had found Andriy and he was perfect. He ran a special agency which offered very special services, and right now he was sitting in his office, feet on the desk, pushing back into the comfort of his old, well-worn reclining seat. He watched as cars swept along wide roads, as reckless and unpredictable as the neon lights that flashed and flickered from shops, offices and advertising hoardings.

He had seen pictures of women before thousands. Most he had cast aside. Some were living, you could see that in their eyes. Some were dead and looking only to re-live lives wasted in purity and childhood guilt, but this one had caught his eye. He flicked the picture over and reread the name on the back: Alexandra.

A pretty face and a provocative thumb pulling down on the top of a black skirt. He had always asked the questions but now she was questioning him. He put those thoughts aside – there was work to do, and he was away. He checked his watch. Seven-thirty, he would just make it on time.

His blue Porsche swung lazily into the sweeping drive of the Hotel Kyiv, the largest hotel in the city, on the crossroad of Oboronnaya and Sovetskaya Streets. He parked right outside: he wanted his car close.

The bar was on the top floor and was all chrome and leather. What had happened to the old run-down dives where real people propped their elbows on the bar and told their life stories to seasoned bartenders? They weren't here and for now, he was left with just this. He didn't much like the chrome and false friendliness, but they served the best martinis and the vodka was cold. He had taken a seat just past the bar and beyond the piano; from here he could see everything, and that was his job.

They were already here; he had spotted them as soon as he arrived and now they sat at the table behind him. He still hadn't seen her face but he knew it was her: Alexandra. There was just something in the way she moved, the perfume (J'Adore), her confidence and arrogance.

They were talking quietly, too quietly for him to hear, but he couldn't get nearer. He knew his chance would come – that had been arranged. Then it happened and he was ready: a commotion and panic. He turned to see the man trying to blot spilt water from his shirt.

'I'll have to go and get this sorted,' he said, then left. Alexandra smiled – she had deliberately spilt his drink. Now was the chance. Andriy swung round and as he stood up he brushed a shoulder with the water-sodden man. They exchanged a glance. Did he know what was going to happen? He couldn't.

'Alexandra?' She nodded assent. 'Quickly, come with me.'

Throwing some old used notes and coins on the table, Andriy grabbed her arm to lead her quickly to the lift. She hesitated, reached into her handbag, took a piece of paper and added it to the debris on the table. 'Ready,' she said, and they raced off. They were down, out and in the car well before he had returned.

It didn't take him long to dry his shirt and use the toilet and he was surprised that she wasn't there when he got back. He looked around the room and then he saw a scrap of paper on the table. Alexandra had written it earlier that afternoon and now it nestled among the notes. He had to read the note again. 'I had to go. Meet me at the apartment as soon as possible.' For the third time, he read the note and left.

Alexandra was quiet as the car raced and her heartbeat was almost as fast. She had agreed to this but now there was a nervous trepidation. It wasn't like the movies. No tearing of clothes as they tumbled into the house, just a search for the keys while Andriy stood by her, watching. Damn his calmness.

The lights had been turned down low and he looked at her. 'As beautiful as I thought you would be. Turn around. No, more slowly. Now get undressed.' There wasn't much to take off; just a dress and skimpy lingerie but Andriy watched as she slowly removed each piece of clothing. A reassuring nod and she again felt the excitement of her nakedness as he watched. There was a rumble at the door as her husband arrived.

'Just do as I said,' Andriy ordered, giving her the reassurance she craved before he headed into the bedroom and out of sight.

As he entered he saw her naked and he smiled, believing that this was a special treat she had arranged – he was nearly right.

'Take off your shirt,' she said. He needed no second invitation. 'Now turn around and close your eyes.' As he did, she wrapped the tape around his wrists, rendering him helpless. She wrapped a scarf around his eyes, making him blind; she gagged him to make him speechless; then she led him into the bedroom where Andriy was waiting. Andriy smiled as they came in. Alexandra pulled down her husband's pants to expose an erect and excited cock but she left him looking slightly ridiculous with his trousers around his ankles. She sat him in a kitchen chair and taped his ankles to the legs. Not a word had been spoken. What thoughts did he have as he sat in that chair? He could hear, but what could he hear? When was she going to come and touch him, he thought? His cock twitched and ached for attention.

Andriy walked up to Alexandra and kissed her, feeling her nakedness as she reached out to undo his shirt, which fell silently to the floor. It was then that her immobilised husband heard a dull moan from Alexandra as she and Andriy locked in an embrace. His head moved to the side as he tried to hear more. He struggled at his ties but he couldn't move. What was happening?

'My darling husband,' she said to the tied man, 'you have been neglecting me recently, you have flirted with secretaries, you have been drinking and gambling and generally you have been a very poor husband. You need to understand that if you don't change then I will change you,' and with that, she took off his blindfold so that he could see her and Andriy. Clearly, he was trying to ask who he was but still, he couldn't speak. 'Now watch,' Alexandra said, 'this could be your future, and mine if you don't change your ways.'

Showing more confidence than she felt, Alexandra walked back to Andriy and threw her arms around him, pushing her body close to his. Then, pulling away from their embrace, Alexandra pulled off Andriy's clothes and admired his sculpted body. Falling to her knees she reached out and took him in her hand. He was large and she slowly started to kiss him. She took him in her mouth, then took more and more until she pushed her head onto him, oblivious to the dulled screams from the chair behind her.

He felt so large, she thought; she knew he was about to climax and she wanted to taste every drop of him. But he pushed her away, lifted her into his arms and lay her on the silk sheets of her bed. Slowly his tongue started to give her pulses of pure excitement and she too was arriving at a climax when again, he stopped. Andriy looked up, moved forward, they kissed and he pushed himself deep inside her.

Alexandra lay back as the waves of heat and excitement flooded through her whole body. Her climax was building again and she felt him getting bigger deep, deep inside her, when suddenly, with a scream of release, they came together.

Alexandra sunk back into mellow satisfaction as she glanced at the chair. He was still tied, bound and speechless, but not blind to what had happened. What was that look on his face? Whatever it was, he was still throbbing and large. He had got something out of it, but had he learned the lesson? Already Alexandra had determined that there would be no release for him that night.

Andriy swept up his clothes and smiled at Alexandra. A smile of thanks or a smile of satisfaction? She couldn't tell. Through her exhaustion, she waved back weakly and he was gone.

13.   TIED

Naturally, I am someone who demands control, but as I wanted to try everything in the belief that opinions only have weight when they have been experienced, I needed to venture into new areas. What good is it to quote other people? So, if I was controlling others – deliberately or otherwise – I needed to understand what it was like to be controlled.

To find the truth I sought, I needed to give myself to someone else and let them dictate my path. I also determined that I would try everything and have every experience.

I had this discussion with Ioana who was on the same course as me. It was under her advice that I started on a more structured research programme, and my first task was to experience what I was demanding of others.

Control, I know, has many components, and I wanted to experience every one of them. There was only one person who I could both trust and take into my confidence. It was Ioana who made the arrangements for the first adventure.

I had been at the university for just an hour when he called. His directions were specific, and so, after a hasty and poor excuse, I was home again by noon. He would be here at an unspecified time, but not before two when I had to be ready and wait without complaint.

I replayed the voice message. I wanted to be sure everything would meet his approval. It was now time and I was fully prepared and a little scared. The high-backed, wooden kitchen chair was placed in the hall facing the front door, which had been left slightly ajar.

I was naked; legs spread wide and held in place by a bar running behind the front chair legs; my pussy pushed forward by cushions behind my back; I was blindfolded, gagged and handcuffed behind the chair. This was the ultimate in self-bondage. I could not move, and the increasing dryness in my mouth was countered by the widening stain of sex juices on the chair slats. Only for a short moment did I wonder what I would do if he didn't arrive. How long would I be here before I was discovered?

Anticipation is the greatest aphrodisiac. How long had I been there? A slight breeze across my already hardened nipples excited every nerve end. Every sense was heightened.

Was he here in the room? Has the door just blown open, making me visible to any stranger walking down the street? Was that stranger now looking at me, wondering if he should take the opportunity that I presented? Or maybe it was not a man but a woman who was having the same thoughts.

The shock of the handcuffs being released sent a palpable shiver through my already hot thighs. Unable to walk, I was dragged and thrown face down on a table. Legs wide, I was exposed, I was wet, and yet still the first thrust into my pussy sent waves of sexual heat through my body. I came first: he quickly followed. Not a word had been said. Then I heard the door close as he left.

I had never seen him and now was no different.

When I arrived at university I had only been with men and never cast a thought about being with a woman. Indeed, if any of my girlfriends at school had made a pass at me I would have run a mile. So when I decided that I should also have the experience of making out with a woman, it wasn't any change of sexuality but simply the need to have a new experience.

For example, men get turned on by cupping a breast, sucking on a nipple and licking a pussy, so don't I have a responsibility (if I wanted men to be perfect when they did that to me) to know what they were experiencing? I needed at least to have experiences with women.

Actually, I would say exactly the same to men. You should want to know what a woman is feeling when she sucks your cock, when you stick it deep down her throat, when you want her to take your cum in her mouth. Only when you have lived with her view of the world can you be great as a lover. You need to have been in her place. If you want to have the best experience yourself you need to have been in her place at least once. Then you can tell her what you want her to do differently or better.

Boys, it doesn't mean you are gay or even bi-sexual. If you expect every woman to take a piece of your anatomy into your mouth, is it so bad that you do the same?

14.   IOANA

Today was to be her own time, a time when Alexandra could explore more fully and more deeply her understanding of power. By now she had been seeing him for nearly four months and she needed some space and time to reflect on where she was; Ioana was the means to that end.

Ioana and Alexandra had known each other from their first days at university, and as much as anyone was Alexandra's friend, she was. They had first met soon after Alexandra had come to Kyiv, in the days when Alexandra was still so unsure of herself. Those were the days when she was still forming the views that are now so strong but then so tentative. She might have had her own apartment, but she retained little else of the core of what Alexandra used to be. They were on the same journey and their paths crossed often, and as Alexandra became more selective of how she spent her time and who she was with, it was Ioana who always seemed to be at the same clubs or parties.

The first time Alexandra had seen her, she ignored her. She chose her friends carefully, and they were few. Their first conversation happened at a roadside café. Alexandra was wasting away an afternoon on coffee and dreams and Ioana just came and sat down.

'Hi, we always seem to be meeting. I'm Ioana.' At first, Alexandra was wary of this intrusion into her time, she didn't want to talk or meet or be part of anyone else's day. It was warm and she was sitting outside, and she was alone.

'Mind if I join you?'

Alexandra just nodded and pointed at the empty seat. Then it all changed.

'How do you control someone? I mean, how do you make someone do what you want so that they really want to do it?' Iona had asked.

This was a question, still without an answer, that Alexandra had been working on for many months.

'Good sex?' said Alexandra, looking up for almost the first time.

'No. That can't last. It goes. There is always someone else who is promising better sex, different sex, illicit sex. No, it can't be just good sex.'

'What about love?' Alexandra had put down her paper and was looking straight into Ioana's eyes. They were brown and sparkled with humour and mischief. Alexandra carefully looked at her and thought that she was pretty, not beautiful, but she was sexy and sensual. Her hair was fair and bobbed onto her shoulders.

'What turns you on?' Alexandra asked.

'Beauty, charm, erotic games, sensuousness, refinement, intelligence.' Ioana said, without hesitation. And then, 'control' after a few seconds' thought.

This caught Alexandra again. 'So, what is control? How do I know when I have control?'

'Ah, that's the journey we are both on and when we have finished we will know.'

Since then, many times, they had sat at roadside cafés over long summer afternoons, talking. She understood the control and manipulation of men in ways Alexandra was still only learning.

Now, as she was in the taxi going across town, Alexandra was thinking about that first conversation. And as she was watching people and cars, she was wondering: *do they know what I am about to do?* She wasn't sure about it herself but she had this feeling that people who stared in at her in the taxi knew.

Some condemn while others are jealous. They want to know why you're not working; after all, it was still early evening. There was a slight autumn drizzle and the wipers moved intermittently across the windscreen, hardly shifting the oil and grease, leaving great smears. How could he see where he was going? Did he know where she was going?

Ioana opened the door of the flat. Alexandra had been here before but never with such a feeling of trepidation and excitement. She had phoned Ioana two days ago and asked if she could help Alexandra explore control in the way she saw it. Imagination was Alexandra's way. If you excite the mind to desire, wanton lust and intimidation, you can have control; Ioana's way was physical.

This was Ioana's apartment and fashioned in her style. It was dark and gothic with a rich intensity that was overpowering. It was lush and opulent, full of passionate reds.

When I arrived, Ioana hardly said a word. I looked at her carefully. She is smaller than me and her breasts are fuller. She was wearing a black basque that pushed her breasts up and close together; it tapered into her slim waist. The sides were cut high and her nipples were visible and erect. All in all, it was disconcerting and added to an increasing concern.

'Hello Alexandra,' she said, with no warmth in her voice. She took my hand. 'Come this way.'

Was fear etched on my face? I tried to be composed but this wasn't the Ioana of the cafés. This was different. How different, I didn't know. Would I find out?

'Get undressed. Take your clothes off.' I felt a shiver of excitement and started to understand. All carefully folded, I laid each item neatly onto the floor and started to feel naked and exposed in a way I had never felt with a man.

Ioana led me to the bed. It was round in shape, and spread equally around there were four leather ties attached firmly to the floor and laid out neatly on the top of the bed. The leather enhanced the richly coloured red silk sheet.

'Lie down,' she said. First, she took my ankles, and with slow caresses along my legs she tied me down. Then she pulled each wrist into position, and they were tied. I was spread out and exposed. My legs were spread wider than was comfortable and fear and excitement tingled through my body.

What would happen?

Nothing at first; she walked around the bed, just looking, taking in the shape on her bed. Was I just a body or an actual person? Occasionally she ran a trailing hand across me. Once she caught my pussy and my back arched in the sudden and unexpected shock, but neither the hand nor the excitement stayed long. Suddenly, I so much wanted her to be tender and gentle, but could I hope for that?

'You haven't shaved your pussy lately. That's naughty. You've been bad. You should have known I would like you to have shaved'.

I was always clean-shaven but even in a few days, some small stubble had grown. I didn't know I was supposed to be shaved. How could I know? This was my first time with her. Yet, still, I felt guilty. I craned my neck to try and see but I was tied too tight.

'We will have to do something about that. You just lie there,' she said as if I had a choice.

I felt her slightly loosen the ties on my ankles, and just like a wedge, a pillow was pushed under my back, projecting and pushing my pussy in the air. Ioana tied ropes to each of my thighs just above the knees. Fixing each rope to the ties holding my wrists, she pulled on each one, forcing my knees up and parting my legs even more. I was on my back, my pussy pushed towards the ceiling, my knees in the air and my legs stretched as wide as they could possibly go. I was helpless to her whim.

Lifting up my bottom, she pushed a white towel underneath me before squirting my pussy with foam. The sound and the touch excited me and I could feel myself getting hot as the cold foam ran around and into my pussy, and after each gush of soap she rubbed and massaged it in further. I could only imagine the circle of white foam around my pussy, but I could feel the tender touch on my labia.

Maybe there isn't much difference between us, for here was my imagination taking over before suddenly I felt the first rough tear of the razor cutting through my pubic hairs. She had started to shave me clean. She was delicate and it seemed that with each stroke her fingers slowly rubbed me to a new sensual high. I moaned slowly to a climax, which she held down by pushing her hand against me. She had finished shaving, and she took a soft towel to carefully wipe away every last vestige of soap.

I felt as though I sparkled like a new pin, but in my cleanliness, my sense of vulnerability and exposure had increased. As if to test my assertion, Ioana bent over and licked at the now smooth skin. Her lips, and then her tongue, explored round and round, but she never quite satisfied my inward lust. Her tongue licked with darting precision as I twisted and turned to encourage her to explore new areas. But I was held firm by the ties and was ultimately frustrated.

I had given up all hope of release when she pulled the lips of my pussy apart and suddenly plunged her tongue deep inside me. I squealed with delight at this new sensation. It was so different from anything a man could do. A man is rough and hard, but she was gentle and soft. In deep and in slowly; slowly and around I felt the soft skin of her cheek against my inner thighs; again I hoped for release but she stopped short.

She eased away and left me lying there in my own thoughts. I was relaxed and my eyes were closed when she returned and I smelt her sweet perfume as she walked around to my head. I thought of her leaning over to stroke my hair and smooth my face when suddenly I felt her pull my hair and lift my head, as a gag was stuffed crudely into my mouth.

I couldn't see what it was, but it felt like a rubber ball. At first, I struggled for air while she tied it tight with straps that went both round and over my head. I tried to spit it out but it was held firm. I stared into Ioana's eyes and saw a sparkle of venom of the kind I had never seen before. It was a hard, uncompromising look, filled with her own delight at my struggles. Was there even a vague hint of a smile on her face?

I wondered what she had in mind for me. What evil, what pain?

But then she started to massage me. I was confused but maybe confusion was part of her game. She covered me in oil and stroked and soothed my body. She took each foot and her hands ran up my ankles to deep inside my thighs. She walked around the bed and, taking each breast, she squeezed and rubbed as each nipple grew harder. Like bread dough, she kneaded my belly. My excitement grew and I was longing for her touch on my pussy again. I wanted to tell her but the only noise I could make was a low moan.

She stopped as suddenly as she had started. I was confused. I was relaxed, the massage had seen to that, but then I was also afraid. I was not used to pain and clearly, the gag was meant to stifle any cries, but was it really meant to give her control? I couldn't speak, I could issue no instructions, I was powerless to stop her, whatever she felt like doing.

Again she left me, and then she returned with six golden-coloured balls, joined together with a black cord held above me so I could take in what she had. Two were the size of an egg, and the other four were smaller. They glistened and clanked together. She waved them above me as I lay on the bed looking up helplessly. How long had I been here? I didn't know.

Moving down the bed and facing away, she sat astride me. It made no difference as I couldn't lift my head anyway, to see what was happening.

Last time it was foam, this time I felt oil being dripped onto me and rubbed along and inside both my pussy and my anus. Two of the balls were eased slowly into my wet pussy, and there was a real joy as I felt them move even deeper inside me, massaging as no cock could ever do. I almost thought I could hear them clink together as I moved and strained against my leashes. Then, suddenly, the other four were pushed deep inside my bottom. This was a different sensation as the four balls pulled and clicked against each other.

I felt Ioana gently play and pull at the cord to massage me more deeply. My moans were deeper and longer as I reached new heights. I was hot, I felt hot, and I felt sensations I had never felt before. Was this because of what she was doing? Would it have been different if he was doing it? Was it because I was restrained? I didn't know and I was almost unable to think as the waves of tension and excitement raced through my body. This was sensuous and deeply arousing – this was not Ioana, as I knew her. She must have seen the pleasure on my face.

The golden balls were left where they were as she returned with a blaze of red velvet material. She just looked and smiled as it was tied around my eyes. Gradually, all of my senses were being taken away. I could not move, I could not talk and now, I could not see. All that was left was to feel.

I felt her hold my breast, and then my head was lifted as what felt like a cord was placed behind my neck. I felt it cross over my chest and then suddenly wrapped around a breast. She tied it slowly. It went round and round as I felt a surge of blood pumping in the breast. The cord was tight. And then she tied the other breast with the same intensity and crude roughness. I felt both sharp pain and a dull ache.

Ioana had not said anything for some time, but then suddenly said:

'Let me tell you what I see. Both your breasts are now tightly bound and hard. The blue of the veins is standing out. Your nipples are erect.'

The ropes were tight; my breasts were painful and tears started to swell under the mask as she turned and twisted some clamps onto my nipples. First one and then the other. As much as I could I took deep breaths, but beneath the pain, strangely I could feel both pleasure and excitement.

What further humiliation could there be for me?

Quickly and painfully the balls were pulled out from inside me.

I heard the crack of tape being unwound from its reel, once, twice, five times in all. She told me to raise myself and I felt the sticky tape on my back. Three pieces were dangling along the line of my back towards my bottom while two went across towards my belly. What was this for?

Suddenly I felt the pain of what turned out to be dildos being inserted – one in my pussy and one in my bottom. They were small and thin and ice cold. Metal?

The first was eased into my bottom and the second into my aching pussy; again the ecstasy and the pain, the exhilaration and the humiliation.

I wanted to push them out and I tried. I usually use my strong pelvic floor muscles to control when a man comes inside me, but now they fought in vain as Ioana resisted them. Long before me, she had known what I would do, and that was the reason for the tape: the dildos had been taped into place. The three strands of tape ran from back to front and two more around to stop them from moving. I could not move, nor could they.

'That will do fine for the moment. I need a break and so do you. I'll be back.'

I heard her steps and the door clicked closed. My breasts, pussy and bottom all ached, but each time I moved a little to ease the pain, the excitement built. I could feel I was coming to a climax again. Could I stand it, could I face it? For once in my life, an orgasm was the last thing I wanted. How long would I be here? I struggled and then the waves of a climax overtook me, so intense, so exhilarating; it shook my body as the orgasm surged through me. Would it ever stop?

Was it an eternity? I can't remember, but I heard the door open and Ioana returned.

'Hmmm, what have you been doing? How are we?' She ripped at the tape as the dildos popped out. She undid the straps around my ankles and I felt her attach new leather cuffs. I moved my legs back together to ease the ache of them being held apart. Then my wrists were released, but again, cuffs were attached. Should I try to move or run? There seemed no point and I just lay there.

'Get up,' she demanded. It wasn't easy, as still, I could not see, but I felt her hand gently come to lead me.

'Stand here.' I didn't know where I was, but I stood as instructed. Ioana removed my blindfold and I found I was standing with my back close to the wall. The gag remained. I looked down as she clipped together the two leather straps around my wrists. My hands were across my belly as if trying to protect a modesty that had already been violated. My hair was damp and limp in strands across my face, knotted together through the sweat and exhaustion. I tried to plead with my eyes for no more but it was clear that there would be no respite.

Again, I looked around the room. It was dark outside. I looked towards the window. The curtain wasn't pulled. Across the street were more apartments, each with a view of me. Was I part of some great elaborate show? Did I now even care?

I was drifting in my own thoughts when suddenly my arms were jerked upwards. Ioana had taken a rope through a ring on the wall above my head, and with my hands tied together, pulled them upwards; a captive again.

She kicked my legs apart and to each ankle bracelet, she attached the end of a stiff rod, which kept my legs spread-eagled.

Tied as I was, I could do little more than watch, and I watched as Ioana undressed. It was seductive and sensuous, exhilarating and sexy. She danced in front of me, she brushed against me, she turned and twisted, excited and tantalised. I couldn't touch her, nor could I touch myself. I so much wanted to do both.

As I looked down, she knelt in front of me. I wanted to believe that she was going to touch me. Instead, I felt the sharp pain of clips – what they were I couldn't see – being attached to the outer lips of my pussy. I was being opened up and explored. The pain was great but still, I sensed the shared pleasure as she kissed deep inside my exposed pussy. Time was endless. I rocked and reared, wanting to scream. Scream with pleasure and cry with pain.

Slowly it died away. I was untied, and finally, the gag was removed.

I started to speak but no words formed.

'Put on your boots and your coat. I will send your clothes around later.

She sent me away naked, more naked than I had ever been.

I sat in the taxi returning to my apartment. I was numb. I didn't know what time it was, I hardly knew where I was.

When Alexandra was back home, she slid gratefully into a deep, hot bath. This was not a cleansing bath or a catholic act of forgiveness. These were not the thoughts that Alexandra had. It was the start of a time for reflection, which would last for many months.

When she was with him she had never really hurt him physically She had played games with him, teased him so that he always thought that he didn't know her. Did she hold onto him only because of his curiosity? When he thought he had drained the last of her, would he go? Where did that strict physical control that she had just experienced with Ioana fit?

Are we naturally either submissive or dominant or can we be both? For now, Alexandra was confused. She didn't know if she would see Ioana again, at least, so intimately. She wasn't sure if she could ever meet her again.

15.   MORE THAN ONE

Maybe through my words, I sound sane and sensible, or maybe you have a different opinion of me, but despite all my bravado, there were times when I did question myself. It was in these darker moments that I had my own dark fantasies.

Because of its darkness, I was very unsure if I should include this fantasy, but as my friends keep telling me, I need to be as open and honest as I can.

I want to show you that you are allowed to have wild and extreme fantasies and there is nothing wrong with them, but if you want to go that step further and live it out, please be very careful. You are about to enter a very dangerous world and you need to be sure of the people you are playing with, and your limits.

Alexandra had always wanted to think of herself as a one-man woman, and she felt she was, but there was always a part of her that wanted to know what it was like to be with more than one man. To be the centre of all their attention was what she craved. She was now single and there was no reason why she couldn't try it.

Her first steps were tentative and thoughtful; very thoughtful. This was a big step. She had thought that two men would be a good start but she hadn't planned on meeting Igor.

Igor was very slightly older and had been single for longer than Alexandra. He had been swinging for a time, and it seemed, on reflection, that it was his smooth words that had convinced her that a larger number of participants would be better. Alexandra and Igor had had sex together a couple of times and he was persuasive; Alexandra agreed to a bigger meeting. Then she found herself agreeing to more than just a group – she had agreed to be a sex slave for them for an evening.

'What does that mean, sex slave?' she asked.

'You allow us to do whatever we want without any objection,' he replied.

Alexandra was both petrified and excited. Is this what she

wanted? Igor said he would make sure everything would be fine and safe. On reflection, Alexandra should have remembered the deep Russian male propensity to be violent. The meeting was fixed for five days away, and as each day passed, Alexandra became more anxious. Then the day arrived. Igor collected her to take her to his home.

'The boys want to watch some football first,' he said, as they walked in. You can serve them their drinks.'

Alexandra thought that sounded easy enough.

'Now get undressed and give me your clothes,' he said.

'What?'

'Yes,' he said. 'You will not be dressed in our presence.'

At that moment, fear and flight were in Alexandra's mind, but Igor put his hands gently on her shoulders. 'It will be ok. I will look after you. Now get undressed.'

With a compliance that surprised her, Alexandra stepped out of her clothes and stood with her hands crossed in front of her, trying to maintain a modicum of modesty. The doorbell rang.

'Get that, Alexandra, please,' Igor shouted.

'Like this?'

'Yes, like that.'

Alexandra went to the door, petrified. She opened it. Two men were there with a pack of beer under their arms.

'Very nice,' one said, as they walked in and went to talk to Igor. Alexandra was crestfallen. They had hardly noticed her. The third and fourth arrived, each with the same apparent disinterest. She watched them settle down on the sofa to watch the television.

'Beers please, Alexandra,' Igor called, and obediently she fetched them all a drink.

'Now, Alexandra,' he said, as she was pouring his beer 'we can't have you just wandering about. Here are the rules. When I point one finger downwards,' and he showed her what he meant, 'kneel in front of me and wait for your next instruction. When I point two fingers down like this, kneel facing away from me, with your bottom in the air for all of us to see.'

He pointed two fingers down and Alexandra turned her back to them all and knelt on all fours, fully exposing herself. Her pussy was wet and she could feel the moisture slowly oozing onto her thighs.

Once she tried to touch herself in between collecting drinks and kneeling, but she received a sharp smack across her bottom.

'We won't have you come yet,' Igor said.

Pizzas were ordered and they soon arrived, although Alexandra was sent to the door to pay the pizza boy. She stood there, naked, collecting the boxes and paying. By now she was used, in part, to being nude among dressed men, but again Igor had found a way to upset the equilibrium. Although the pizza boy (and Alexandra could see from the bulge in his trousers, that he was actually more a pizza *man*) tried to prolong the encounter, it was Igor who delayed her as he fumbled for change.

They sat at the table to eat. Alexandra was hoping she would be offered some food.

'Can I have something to eat, please,' she asked?

'Get under the table,' Igor said. 'You can eat our cocks, one by one.'

Alexandra wondered if she was really doing this. Was this really her? But it was like a drug, and she crawled under the table to do as she was asked. She could hear the voices and the laughter but see only legs. She had to start somewhere and she reached up to undo the trousers of one man. She undid his belt and lowered the zip, and could feel his cock getting hard as she pulled it out, but she couldn't tell if he was showing any other reaction. Did his friends know that she had started with him? One by one she sucked each cock, and just as she thought that he was going to come, each pulled away.

'Right, Alexandra,' Igor said, as they got up from the table. 'We don't need you for the moment, we need to get ready. You wait here. But we need to make sure you don't play with yourself. Give me your wrists,' and with that, he tied them behind her back. 'And you don't need to see what is happening either,' and he put a black hood over her head and lead her to the corner of the room, where she was left.

Had she been able to see, she would have seen them shower one by one, and put on black hooded robes so that she couldn't tell one from the other. She would also have seen that they were pulling back the carpet to reveal a small trap door.

Alexandra's mask was taken off and she saw the five, robed men. She was shocked and her knees buckled a little at the eerie sight. Igor led her to the trap door, knelt her down carefully and undid the rope on her wrist.

She looked as the trap door was opened and her head was pushed into a small rectangular space hardly larger than her head, lined with wood. She felt a wooden fitting like medieval stocks being closed around her; she heard a metal bolt locking it closed; she was trapped.

She pulled at the trap door but she couldn't move. The space was claustrophobic. Fear, anticipation and excitement surrounded her. Alexandra was kneeling with her head in a box below the floor that forced her back straight up into the air. She tried to move her head out; she couldn't. Her legs were being pulled apart and she felt clamps on her ankles and calves and then her wrists were fixed so that she could not even squirm.

Alexandra tried to imagine what the sight was for the hooded men. There was a headless body with a wet pussy and arse facing them.

The first penetration was deep and rough. As each man took her – and sometimes it was two at a time – Alexandra moved to a state of detachment. Her body was being used, and often used roughly. There was more pain than stimulation, as through the tears her thoughts detached from her body and she saw herself being abused. Reluctantly, she climaxed. They came deep inside her, and yet still they carried on. Alexandra lost track of time. How long does it take five men to satisfy their most basic of all carnal desires, she thought?

The penetration finally stopped and, with relief, Alexandra heard the bolt being withdrawn. The trap was opened and she was being pulled out. She was stiff from being tied so awkwardly and nearly fell as she tried to stand. She knew that with the tears her mascara would have run and stained her face, leaving her at her most unattractive. But for once she didn't care about that. Her thoughts were now solely to find her clothes and get home to a bath.

So that is it, she thought, I have tried it; being used like a slut.

She was collecting her thoughts and hoping to collect her clothes, as she was carried and laid on a table. She no longer had the energy to resist and did not even need to be tied to keep her there.

They took her again. She was penetrated in both her pussy and arse at the same time, and the grinding became intense. A cock was thrust down her throat and she found one cock in each hand. Slowly she moved her hands. Five cocks and Alexandra. One by one with her hand the men all came, the last ones over her face.

'Get dressed,' Igor said. She obeyed. 'Here is money for your taxi. I will call you tomorrow,' and before she really had time to think, she was in a car, wiping the cum from her face and hair.

Once, Alexandra thought, just once. But never again.

Alexandra

IV. MIKHAIL – HIS STORY

I was very mean to Mikhail, but in his own way he needed to be treated like that, and even today I wonder if it was very cruel of me. However, that is who I was, and there is no turning back the clock and wishing for different days.

These are not all current thoughts because even then I tried to put myself in his shoes, to wonder how he felt.

I have never liked weak and subservient men. I like 'real' men; I like romantic men; and I like men with a strong, independent streak who know what they want. It doesn't matter if I am in Kyiv, London or around Europe, I can't stand pathetic, cowardly or wimpish men who, to my mind, literally have no balls!

With strong men, there is a wonderful battle of the genders which is both intellectual as well as physical.

Don't get me wrong, I do also like romantic men and romantic moments; I like sitting on the sofa, cuddled together, watching a film; I like shopping together; I like it when he says he loves me and wants to make love to me; I like it when we shower together and he wraps me in a towel and carries me to the bed, but sometimes that is not enough.

It was around this time that I discovered that I also like to be in control. Even in the relationships that lasted any length of time, there were always those moments when I enjoyed being in control of my man. I like to tease, tie and sometimes even cause pain to my men. It gives me immense sexual satisfaction, and I get a real high from the control I exert. I like to be the one in a relationship that sets the sexual agenda.

These feelings were at their strongest and most powerful at that time in Kyiv, and Mikhail was the focus of all my desires. It was in this mix, during those years, that Mikhail was the recurring theme of my life.

I didn't want to emasculate him and have him follow me around like a lap dog. I didn't want him to stop being the strong alpha male in his other activities, it was just when it came to sex that I took control. I was never bossy, domineering or even a dominatrix in our public life because this wasn't a fetish, just the way I felt about sex. Particularly at this time in my life and in this relationship, this was the way I was, and it was the only way I could even envisage a long-term relationship.

As a good psychologist, I have undertaken an analysis of myself, considering if I was protecting myself from something or if it was simply a sign of how I deal with men in general. It is not. It is simply a preference and nothing more should be read into it.

I adore men who love me so deeply and passionately that they will do everything they can to make me happy, and if submitting to some of my wilder and more painful moments is what they have to do to show me their love, then that is wonderful. In fact, the less they actually like what is happening, the more I love them for their submission.

Mikhail was such a man. Strong in body and mind, he was a successful writer in Kyiv. For a moment I thought I loved him – I know he loved me – but then I pulled back. My rules hadn't changed and I still needed to work on my master's degree, I had my modelling and I didn't want any extra obligations.

Our relationship started gently but became serious, and for a time we lived together, but soon I realised he was a jealous man. He could be out without telling me, but he wouldn't allow the same for me. I would have been faithful if he hadn't tried to pin me down and promise faithfulness. I rebelled and tried to exert my own control.

It became a battle of wills and one that he was always going to lose. The experience of whips and candle wax were, for Mikhail, far less painful than the thought processes and power I exerted. He will tell you that the most painful moment was when I stopped seeing him, but that, as they say, was his problem, not mine. I had other ventures and roads to follow.

I now feel a little sorry for Mikhal who just happened to be the man in my life at that time because, in hindsight, it was less obvious at the time, it is now easy to understand. I needed to explore a full range of fetish activities and those areas of sexuality that are outside the norm of most people. After all, isn't some form of fetish at the core of all fantasy?

I needed to know and to quench my thirst for this knowledge, I had to give up some of my preconceptions and role in life.

In those selfish moments when I decided that a relationship was finished, I didn't spare much of a thought for my partner. Should I have? I don't know, but I did once in a while try to see it from their perspective, although it made me no more compassionate towards them!

Soon my academic and personal interests collided again, and once more I took the selfish line. I still saw Mikhail, but I found that the more he wanted me, the more I needed to control him.

These are his stories and words.

Alexandra

16. A FOREST QUEEN

I am never sure what my Queen has in store for me, but I always do as she wants; so it was with excitement, more than trepidation, that we drove off in the car. She had already warned me that today she was feeling like she was my Queen and would give me naughty instructions.

We drove out of town and towards the countryside, then into the woods. We parked and she took her rucksack and said, 'follow me'.

We chatted about nothing much as we walked deeper into the forest along a path, nodding greetings to other ramblers before we turned off the route. Then she stopped about 10 metres off the path. My Queen stopped, turned to me, and said, 'get undressed, everything'. There was nothing else for it at this point but to do as I was told. She took my clothes and put them in her bag before taking out her rope.

Throwing the rope over a high branch, she tied my wrists and pulled them above my head and then each ankle, so that my legs were spread wide. As I looked I could just make out the shape of others walking the path we had just walked. She took the gag so that I couldn't speak, and then my Queen blindfolded me. Naked and suspended, gagged and blind, she whispered in my ear.

'I'm going to get a coffee and maybe something to eat. I'm sure you'll be alright here. After all, you aren't going anywhere. I just hope I can find you again when I come back!'

Alexandra

17. SHE TEASES ME

I am sitting at home with Alexa. We have had our dinner and are now sitting on the sofa. The television is on but is hardly being watched as I am telling you about the problems at the gym. You listen; you laugh a little, and when I have finished my story you get up, saying you have to go to the toilet. It is natural and I hardly notice, except when you come back you're wearing that naughty look in your eye and you're carrying an upright chair from the kitchen.

Putting the chair right in the middle of the room you say 'Mikhail, get undressed and sit here'. I know better than to question you or ask you why or what you are going to do, so I do as I am told and sit down.

'Now, hands behind your back.' Doing as I am told, you clasp them together with your handcuffs. 'I just don't want you to play with yourself,' you whisper in my ear.

I nod, relieved that it seems I am not going to be smacked.

You stand in front of me, close enough for me to touch, stroke or caress you, if only I was free to move.

As you kneel down in front of me and look at my crotch, seeing my quickly growing cock, I close my eyes in anticipation of your lips and mouth taking me. But I feel nothing and I look at you. You are still just inches away from me.

'I know what you want, my darling,' you say, 'but not tonight,' and that only makes my cock even harder.

Standing in front of me, and with the background music soft and the candles casting a gentle glow, you slowly do a striptease. It is a long and sensuous tease. A blouse is removed and then a skirt and you are standing in only silky, skimpy lingerie, black stockings and high heels. All the time you are teasing my cock; nearly touching it; nearly holding and pulling it and nearly sucking it, but each time you stop when you get close; each time my cock grows harder while the frustration intensifies. It is throbbing and hurting and I wonder if I will come without even being touched.

My eyes are fixed on you as you remove your bra. I look at your breasts and beautiful nipples, and as you move close to me I hope that I will be allowed to suck them, but again you take away the ultimate pleasure. The only touch is once when you drape your bra across my cock and watch as it jumps and twitches as if it had a life of its own, but you stop. You don't want me to have so much fun!

You are wearing the skimpiest of sexy knickers. I look hard at you and I think they might be just a little bit transparent and I believe, more in hope than in reality, that I can see your pussy; but it's all wishful thinking.

I was going to say that I didn't have to wait long before you finished the striptease, but that would be a lie because the tease continued.

'Please undo my hands so that I can touch you, kiss you and make love to you,' I say.

'No, if I did that you would only play with yourself and I want you to concentrate on me. Now watch carefully,' you say.

What else could I do? You are right, that is what would happen, so I try to ignore the pressure building in my balls and my twitching cock.

Finally, you remove that veil of flimsy material and I see your beautiful and very wet pussy. I so much want to lick it and my cock so wants to enter it, but there is no hope of that. As you stand in front of me you play with your pussy, touching your hard, wet clit. I know what is happening. You are going to have an orgasm and I can only watch and have no part. I can only watch as your fingers dig deep inside your pussy.

I see the signs as your tummy tenses, your eyes start to close, your legs start to quiver, you start to moan and suddenly you thrust your pussy close to my face. Am I going to be allowed to lick it and make that final moment special? No. Instead, you have an orgasm, a special orgasm, and as you explode you squirt onto my face and into my mouth.

You sink onto the floor trying to compose yourself. I can hear your heavy breathing.

'Let me go so I can hold you,' I ask.

'What, with a cock as hard as that? As soon as you're free you will chase me down and make passionate love to me and make me come again.'

Then you add: 'Hopefully!' And with that, you undo the ties.

Alexandra

18.   ONE HOUR TO BE READY

Alexandra would send me a simple text message. It would say, maybe, 'be ready in one hour'. I would shower and take out the few toys we had: shackles, blindfolds, ropes, whip, candles and a strap-on. There were others that she used by taking normal household bits and pieces, but you will have to use your imagination for those. I would kneel, naked, in front of the door, wearing a blindfold. I would wait to hear the turn of the key with trepidation. What mood would she be in? Would she be hard on me? I don't like pain. I don't do this for pain, I do it for love, but I will do whatever she wants to show that love. I would hear the steps towards me and feel the run of her fingernails across my back.

'Good boy,' she might say. 'Stay still, I will be back. But we had better make sure.' She would stand me up and tie my hands behind my back. And there I would stand while she prepared herself. I couldn't see but I knew what would be happening.

She would shower and change. Probably – or hopefully – she would wear crotchless knickers, black fish-net stockings, and a basque which held her breasts firm and maybe expose her nipples. Her hair would be drawn back tight and her lips painted a dark, full red. Of course, I could not see until the end when we had finished, as throughout I would be blindfolded.

But I could imagine, and the imagination combined with apprehension would make me hard. Whether she wore panties at this stage, I could not tell. Sometimes, after we had finished, I might see a pair of discarded silk knickers, but not always. But then there were the high-heeled shoes. The floors were marble and it was the sound of them returning that meant the start of my ordeal. Then I would start to flinch, waiting for the first touch. Would it be gentle, a hand drawn across my belly? Or the whip across my buttocks? I would never know.

What happened next would depend on her desires and imagination, but let me tell you about one particular day.

With my hands still tied, she used the soft whip first on my back and then my thighs. I could tell she was in a hard mood today. This was a warm-up for worse to come. It's not always the feel of the whip that hurts, but the thought of what is to come. You can hear the movement before it hits and the body moves away.

'Come here,' she says, as she leads me across the room. My hands are untied. 'Lean forward,' and as I do I feel the chair on my belly and my hands are retied to the chair. I know what is coming. I am standing, leaning forward, resting on the chair. I can't hear, but I know what she is doing: she is putting on the strap-on. I expect that next, she will take the lubrication to make it easier for me, but instead, I am smacked. It is hard. It happens again and again. It hurts but I am not allowed to stop her. We have a safe word but if I use it I will have let her down and then I feel the pain in my arse: no lubrication. She's wearing the strap-on. It goes deep and presses on my prostate and bladder. The very first time it was so painful I screamed out, but with time I can take more, and she even bought a larger dildo. I don't know how long it lasts but I'm pleased when it stops.

Untied, I am again moved around the room and told to lie on the large coffee table we have. I feel around and find a way to lie on it. My legs and arms are again retied to each table leg. I cannot move. And now I can smell the smoke. She has lit a candle. I hope it is a white one. The coloured ones are so much hotter. And then the first drip on my chest, it moves down the belly and closer to my cock. I know that pain. I can take it unless she pulls back my foreskin and drips wax on the tip of my cock. That is almost unbearable.

Now the whip again, first across my thighs and then on my cock. It is hard and she flicks and whips at it, causing it to twitch. I know what will happen. It will bruise. It will be black and blue, but I can take that because for the next week she will look at it, stroke it, kiss it and say 'poor cock'. But the marks on my thighs? They will persist and she knows I will only go to the gym if she is with me so that when anyone sees them they will know that I am with my love and she is the person who gave them to me.

Then the first part is over and I know that all will be well, I have survived. She will tease my cock, pulling and playing with it and scraping off the wax playfully. She will suck it and take it deep. She can deep throat even when it is fully hard and I know she will take me. Then I will hear the strain on the wood as first she stands on the table and then slowly lowers herself onto my hard and throbbing cock. Faster and faster until I hear her moans start to build. I still have to concentrate because there is little stimulation for me in that position and I have to stay hard. Faster and faster and I can feel her pussy almost try to pull my cock deeper into her, then that moment as she orgasms hard.

I am not allowed to come until she had finished. In fact, I think that is generally a good rule and I have learnt to hold myself until she has orgasmed many times. The only problem can be that by the end of holding it in for so long I cannot come, but I don't mind that if she's happy.

She is kind to me, even in her special moment, and again she takes me in her mouth and makes sure the end is happy for me as well.

I am untied, unblindfolded and I try to stand. It is not always easy as my joints have stiffened.

We shower together and she washes the last of the wax off me. We kiss, we dress, and we look into each other's eyes. I see the love in her eyes and she sees the love in mine, along with the pride that I have again done the most that any man can do to show his love.

Alexandra

19.   THE LOUIS VUITTON HANDBAG

Again we woke to a rainy day; although it was still warm the sky was overcast and covered in cloud. It made the day feel heavy with humidity. We peeked out of the duvet and knew that picnics and walks were out of the question. What to do? You looked at me with those pleading eyes, 'can I have a coffee darling?' you say. 'Please make me a coffee, Mikhail.' Even if you hadn't asked I was just about to do that, so I wandered off to the kitchen while you turned over to go back to sleep.

It's fun being able to stay in bed and after the coffee and fruit, we decide that much as we really want to stay there, we really have to get up. The rain and humidity do not encourage much activity. We can't even bother to get dressed, and wrapped only in towels we sit in the kitchen and make some breakfast. As I sit at the table and watch you walk about, totally relaxed, I am in total awe of you.

'What are we going to do today?' I ask, scratching an itch.

'From looking at you,' you say, 'I know what you want to do.'

I didn't mean to, but my hand had wandered down to my already growing cock. 'You always make me excited,' I said, 'it is your fault for being so beautiful; but what are we going to do?'

'I know,' you say suddenly, 'I want to make a video today and I have a special idea.'

'Okay,' I say, knowing that it is always going to be fun, whatever plan you have.

'You just stay there and enjoy your breakfast while I go and get things ready. Don't peek in the room; I want to make it a real surprise for you.'

Maybe rather stupidly I trust you totally, and so I finish my toast and marmalade, check the news on the internet and relax, waiting to be called. But when I'm finally called to the bedroom, the surprise is complete. The video camera is set up on a tripod and you are dressed in not very much other than tiny knickers and a mask!

'Stand there, my darling, and smile, because you are on a live cam feed.'

'What?'

'Ssshh, don't worry,' you say, as you walk towards me and wrap a rope around my wrist. 'I have logged us onto a website and we already have an audience of over a hundred waiting to watch you behave properly for your Queen. Don't let me down.'

There is nothing I can do as I face the camera. You have tied both my wrists and pulled my arms wide and fixed them. You have done the same with my ankles and legs so that I am standing there like a starfish, facing the camera; there is also an audience waiting for me to be used.

'I must check our audience and see what they think,' you say, 'because this is a special show and they will decide what I should do to you. What do you think of that? It's a kind of request show.'

I am about to answer when you say, 'Wow, we already have over five hundred people watching and some very good ideas. Here is the first one. They want you to be gagged,' and that is what you did. You took off your panties so very slowly, playing to the audience, and then stuffed them into my mouth before wrapping tape all around my mouth. I was more worried about breathing than talking!

'Oh. I don't think we can do that one. A man here wants me to kick you in the balls ten times, as hard as I can. But we can do this request,' and you walk towards me before tying my cock tight, separating my cock and balls before hanging a weight which pulls them down. The pain is excruciating.

I hope you remember that stopping the blood flow can cause permanent damage to my cock! You will suffer just as much as me if it falls off.

'What next?' you say, back at the screen. 'Mmm, I like this one. Darling, we now have over eight hundred viewers. Now, I am sure you will enjoy this one.' Again you come towards me and take hold of my cock and start to massage it so that it grows to nearly full size and then you take the urethral probe – the largest one we have – and slowly push it into my cock. Ooohh!

What more can you do to me? My balls, which are being stretched and pulled, are aching; my cock is aching from being tied tight and having a probe stuck down it. I know I will soon find out what else you will do, and I watch you as you sit at the computer and type and share ideas with our growing audience of online viewers.

'You will like this one, darling,' and you take five small elastic bands, and one by one, from balls to the tip, you fix them tight around my cock. They restrict the blood flow, even more, making it larger and even more painful. Look at my clock please, darling, I don't want to lose my cock.

'We have another idea and we have all the bits. It is time for a bit of electricity!' you say, but I am not sure it is such a good idea. It depends on what intensity you use. You get out the box and put the electrodes on my cock: one at the tip and one at the base of the shaft. I know what it's going to be like. Well, that is, I already know what it is like, but not with all these ropes, bands and weights on me at the same time. If the pulse is low it is mind-blowingly pleasurable, but if the pulse is large it is very painful. I should have guessed. This is head-on painful.

You leave the pulsing going, as you return to the computer. How long has all this been going on? I don't know, but it is a long time. What else could you want to do to me? I look hopefully in your direction.

'That's it, my chocolate muffin. We are finished. I have reached my target.' I see you close the PC, come to me and start to untie me. My cock and balls both hurt, but as you take off the gag I manage a few words. 'What do you mean you reached your target?'

'You don't think I did this just for fun? I was getting tips from our audience. They were paying us. We made a lot of money. In fact, we made just enough to buy the Louis Vuitton handbag I have been looking at. Come on, darling, have a shower and you can take me out to buy it. You are very special, doing all that for a handbag!'

I wore very loose pants and limped all the way around the shopping centre, only stopping to buy a Pepsi so that I could take some Aspirin!

Alexandra

20. DISCARDED

Mikhail hadn't yet had a shower and hadn't shaved. Although it was still mid-morning and he had been awake only an hour, he had hardly slept during a restless night, so it was not surprising that he was looking dishevelled. He had pulled on jeans and a T-shirt and was wearing at least two days' worth of beard growth. He had had his breakfast and managed to settle at his computer ready to write, but the words did not come easily; he had not properly shaken off a bad night's sleep.

There was little reason for this sloppiness, other than the general malaise of frustration. The weekend was nearly over and not enough progress had been made, and the novel had been lying dormant for too long. There had been too many distractions and he hadn't been able to concentrate.

Whenever he turned on the computer he would hope that today would be the day when she would write to him again. But as the PC flickered into life, he quickly saw that she had not written. There was never an email, but he would see her face filling the screen on the computer screensaver. Her picture changed to yet another; this time in a bikini. It changed again and there she was, always looking at him, tempting and taunting him. She was close but never close enough.

He wondered if he should remove the screensaver to give him some space and time, but decided that it would be like cheating on her. To take her image away would be the same as putting another woman in her place. 'No,' he said to himself, 'that will have to stay.'

He had coped well with Valentine's Day. He had found ways to cope with being alone, and learnt that by not going out too often he could become inured against the effects of the world of romance all around him. He had almost decided that other than her, there would never again be anyone else in his life.

The first time they had met was in Kyiv, but he left her with few hopes and fewer expectations. Then they had met again and now he needed to know where their lives together would take them. He wanted love. He wanted her love. He enjoyed being in love and he had even thought of giving his love to someone else, but the thought of having his heart broken frightened him.

The weekend had not been busy. On Friday evening he had had a few drinks with friends, holding back on the temptation to relieve his frustrations alone in bed, and then on Saturday, he went to lunch with others.

Among them were both singles and couples, but it was in company that he felt most alone. He looked at the couples around the lunch table and desperately wanted her to be there. He wanted her. He wanted others to see her, talk to her and understand why she was so suddenly so important to him. He wanted to hear her laughter and see her smile. He wanted to leave with her, to go back home with her and then make love to her.

As the food was served and the conversation chattered, his mind was elsewhere. If she was here, he thought, we would go home, and then we would sit and talk about all that had happened. She would smile and say that so-and-so was funny, or she was nice, or they were annoying. He would make them both tea in the kitchen. She would come up behind him and put her hands around his waist and rest her head on his shoulders. He would tell her that she was very pretty, and in fact, she was the prettiest girl in the world; as she heard those words she would hold him just a little bit closer.

'Have I told you today that I love you?' she would say.

'Not since we woke up and I said that I loved you,' would be his answer. He could easily imagine the rest of the conversation. She would say, 'I love you,' and he would turn around and look deep into her eyes and kiss her. The kiss would be long, deep and fully reciprocated. With his arms around her waist, holding her close and looking straight into her eyes, he would say, 'you are the most wonderful person and I love you, and I am the luckiest man alive. I am old and have so many faults and you are young and beautiful. Why you choose me I will never understand, but I say a prayer of thanks to God every night that we are together.'

'Don't ask why,' she would say, placing a finger on his lips, 'it was just what was decided for us.' And as they kissed, their hands would move and explore each other's bodies.

He would outline the shape of her waist and his hands would rest gently on her bottom; as their kissing became even more passionate there would be an inevitability of what would happen next. As she undid his shirt buttons, he would lift her and place her gently on the kitchen table. He knew she did not wear panties and as her skirt rose up she would be pulling at his trousers, and soon they would be absurdly down at his ankles. From the very first time they had met, she had made him excited, and he had learnt to cope with the continual bulge in his trousers. As his trousers fell to the kitchen floor he would already be hard and erect.

And so it was on that Saturday as he sat at a lunch table with eleven other people, that again he had an erection as he thought of making love to her on the kitchen table.

'Do you want some more potatoes?' someone said. With thoughts of her running through his mind, it was an incongruous question, but the reality was that she was not there and he was alone. At that moment he felt lonelier than at any time in the past.

His Sunday drifted on. He showered and dressed, believing that if he sharpened up his appearance, his mind would clear and he could write. Where was he in the novel? Maybe he could write a love scene for the book and help his patient characters in their own frustrations.

When he placed his characters in a remote wooden cabin in the snow of a European winter, there was a large roaring fire and he saw his heroine lying on the sheepskin rug. She was naked and her beautiful body looked at him, drawing him closer. He leant down towards her and did the one thing he knew she liked almost more than anything else. He licked her pussy. He ran the tip of his tongue onto her clitoris and then sucked at it, pulling it gently into his mouth, before his tongue explored deeper into her. Her body arched as the heat spread through her thighs and into her body. There was a moan. He looked at the muscles tightening as a hand grabbed at his head, pulling him further into her. Then she came with a screaming orgasm.

They would relax a little as she recovered before taking his cock deep into her mouth. She had learnt how to deep throat and take all of him in without choking.

He was trying to write a scene of love and so the lovemaking was both passionate and tender. Each was aware of the other and trying to make it as good as they could for each other. This was not to be a five-minute affair, but a statement of love as bodies intertwined. But as he wrote the characters all became confused and it was always Alexandra and him. 'Try and concentrate,' he thought. Maybe he should write a lustful sex scene. That must be easier.

What would it be? He had his main character take a phone call from his heroine.

'Come to the office at one o'clock and we will do something for lunch,' she had said, so he headed off to meet her. 'Maybe it's some shopping or just a coffee,' he said to himself. She, like him, wanted them to be together, so she was there in the car park waiting for him.

It is good to spend time together, he thought, as he drove in and parked next to her car.

She had also seen him arrive and beckoned him to open the large back door of the 4x4 Mercedes.

'Get in here,' she said, and he recognised the tone in her voice. This was not shopping. 'Take off all your clothes.'

With anyone else he might have objected or laughed but there was a forcefulness that could not be denied and he climbed in and started to undress as she followed him into the car. Reaching into a bag she pulled out rope: a bright red rope.

'Lie down!' and he did as he was told; then she tied him, spread-eagled, in the back of her car. As he was in open view he hoped that the slight tint in the window would stop anyone from seeing him naked and restrained.

The back door closed, and the front door opened. She got into the car, started the engine and away they drove. The thing about tinted windows is that you can see out and hope that no one else can see in, and that is exactly what he hoped, although there was excitement in the possibility of being publicly exposed. So as they drove he lay there, naked and uncomfortable, as she turned corners and stopped and started at traffic lights. At one point the traffic lights were red and they had pulled up next to a bus. As he lay there he could see all the people in the bus looking around and some at the car – her car, with him tied and naked in the back. Could they see him? What did they think?

They stopped once more and this time he heard her get out. Then the back door opened and by just lifting his head he could see they were in a park. In the distance were people. She climbed in; kneeled next to him; checked his ropes and was satisfied that all was still okay.

'First, I want some photographs,' she said. She stood over him, camera in hand, and he could hear the shutter snap open and closed. She stepped out of the car and took more shots, while he could do nothing other than just lie there.

'And now I want to fuck you and then maybe I will throw you out into the park for anyone else who wants you. You would like that wouldn't you?'

His hero didn't know how to answer that. It was both yes and no, but he didn't have time to think as she lifted her dress, pulled aside her knickers and guided his cock straight into her pussy. She moved up and down; faster, then slower, then faster again. The door of the car was still open and if anyone had passed by they would have seen them screwing and heard their screams as they came together.

He looked at the computer. He had not written a word, realising that all his characters had merged and that the girl in all his thoughts was her.

She had enveloped him and become his focus. He knew that he wanted her and wanted to be with her all the time. He wanted to phone her and hear her voice. He needed to be part of her life and he wanted to know that she also thought of him during lonely weekends.

She had said that he had to be an adult and sort out the problems. She was, of course, right. She was always right and that is why he was so quickly and absolutely drawn to her.

Sunday night was drifting into Monday morning and the start of a new week. He felt tired and the television was droning into late-night mediocrity. His bed waited, with only the comfort of dreams of her. Tomorrow was another day, and each day brings new opportunities and new challenges, but there is always one certainty: Alexandra's perfection.

Alexandra

V. FUN WITH ADAM

It was 2004 and I was twenty-three when I finished my master's degree, but still, I continued at the university, staying on as a doctoral candidate. The work was hard but it was an easy life because I loved what I was doing, but I knew I had to stretch myself. So, in my second year, I accepted an offer of a two-year research award in London.

Of course, with my modelling, I had been out of Ukraine, but living in London was going to be a whole new – albeit exciting – experience. If moving to Kyiv was a big step (because it was so much larger than anything I had known), London was a whole lot more, and a real shock.

It was the autumn of 2006 when I arrived at Heathrow.

First I had to find somewhere to live and the university accommodation service had given me the addresses of many apartments they thought I could afford, but they were wrong. They must have thought more of my grant than I did. Of course, through my modelling income, I suppose I might have become accustomed to having the good things in life, including accommodation, but what was on offer was not what I had expected. I was poor and London was very expensive. I had always seen my modelling income as my reserve savings and never to be relied upon for basics; I was never going to use that.

Anyway, most of the flats I couldn't afford. Of those that were left, few inspired me, but I had to live somewhere. Finally, I moved into a flat in a block in East London.

Starting in London was like being a new undergraduate in Kyiv all over again, except London is so much larger and impersonal that I would sit in my room on those first days wondering why I had ever left home. But I was here and I had to make the best of it.

My English was good enough for a casual conversation but not for the studies I was about to embark upon, so I had to quickly improve this skill. As always, there is a story to tell.

Alexandra

21.   HELP WITH MY HOMEWORK

It was still her early days in London and it was at the start of Alexandra's English studies.

The storm may have passed, but the weather still hung heavy on Alexandra. Ukrainian by birth and Ukrainian to the core, she was now an alien in a foreign country. She may have many degrees at home, but to continue her studies here she needed to learn English and pass the exams.

She had a third-floor flat in the East End and it was sparsely furnished from a second-hand shop. As she sat back in her chair, staring at the computer on the table with its siren call of another test to be submitted, she realised it wasn't the weather that made her feel so low; it was the threat of another looming deadline that weighed heavily on her spirits. The realisation of the depth of her problem overtook her. The workload and the timescales did not match. She needed help, but where could she look? Friends from the language school were of no use. They were under the same pressures as her and their English was probably worse. She needed a native English speaker. A native English speaker, she thought, that means an Englishman; and she knew one of them.

Matt lived alone in his flat just two floors above her. He had moved to London many years ago and was more than twice her age; but whatever, she thought, he was English. They weren't real friends, just someone she met in the lift or passed on the stairs, but he was always kind, with a sexy twinkle in his eye as he teased and flirted with her when they met. He had invited her to share a coffee at Starbucks with, he said, the promise of extra compliments. She had laughed as he said it in his very English way.

Once, in a light-hearted moment, as they met with groceries on the stairs, he had held her arm lightly to draw her closer and told her in a spirit of secretiveness and indiscretion that they should run away together to escape the tribulations of this world. They parted with a European kiss on her cheek; just as it was back in Kyiv. Yes, she thought, Matt would help her.

'Matt,' she said on the phone, 'it's me, Alexandra, from downstairs. Can you help me? Pleeeease?' she said, drawing out all the vowels to extract the deepest sense of need, 'please can you help me?' She explained her quandary.

She knew he would say *yes*, and so there was no surprise when, five minutes later with his PC tucked under his arm, he knocked on her door. In detail, she explained her problem. 'Would he,' she asked, 'take some of her English exams for her?' He listened both sympathetically and attentively. He complained just a little, citing the English values of honesty and fair play, before caving in. Then they doled out the tasks.

He sat at one end of the small wooden dining table, with Alexandra at the other, as they started to work. More than an hour passed and the tasks were slowly being ticked off, and the pressure eased enough for Alexandra to take a break and make them a drink.

'Coffee, Matt?'

'Fantastic,' he said, still working and not lifting his head from the computer. Alexandra went to the kitchen, made the coffee and returned, and even then he did not look up as she carefully and quietly placed the coffee at his elbow.

'Thanks, darling,' he said, without any self-consciousness.

Darling Alexandra thought. Was that simply an English affectation or was he betraying his subconscious thoughts as he concentrated on the work? Alexandra sat and looked at him more closely.

Despite the age difference there was something in him that was sexy and she thought that maybe an affair with him would be fun. *Stop it*, she said to herself. *You have work to do. Concentrate on that. And anyway, you already have a boyfriend, even if he isn't much use. His performance in the bedroom was definitely subpar.* But the naughty thought of Matt still nagged.

In one of his moments of confession, Matt had once said that he had made a porn film to support his early work struggles. He showed no embarrassment and said that it was easy. 'If any of my friends tease me for being in it, I will tease them for watching it,' was all he would say.

Alexandra had laughed and told all her friends that a porn actor was living in her block. It always resulted in laughter. She had never searched the web to see if any of his films were there, but here, tonight, he was in her room; and, with Matt's help, she was ahead of schedule with her homework. Maybe she could take a peek and do a search now?

She tried to casually turn the screen away from him just an inch, so there was no chance he could see what she was looking at. She turned the speakers off. Here was the site and there was Matt with two beautiful girls. They stayed dressed but he was naked. Alexandra looked over at him, still working for her. The girls laid him on the bed, stroked and caressed him, and Alexandra saw his cock get larger and larger as each, in turn, took him deep in their mouths.

'What's wrong, Alexandra?' His words startled her.

'Wrong? Nothing is wrong. What made you say that?'

'Oh. It was just the look on your face. It was as if you had been surprised by something. You know, these English texts aren't that exciting.'

'Yes, I know. Sorry, I was miles away. I was in my own thoughts for a moment. Sorry,' she said, but her real thoughts were elsewhere as the video kept rolling and she saw him again disappear, deep into their mouths.

'No need to say sorry, Alexandra.'

'No, you're right; but I will have to find a way to say thank you for all this, Matt.'

'I'm sure you will find a way. You are so inventive,' and he returned to his tasks, but for Alexandra, it was less easy because every word she saw on the page conjured up that video of Matt.

She read the school text some more. *...Elizabeth gently roused her knight from his sleep...* If I was Elizabeth, she thought, I wouldn't rouse him from his sleep, I would make sure he was aroused in his sleep.

She slipped into a daydream. Matt would be her knight. He would have just returned from the crusades, recognised as a knight of great heroism. She would be his princess and he would be her knight, asleep, naked in her bed. As he lay there, she wanted him to wake; she wanted him, and she wanted him aroused. She slipped off her nightdress and as it fell to the floor she caught a glimpse of herself in the mirror. Stunning, beautiful and naked, with her small and pert breasts, long legs and the mound below her flat belly acting as guardian to her most beloved area. Slipping into bed next to him, she ran her hands across his chest and felt it rise and fall in a deep sleep. She was becoming impatient. He had been away all these years and now she wanted to be conquered, she wanted her walls climbed and mounted, she wanted to be invaded and taken. Her hands moved down to his thighs and caressed his cock. Just one hand at first, but as it grew, both hands were holding it. Then Alexandra, just like the girls in the film of Matt she had just seen, pushed the sheets away, and without any attempt of finesse, she took him deep in her mouth.

Yes, she thought, I would arouse him in his sleep.

Matt woke her from the dream. 'Stay with it, Alexandra. You are drifting away. We need to get this done tonight. Actually, it is very hard. Do you think it is hard?'

Matt was being serious. Alexandra looked across at him sitting at the table. She hadn't noticed he was wearing tight dreams. *Damn it*, she thought, I can't even think properly. It is not tight dreams but tight jeans.

Maybe it is hard; maybe it is being constrained in those tight jeans. Is that why he's squirming on the chair as he works? Maybe that large dick is pushing and struggling as it tries to live its own tight dreams. Maybe it knew that Alexandra would be a tight dream?

Now she wriggled and twisted on her chair as she started to feel that moment when her pussy moved from being a benign yet integral part of her anatomy to becoming the core and very centre of her being. It was as if every other nerve shut down, allowing her pussy a monopoly of her senses. And she knew she was a tight dream. She knew she was a haven for that monster. She knew she would capture it in her pussy and hold it tight, squeezing out every last drop of his seed. As she had these thoughts, the warmth in her pussy increased and the joy of the wetness developed.

No longer a dream, this was real. She was getting excited but still, there was work to be done. How would she see this through to the end, and where would it end? However hard it was, she finally returned to her English comprehension. This time it was a piece on vegetarianism and the sins of eating meat. A true carnivore was appeasing the vegetarian.

Only eat an animal you have known personally, the text said. Ah, she thought, I wonder if Matt feels the same? He has known me personally, if not intimately now, for over a year. I wonder if he would eat me? Maybe he would take me to the bedroom. Make me stand still and slowly undo each button on my blouse to expose my breasts, because, of course, I never wear a bra. Maybe he had seen my nipples become more erect each time we met on the stairs. He would walk around me and undo my skirt and watch it fall to the floor, before dropping to his knees in front of me and slowly pulling down my panties, leaving me standing there in just stockings and heels. He would make me step back and push me until the edge of the bed made me fall backwards, and as I fell, my pussy would be facing him and he would open my legs and push his tongue deep inside.

Even as she sat still trying to work, she could feel him; first inside her and then slowly moving around her clit. She sat back and her hand was moving towards her thighs when she stopped herself. He was still here and she was about to masturbate in front of him. *Stop it, Alexandra!*

It was not easy to stay focused and concentrate, but over the next half hour, Alexandra managed to work almost as diligently as Matt. Then there was the next distraction.

The comprehension test moved on to an interview with a fading Hollywood star. *Question: When you were in Hollywood did you ever come across Marilyn Monroe?* An innocent question, but what if Matt were questioned about this evening?

Question: Did you ever come across Alexandra when you were in London? Oh, if only he would. Maybe when he had finished eating me out, and I had taken all his cock in my mouth and the jeans had met their tight dreams, then would he sit astride me? I would watch as his hands moved the skin on his cock backwards and forwards and his face contorted as he reached a climax. I would feel his ball sack get tighter as that moment of release got closer, and then he would smother me in his beautiful cum. It would squirt across my face and run down my cheeks and I would try and move my head to catch a rivulet of cum in my mouth so that I could taste that wonderful saltiness of life. Yes, Matt could say he had come across Alexandra while in London.

Finally and at last, Alexandra thought, the work is done. Matt had finished most of the tasks and her efforts were more visible by the stains on the chair.

'Well, that's all done,' he said, and as he stretched out his phone rang. He listened and nodded at the conversation and then said, 'Sorry. I can't now. I'm rather tied up.'

He hung up the phone and then looked up at Alexandra. 'A friend wanted to meet for a beer,' he offered as an explanation, and Alexandra nodded; that was when Alexandra had her idea. While Matt finished off and closed down his computer, she went to her bedroom and brought out a little bag which contained all her toys.

'Matt, you have been my hero,' she said. 'I wouldn't have got through tonight if you hadn't been here.'

'It was nothing,' he said, not knowing that even as she heard his words she knew it was a lot more than nothing. The memory of his video was clear in her thoughts and she knew, for sure, it was a lot more than nothing; it was the thought of his size that had sustained her all evening.

'Do you have to go? Can you stay for a while? I would like to say thank you and give you something to drink. Can I tie you down to that?' she asked.

'Alexandra, you can tie me down to anything, anytime you like,' he said, not fully realising how prescient were his words.

'I'm glad you said that,' she said, 'because that is exactly what I had in mind. Now, stand up, Matt.'

He didn't know quite why he stood so obediently. Perhaps it was the sudden tension in her voice, but stand he did.

She took an arm and pulled it behind his back, grabbed the other and clumsily managed to tie his hands behind his back. To be honest, if he had wanted to resist or even undo the rope it would have been easy, but he went along with the play. She teased him at first by undoing his shirt and he protested that there were other ways to show her gratitude. A drink, he said, would have been quite enough, but she knew this was far better for him and her.

Alexandra stripped him, and over the night without resistance she tied and retied him, used and abused him, reliving each and every one of the fantasies of the evening. He was every bit as large as he looked in the films. Throughout the night, until the early hours, Alexandra continued with her plans. She sat astride him to fuck him and feel him deep inside her. She sat on his face and made him eat her, and finally made him come across her face.

In return for this favour, Matt often helped her with her studies, and it was no great surprise that her grades continued to improve!

Matt was brilliant with me and soon my English was getting so much better that from then on, I could move forward very quickly. I was making new friends in London and was introduced to the London scene in all its variety.

It was so different from Kyiv where I could be the Queen of the clubs. In this maelstrom, I no longer had to pose as much and I took the chance to be ordinary!

Alexandra

22.   THE RUGBY CLUB

With time I was becoming integrated into British and London life, both academically and socially, and I was having a good time. I loved London and all that it offered. I had good friends and occasional boyfriends with regular but uncommitted sex.

I made good friends and one of these was Mandy, who was also a doctoral student. One weekend she took me to watch a very British sport – rugby – and that soon became something very special, as well as the source of new boyfriends.

Alexandra was becoming more used to her life in London and experiencing many of the delights of life in a western capital. There was work plus cultural and sporting activities to enjoy and experience.

She hadn't wanted to come to watch the game on a cold winter's day, but her best friend Mandy had insisted. Mandy's new boyfriend played rugby and she wanted the company of her friend.

They had travelled in Mandy's little car through the London suburbs and had stood watching the game, while Alexandra tried to find something of interest. She really felt that this was a waste of an afternoon which could have been better spent doing many other things, including working.

The game was near the end and this was Alexandra's first time at a rugby match. She was cold and decided that she was not much interested, but then again, there were 30 young men in shorts running around, so there was a peripheral benefit.

Alexandra didn't understand the rules of the game, but the participants were athletic and strong and she liked the physicality. They ran fast, they tackled each other with a crunch. They were what men should be, and they did look so good in those shorts. She admired the muscles, big shoulders, strong thighs and those sexy bottoms as they sped past her down the touchline. Although they were increasingly covered in mud with their better parts hidden, Alexandra could start to see some benefit in this way of spending a

Saturday afternoon.

As the game drifted to the far side of the pitch, Alexandra started to dream. Mandy had told her that after the game the men's changing room had one big white tiled bath which they all shared.

'That can't be,' Alexandra said, 'these guys are straight.'

'It's true,' was all Mandy would say, and although she couldn't believe it, Mandy again reassured her. 'Richard told me. They have one big bath and they sit in there talking about the game. It's true, Alexandra, it really is true.'

Alexandra started to imagine wandering into this room. She saw showers around the outside and the big white tiled bath, and slowly into her mind formed the vision of 30 young men, all naked, laughing, showering and washing, with soap and shampoo rolling down their muscle-covered bodies. And as she dreamed, she saw herself naked and stepping into this room of naked men and then into the bath. There she was surrounded by the cream of manhood. An arm pulled her closer and another started to touch her and soon she was in a deep and passionate embrace, as hands were all over her. She felt down below the water and reached out to find a now erect cock in her hand.

Despite the cold in the air, her dream was making her hot and wet. She imagined how she would have sex with each and every one of them, right there in the bath, knowing that all would be wanting her. She was on her back in the steamy bathroom. There was a cock deep in her pussy and one in her ass. There was one in her mouth and one in each hand and there was a queue to take their place after each had come.

Standing on the touchline in a world of her own, her eyes were closed and she was starting to shake with excitement.

'Alexandra, watch out!' Mandy shouted. Alexandra came out of her trance and saw a hoard of players coming in her direction. Which way to jump? There was hardly time to think, and she didn't as she was knocked aside. She lay there, winded and bemused.

'Hey, sorry,' he said. 'Keep your eyes open next time,' and he was away, back in the game.

Mandy helped Alexandra up and cleaned the mud off her coat as

Alexandra cursed at those oafs, more for spoiling her dream than for knocking her over.

The game finished and Alexandra and Mandy wandered off to the bar. 'They will come along after they've cleaned up,' Mandy said. At least Alexandra was starting to get warm again but she wasn't so sure she now wanted to meet any of these stupid men.

'Hi Mandy,' a tall guy said as he walked in. It was Richard, her boyfriend. He was followed by the crowd, chattering and pushing at the bar to get drinks.

'Hi Mandy,' Richard said as he kissed her on the cheek, 'who's your friend? Is this Alexandra, the girl you were telling me about?'

'Of course; Richard, this is Alexandra, she is Ukrainian. Be nice to her.'

'Of course, I will,' he said, and he took her hand and kissed it with a mocking bow of his head. 'Here, let me introduce you to some of the team,' and he called over one of the taller and lither men.

'Alexandra, this is Adam. He is one of our stars. Did you see that try he scored today? Pretty special, if you ask me.

Sometimes when two people meet there is chemistry, and when you are both young, that chemistry can often be sexual. There was immediate sexual chemistry between Alexandra and Adam. It was immediately clear to them both, and even Mandy could see something happening.

'Hey Alexandra,' Adam said, 'you were the one that got knocked over on the touchline. Sorry about that. Got to keep your eyes open if you watch rugby,' he said.

Alexandra looked at him. 'No trouble,' she said, 'it was probably my fault.' Mandy gave her a sideways look. That hadn't been her reaction two hours ago.

Adam returned to the beer and boys but kept throwing Alexandra glances which were coyishly returned. He came over to her.

'I'm sorry. I can't stop looking at you. You make me feel so horny. I know you feel the same,' he said.

He wasn't being especially perceptive because she was already feeling weak at the knees and she could feel the redness at her neck as sexual excitement built. She nodded.

'Come with me,' he said, and he took her hand and led her through the door labelled changing rooms and into a large bathroom.

There it was. It was real. A very large bath – surely fifteen or twenty guys could bathe in that at the same time, and suddenly her dream returned and she knew then that she was about to have sex with him – right there and then.

He reached out and pulled her close to him. They kissed deeply and his arms went around her waist. Her feet came off the ground as he held her tightly.

Their passion increased and clothes were almost ripped off. She felt each muscle on his body as she ran her hands all over him. He pushed her back against the wall and she felt the cold of the white tiles on her naked back.

'You're cold,' he said, and he reached out; there was a sudden rush of hot water from the shower, and under the steaming spray his kisses covered her whole body. He kissed her lips and neck. He kissed her breasts and body. Her hands traced every curve on him. She turned to face the tiled wall and on her toes, she grabbed at his engorged cock and pushed it into her pussy.

He pushed deeper and deeper while Alexandra arched her back and thrust out her hips to take more of him. His hands were on her hips, pulling her onto him. Their passion increased and he thrust deeper and harder. The heat in her thighs grew stronger, and in a sudden moment of ecstasy she gasped and they came together.

She let out a long moan, turned and sank back down, deep into his arms, as he held her tight.

Watching rugby was going to be alright.

23. STRIPTEASE

This was the start of my next great romance, and soon Adam and I were, as they say, 'an item'.

I loved the pubs and clubs, London buses and even the tube, which so many Londoners seem to hate. When I had spare time I explored old lanes and roads, ancient buildings and galleries, and all that London has to offer; it is a wonderful city and probably one of the greatest capitals.

However, I was no longer the queen bee I had been in Kyiv, where I could hardly go out without being recognised; but in many ways, I found it better and easier than being a large fish in a small pond. As I grew emotionally I had a more rounded view of the world. I didn't have to be the centre of everything, just the centre of my world. However, that didn't mean that I had lost any of my self-confidence!

One thing I wouldn't allow to change in London was that every year for my birthday, ever since I was seventeen, I have treated myself to a birthday adventure, and that's how, for example, I did my first parachute jump. I always set out to do something that I would never otherwise do without the stimulus of a birthday surprise. That had been my creed all my time in Kyiv and so I saw no reason to change my approach in London.

Sometimes I do really sexy things for my birthday adventure...

It was my birthday and it was when I was in London that I decided that I was going to be a stripper for a day. I can't remember why I chose it, it was probably some romantic gesture, but I know it was really all an excuse. I knew I would be excited by the thought of lots of men watching me, but they were also paying real money for the privilege. There is something really exhilarating for me in that thought.

There's a pub near where I live in East London that has strippers every night (they are also there on Sunday lunchtimes but I have always found that really odd). I had never been in there to drink but, as it was on my way home, I had seen the sort of guys that were there. It wasn't just dirty old men in macs. I had seen business guys after work and builders from the local site. These were my fantasy guys. These were the guys that were going to give their money to me for my version of sex.

Normally I'm the quiet sort with 'nice' boyfriends, but when I was whistled at walking past the building site, I got hot thinking about the builders. I had thought of flashing them but never had the courage. That's why I chose a local pub. The thought of these guys seeing me again really turned me on.

I didn't know what I had to do to get the stripper's job for a day. I thought I should have some sexy outfits, so I spent the weeks up to my birthday buying the sort of clothes I would never normally wear: a thong so skimpy that it left nothing to the imagination and a bikini top so small that it just covered my nipples. These seemed like the right things to wear, so I put all of them into a small bag and set off from the university at five o'clock for my birthday adventure.

There was a moment just outside the pub when I nearly gave up. It suddenly dawned on me: how far would I have to go? In my naivety I had assumed that with licensing laws and all that, I would be able to stop at my bra and panties, but what if I had to go further? There I was, right in front of the door, still unsure, when a group of guys arrived; and well, they sort of pushed me in.

Inside it was dark. Of course, all the windows had been blacked out to stop prying eyes. There were a couple of rather bored men at a pool table without an eye for a pretty young black girl, wearing tight shorts and a skimpy top, dancing to loud music on the stage. The stage was large and brightly lit, and I turned to watch for a moment. She whirled around a pole, at one time swinging both her feet off the ground. My God, I hadn't thought I would have to do that, but I was in and now and I wanted to push ahead.

'Can I work here tonight?' I was asking a guy who seemed to be in charge behind the bar.

'Are you booked?' I felt stupid. Of course, girls don't just turn up: the acts are booked in. Behind me, sitting in a corner beside the stage were three scantily clad girls. The black girl was off the stage and thankfully she still had most of her clothes on.

'No, but I want to work tonight. You don't have to pay me, I'm doing this for fun.'

'You'll have to speak to them and see what they say'.

I went over to the girls and explained to them my 'adventure'.

'Fine,' they said, 'but any money you make you'll have to give to us'.

Not unfair, I thought; after all, this is their living. 'You'd better go on next before you change your mind. Go and get changed.'

So there I was, ten minutes later, dancing in a bikini top and thong to an audience of twenty men. I tried to remember what that black girl had done. I swung around the pole, cupped my tits and thrust them together as I leant forward. That's what they'll want – a good cleavage. It wasn't very polished, but three minutes later I was off stage – I had finally done it.

The pub was filling up and by the time my turn came round again, there must have been nearly fifty there, including the blokes from the building site.

Watching the other girls, I had learnt some of their moves, but also the acts were getting stronger. My knowledge of the licensing laws was clearly not very good. By now all the girls were topless at the end of their act and one had even pulled her knickers aside, and given a quick flash of pussy to the guys who were now sitting beside the stage. Even the pool players occasionally looked up.

Soon I was topless. I was on the stage, doggy style, thrusting my pussy and arse into the faces of unknown men hardly five feet away from me. I know stripping is supposed to make the guys horny, but what was it doing for me? I was getting more excited all the time and could feel myself getting wet, and I don't mean with perspiration from the exercise and stage lights.

I hardly heard the music stop. I collected up discarded clothes and returned to the side of the stage with a huge grin on my face. This was more than fun.

'Jug time,' said Sandra, one of my new friends.

'What?'

'We get paid a bit by the pub, but this is when we collect tips from the punters and make some real money. Remember: the sexier you are, the more they'll give.'

I was about to put my top on when Sandra said, 'No, leave that off, we'll get more. You start at that end,' she said, placing a pint glass in my hand.

So there I was, walking through a busy London pub wearing nothing but a tiny thong and high heels, asking guys to pay to see my body. I started nervously but soon got into the banter (maybe the gin and tonics I'd been drinking to calm my nerves helped).

As coins hit the glass my confidence increased. I pushed myself into groups of talking men.

There was a time when I was in the middle of a group of six or so guys, nearly naked, with tits pressed up against a guy, teasing and playing with him, my hand on his cock, persuading him to put more money in the jug. I felt a hand on my bum. Any other day I would have turned on the pest. Today I let it rest before slowly moving it away. I laughed to myself. Maybe it should be called a grope of men.

Then it was the builders. I pressed my way into their group. I like builders they always seem so hunky and gorgeous. This was heaven. I stood close as I solicited them for money. I was getting brave and pushed up against them, one by one, letting my thigh and sometimes my hand rub against their cocks. I could feel them grow in front of me.

As I said, I had never been to a pub like this before and I didn't really know why we were collecting. I assumed it was a sort of thank you for more of the same. Not many minutes later I knew differently.

After Sandra, it was my turn again. And Sandra had set the mark.

It was a five-minute slot and Sandra had put a Barry White song on for me. One minute in and I was already naked, apart from the high-heeled shoes. My top had gone and so had the thong. The stage-side seats were full as my legs were spread wide to the audience. My builders were in the front row. Once, walking past their building site, I had thought about flashing them – but not like this. As I rubbed my clit gently I saw them, as one, move their hands to their dicks. I was lying on the stage as I tentatively pushed first one, then two fingers into my now wet pussy. Doggy style, I pulled my ass cheeks aside to show them all the pink and slightly engorged lips of my pussy, increasingly moist and hot.

I could feel the intensity of all the eyes watching me. A quick glance and I saw the game of pool had stopped. The music had finished and my grinding slowed as I heard the applause. Not long, not loud, but applause. I had turned them on.

There were two more jug collections and Sandra had me out with the punters, collecting in nothing but my shoes: naked to the core. If anyone had ever asked me to streak or even sunbathe naked, 'no way' was the answer, but here tonight I was walking confidently and brazenly around a London pub wearing not a stitch of clothing, collecting money from unknown men. Tonight I was their whore.

Two more collections meant two more shows. I was into this now and I sort of knew what they wanted. More importantly, I knew what I wanted. Sandra had given me her bottle of baby oil which I had spread freely on my tits and then my pussy. I was as horny as hell as I rubbed my clit and fingered my pussy. They might have thought that the end was all faked but I can tell you it wasn't. At the end of my final show, I came in a screaming loud orgasm that had been building up all evening. I writhed, twisted and bucked as the music died away. I was awash with heat and oil but even then not yet fully satisfied.

I thanked Sandra for her help, guidance and patience. She said I was a natural and should think of this for a living. I said it was a one-off. She said they had made good money. I said I was pleased and I might come again to watch their show. After all, these were now my co-workers and friends.

I dressed and left the pub, turning only to think that this was probably my best adventure so far when I heard the whistle. I knew that whistle. I had heard it at the building site.

There was a van across the road and three of the builders were leaning against it. It was an impetuous instinct, bred out of the exhilaration of the night, that made me walk across to them. I was still horny and excited and didn't want the evening to finish. That evening I was a slut, I had shown them everything and they were the most intent of my audience. My words were said unthinkingly.

'Let's get in the back.'

With no further encouragement, they opened the back of the van and I climbed in. There was just enough room amidst the rubble and mess for the four of us to stand up. While they surrounded me I slid to my knees and undid the belt and trousers of the guy facing me, and pulled out his cock. With little foreplay or subtlety, I drove it deep into my mouth. As I sucked I reached around to find two more growing dicks in my hand. I jerked them off and moved my head to take each in turn. There were now three rock-hard dicks for me to play with. Each was worked to increasing levels of excitement as I sucked and pulled on them. Then, with moans and groans, each one came, and a milky froth of cum was running down my face. They pulled away as the cocks went limp in my hand.

There seemed little to say. My night was done. It was no longer my birthday. I wiped my face on a cloth given to me, opened the door of the van, and left. I can't remember if I said bye, goodnight or thanks.

24. IS THAT A SAUSAGE!

I have become fascinated by the thought of public sex, which means we are having sex with other people close by or even visible to prying eyes. I have these fantasies often when I am out and about. I look at a shop's changing room, a parked car, an empty park bench or a restaurant and I just seem to start fantasising about sex. I am going to have to do something very soon about this so I can move on.

I'm not sure that we choose the restaurant very carefully, so maybe it's just by chance that everything is right. Other people are eating and enjoying their food but it is not too busy; conveniently the tables are large and spread apart, there's a large tablecloth and, most importantly, we feel horny!

We sit next to each other as we order, talk and eat, and it is while we are waiting for dessert that I put my hand on your cock. In fact, it was an accidental brush as I reached across you. It was not deliberate, but it immediately makes you hard and I notice that – I always notice when your cock is hard. So, playfully, I rub you just a little bit more.

'You what?' you say, 'you want me to take my cock out so you can see how hard it is?'

'Yes, my darling. I want to see if you still lust over me as much as you love me. I want to see your beautiful hard cock,' and I sit back, waiting for you to do as I ask.

Of course, you huff and you puff, but your protestations are not enough, and of course, you do as you are asked. So there we sit as I slowly massage your cock, which is hardly hidden by the tablecloth. Soon it is nearly too much for both of us. I feel hot and I want more than just the feel of your cock, and looking around and waiting for that moment when no one is watching, I tell you to slip down off the seat and under the table to lick me. I love the feel of your tongue on my clit and pussy and I wriggle a little. Then, from under the table, a hand appears holding up a pair of small panties – removed while you were licking me.

You lick my pussy and then my clit, and slowly put two fingers inside me, easily finding my G-spot. It's a shame that you can't see my face because I know it is covered with both a big smile of pleasure and a very poor attempt to hide the growing excitement and the powerful feelings building inside me. Your fingers move faster and faster, knowing fully the expected outcome, and I feel the orgasm building as you push harder on my G-spot, which explodes in orgasm and juice. There's a groan and a moan as I vainly try to hold back the noise, but still, there's no mistaking what is happening.

As you return to your seat I see that your face and shirt are soaking wet with all the juice from my pussy. I don't know why, but it makes me laugh. I shouldn't, but you do look as though you have been out in the rain.

I tell you that you should go to the bathroom to tidy yourself up and let me regain my composure; although there is really no way that I want to be composed.

I think about it and I want to stay excited; then, while you are in front of the sink washing your face, you hear the door open and looking in the mirror you see me standing there.

Without a word, I grab your hand and pull you into a cubicle. We need to finish what we have started!

25. DRESSED FOR NOTHING

It has been a hard day and I'm planning to meet Adam for a drink straight after work. Being in a naughty mood I have made some very special arrangements, so before I leave the office I have to go to the ladies' room to get ready. I'm already nervous; this is the first time I have done this but it doesn't take long to prepare. Soon I have my coat on, wave goodnight to my co-workers and I am ready to set out.

We have arranged to meet in a busy bar, and as I sit on the bus going across town I'm so excited and desperate to see you. It may only have been a few hours since we kissed each other goodbye to go to our respective offices, but as ever, it seems like a lifetime.

The bus stops, the doors open, and I walk the last few hundred metres to the bar. It's cold and there is a chilly wind blowing, but as I think about your surprise, already my pussy is hot. I'm sure everyone is looking at me as I walk along the pavement as if they know already what is about to happen.

Oh, my man, I really do hope you like my special treat. I am sure you will because already it is doing wonderful things for me.

I am a little more nervous now as I open the door of the bar. I wait for a moment and look around; then I see you standing alone, so I push my way through the crowd to join you. You are such a gentleman and I like the way you walk to greet and kiss me. I am pleased to see you again. You look so gorgeous and I have missed you.

'Hello Alexa, what would you like to drink?' you ask. 'Give me your coat and I will hang it up.'

'White wine please, darling,' I say, 'but I think I will keep my coat on. I am still cold. Wait until I have warmed up just a little more.'

With our wine, we move to a table in a quieter corner of the bar and sit close to each other. I am so much in love I can't take my eyes off you.

'Adam,' I say, as I turn to look straight at you, 'I have a special treat for you.' I can see the look in your eyes and I know what you are thinking when I say this. You will think that I have brought some handcuffs or something else to play with you in a public place. I have done that to you so many times before.

'No darling, this really is a treat for you, and even thinking about it has already made me wet with excitement.' As I say this, I undo a couple of buttons on my coat and watch as your jaw drops when you see that I am not wearing a blouse or a bra. You can see my breasts and erect nipples.

'You came from work dressed like that?' you ask.

'Not just like that, but like this,' I say, as I undo the rest of the buttons on my coat and he can see that not only am I not wearing a blouse or bra but I don't have a skirt or lingerie either. In fact, other than hold-up stockings and boots, I'm naked under my coat. As you look you are staring at my breasts and my pulsing and now exceedingly wet pussy.

'Wow,' you say, and then go quiet for a moment as you take in what you see. 'That is putting a real strain on my trousers.' I look down at his crotch and see the bulge of his cock, hard and aching to get out; but this time it will have to stay locked away until later.

'I can see that darling, do you think this will help?' I ask as I pull the coat wide open – just like a flasher. You laugh a little nervous laugh, smile and I ask, 'Adam, do you think I am overdressed?'

I know I am, but there is no sensible answer.

26.   PRECONCEPTIONS

As my life moved forward I was spending much of my time interviewing women to learn about their deepest desires and fantasies. It was a sensory overload that fuelled my own thoughts and fantasies.

I would often wonder who I was, and when, with experience and living, I would really start to rationalise all that was happening.

Reflecting on who you are is very important for a sane life.

Preconceptions. We all have preconceptions. We look and we see what we expect to see; that is how magicians make magic.

Out of the station, turn left, walk for fifty yards and take a right. I am wearing my smart business suit, my hair pulled back tight on my head and heavy-rimmed glasses; so what am I? They look at me as they walk past. What do they see? A businesswoman going to work? I am going to work. I think about the word 'work'. I am confused.

Many people are on the street. It is morning and it is like a scene from one of the stories in the magazine I was just reading; an isolated woman in a crowd; a woman with little purpose in a sea of apathy.

Two men walk past me. One taller and fair and one shorter and dark; both handsome, and for a moment I see it in their eyes. They imagine us all together, naked, entwined in a sweaty mingling of arms and bodies.

That is a preconception. Men look at women and they think of sex. Women look at men and they think of security. They pass me, one on each side, and I turn to look at them, to follow their eyes and prolong their dream. They have both turned to look at me. We smile but walk on. There will be others.

If I am confused, then, so is everyone else. I want a cigarette but I don't have any with me.

A boy, a teenager, walks toward me. How old? Maybe fourteen. Blue jeans, white trainers and a hoodie; a normal boy. I stop him, whisper in his ear, give him a ten-pound note and point at the shop across the road. He nods and runs across the road and returns two minutes later with a packet of cigarettes. He hands them to me. I say thank you and smile. He has broken the law and I have my cigarettes. Youths need to be instructed and lead towards rebellion.

It's all about preconceptions. Age is a preconception.

Leaning against the wall I take a break, to prepare myself for work. I stop to light a cigarette and take a deep breath of poisonous air. I always need to prepare for work. I check my phone to re-read the message and check the address. It was a simple message, calling me for a project and a meeting in the office.

Again I walk; a left and then a right, and I reach the door, a large unassuming door onto the pavement. I push at it and walk up the steps as if I have been here before and done this many times. It is a grey and inconspicuous picture. I know the routine. First the interview; I know all the questions and all the answers. I push at the door and walk in confidently. Confidence is another preconception.

I see the desks in a row but no one is seated there. I look towards the window and smile. Standing at the window, talking, are the two men I met on the street.

'Hello again, take a seat,' the taller says. I do as he asked. Obedience and control are other preconceptions.

'We want to ask you some questions to make sure you are up to the job,' the taller man says.

'Do you mind if we film this as we talk? We need a good record,' the shorter man says.

'Of course,' I say, 'go ahead,' and they finish setting up the camera and the lights. They take their time and are fussy, and I think that if they wanted to film this they should have brought some expertise. I have no concerns about extra people being there. I like to get this sorted out in one visit. And finally, we sit facing each other.

The questions come from both of them in rapid-fire mode. 'How long have you been working at this? How did you get into this business? Why did you start? Who have you worked with? What can't you do?'

With all my rehearsed answers it is easy. I answer in automatic mode. 'At this job, about three years. I wanted new experiences. You only live if you have direct experience. I have no truck with the prudish. I like to challenge pre-conceptions.'

I do not need to concentrate, and as I answer, my mind is far away. As they quiz me I remember our encounter on the streets and think of sex. I see them naked through their clothes. Two naked men opposite me and I think of the control they are trying to exercise. Clothes give them control. Why don't they do the job properly and strip me and tie me tightly with rope, blindfold and spread-eagle me, and then they could ask me the same questions. Then I would answer truthfully.

We are all in bondage to our preconceptions and history. I am trying to break my mould to give myself the freedom to be me; so put me in bondage, and I will give the answers that would excite the psychiatrist. But they don't and I return to their world of predictable questions. We sit looking at each other in a long moment of silence that I refuse to break. They look at each other.

'Give us a moment. We need to talk. We will get a coffee. Do you want anything?' the taller one says.

I nod. 'A coffee, please.' I have been here before. I know what they will say. They will want to see really how good I am. They will want to test me. Why couldn't they just say it? But they stand and leave me and I watch as they stand by the window talking. One lights a cigarette. I want to join him with a cigarette but that would challenge all his preconceptions. I watch closely as he puts it in his mouth and then as the smoke slowly curls away from his lips. Would he like to see me smoke with rounded, pouting, red-lipsticked lips? I see his lips move. I know what he is saying. I don't have to hear.

'It wasn't our plan, but we need to see how good she is. If we are going to work with her we need to know if she's really got it.'

The rest will be more blah blah blah. They know what they want but it needs justifying. They need to justify their lust. I have heard all this before. It's always the same. I am always expected to perform. They talk. I stop listening and let my thoughts wander off again.

I think about business as a primaeval competitive contest with winners and losers. I think about sex. I always think about sex. I think more about porn. This is porn a woman and two men. It is not about love or sex, it is about a job which has to be done. Business is a job that has to be done. Sex is a job that has to be done. We are tied by it and we are all in bondage to what has to be done; we are in bondage to the preconceptions of others.

I know I am in bondage. I am tied and I cannot move. I am being used. I am being abused. That is what I do. That is what I am. There are few choices in bondage. I am naked and tied. I lift my head, and as I do, I see him walk naked and masked towards me. He places a crown of thorns on my head and ties a rope around my breast. It becomes engorged as the blood flows in and can never escape. Blood captured and bound and in its own bondage. He lies on the floor and the ropes fall off me. Am I going to have sex with him? Do I have a choice?

'Let me get the camera,' he says. 'I need to film this.'

'Now. On the count of three, fuck her; one, two, three, action.' I start to fuck. It feels good; I don't want it to stop; it is the ultimate release from bondage.

'Ok. Now I want a cum shot,' he says.

'And an orgasm from me?' I ask. 'I want to be released.'

The tall one looks at me. 'She can't,' he says, 'she's a doll. Can't you see? She is not real.'

From above, far away from my body, I look down. It is all fake. I am just a plastic doll. It is like this in all of life. What you think you see is never there. What you think you have is a mirage. Life is a big magic trick. Just one more case of seeing what you want to see.

'And me?' I ask. 'Can I have some release?'

'No, not you. We will fake it.'

I look at the doll and feel sorry for her. Always used and always abused. She is in her own bondage. I look deeply at her and I want her to be real and feel and not suffer. I see the pity and shame in her eyes and I am sure there is even a tear.

Finally, they finished their conversation and they return to me.

'We have decided and we just need you to do two more things for us. Will you read this script?' They hand me a piece of paper which I read as the camera rolls.

'Soon we were all naked on the bed, and they were kind enough to make sure that in their shared passion I wasn't totally excluded. The early evening turned into a late night. As I left them they were still naked, arms around each other, waving at me from the door.'

'And so?' I say.

'Now we pack up. Take a break.' I wander towards the window and light a cigarette. He comes and stands next to me, silently takes my cigarette and starts to smoke, dropping his head on my shoulder.

'And now?' I say.

He turns and looks at me. 'You will get a positive recommendation from us. We are sure you will do very well in the job. There is just one more thing we want. I nod with satisfaction.

I watch as they pack everything away. I am again tied to the wall with a camera rolling and fixed on me. I hear them leave, the lights switched off and the door slammed shut.

Alexandra

27. WORKING IN PORN

It was another birthday and in the build-up, I was thinking about sex and pornography – as every good woman does!

The stereotype from twenty years ago was that women don't have fantasies and that it was totally a male preserve. Some men may deny that they fantasise – don't believe them, they do. That is why scantily clad women still inhabit newspapers and advertising hoardings.

Twenty years ago many women might also have denied, even to their closest girlfriends, that they fantasised; but from all the research, we know that it was a lie. Now we know that for sure. If only measured by the huge sales, and therefore, presumably, the use of, vibrators and dildos. Did you know that one UK chain sells over a million of the Rabbit dildo each year! I can't believe that women would use their dildos with a totally blank mind.

There is, however, a difference between men's and women's fantasies. Ours are usually far more subtle, clever, erotic and emotional than any man's. That shouldn't surprise anyone because women are far more subtle, clever, erotic and emotional than any man.

Men don't understand this because sadly we still live in a world dominated by men's perceptions that assume, for example, that women share the same porn-driven fantasies that they have. That is wrong and why I wanted to share with you a real woman's fantasies.

As you may have read already, on my birthday I always try to do something different or unusual; it makes me feel younger. I have been a stripper and I have worked as a maid in a brothel, but for this birthday, with the help of good friends, I managed to spend the day on the set of a porn film.

Okay, I will own up. I have friends who work in places you wouldn't expect and I do have a friend in that business. He is a cameraman and he said he could get me on the set for a day. I was excited. Of course, I prefer to have sex than to watch and after a while, I find porno films boring, but the thought of watching one being made was totally different and exciting.

Damien, my friend, said that the production company had rented a large house in the Surrey countryside; it would be a midday start. He and the lighting guy (who was also our driver) had to be there early to set up, so in a white van full of cameras, lights, microphones and booms we were set to leave London at an unearthly hour in the morning.

What does a girl wear to a porno shoot? Well, first of all, I wanted to look good next to the actors, but then I didn't want to look too much like one of them; so it was good and classy makeup, a tight white T-shirt, boots and blue jeans. That, I thought, would make me at least look like the crew.

We were there just after ten o'clock, before the actors, so Damien and his mate could set up the lights and sort the camera positions with the director, and that was the first shock of the day.

I had always had an image of the director of a porn film as an old and slightly sleazy guy, but no, I was wrong. Women do direct porn and this film was to be directed by a woman. Nattie was the director. Maybe mid-forties, and thankfully dressed just like me in jeans. Damien introduced us, and as we chatted we seemed to hit it off straight away, but that was not for long because there was work to be done. Nattie and Damien needed some test shots to make sure the lighting was right and it was Nattie who asked me if I would stand in, as the actors hadn't arrived yet.

'What?' I said. 'Me? Do porn? Sorry, no.'

'No,' Nattie said, 'just go to the set and we will take some shots. You don't have to take off your clothes. This is not porn, this is just a camera test.'

Relief. Nattie sat in front of a monitor and Damien filmed while they moved and adjusted the lighting.

'Move a bit,' shouted Nattie. 'We want to do some tests.'

'How do I move?'

'Sexily,' Nattie replied, as she came from behind her monitor and gave me the largest dildo I have ever seen. 'Play with this,' she said. 'Hold it, stroke it, even lick it. It will help us with the setup.'

I looked at the dildo. In many ways, it was like a normal black penis with vein lines and a tip, but it was enormous: much, much bigger than anything I had seen in real life. I studied it and ran my fingers up the shaft to feel the texture, which was smooth. I was so fascinated by it, that I turned it round to look at it from every direction. I licked the end to see how it tasted. It was mesmerising.

'You're a natural,' I suddenly heard Nattie shout. 'You should do porn. Get all that, Damien?'

I looked at them. 'What do you mean?' I asked.

'You will see when Damien shows you the film.' Nattie was laughing lightly. 'It was a test shoot so of course, the camera was running. We have you and that dildo on film. If all the actors were that interested in the dildos and cocks, we would make mainstream porn and not the B-rated stuff we do.' Damien was smirking. I know what he had in mind for that film, and I noted that I had to remind him later that it was to be given to me or destroyed. I wasn't going to have a soirée with my friends broken up with a film show, with me as the star.

Finally, the actors were beginning to arrive. The three girls, I noticed, were generally small in build, but consistently had breasts that stood out beyond anything natural. The men looked normal but that is only if you spent your life in the gym.

'Nattie,' I asked, 'is there a script or anything, or is it just a film of people fucking?' I didn't know how else to describe it.

'Well, we do have a storyline, but the actual script is all printed on one sheet of paper. There isn't too much dialogue.'

'So what is the storyline? I asked, feeling rather stupid. Maybe she thought I should know.

'Well,' Nattie checked papers on a clipboard. 'It's a girl with a girl and then guy-girl normal, a guy with two girls with anal, then...'

'Ok Nattie, I get it. It's all about fucking.'

'That's it,' she said.

I looked around and counted up the actors. 'So,' I said, 'it's three girls and five guys.'

'That's it,' said Nattie. 'The other two girls are the fluffers.'

'There aren't another two girls,' I said, and asked, 'what is a fluffer?'

Nattie looked around as she was replying. 'A fluffer,' she said, 'is a girl that makes sure the guys are ready when we need them, with a BJ. Fuck. Where are the fluffers?' she shouted, to no one in particular.

She left me at a pace that made me realise that something was wrong. She talked to the actors, she talked to the production assistant and then she talked to Damien. Then she talked to everyone again.

She walked up to me.

'Alexandra,' she said, 'we have a problem. The fluffers get the guys hard and keep them hard between shots. Without them, we won't finish today, and we don't have the set tomorrow. Without the fluffers, there is no film.'

'Ohh,' I said. 'That sounds rough. How can I help?' Looking back on it now I can see I was very naïve.

'Damien told me about your birthday adventures. Will you fluff for us?'

I looked at her in disbelief. What should I say?

'Do I know how to fluff?' I couldn't think of anything better to say, momentarily wondering if fluff was actually a verb.

'Do you know how to give a blow job?' she asked. Now, I pride myself on being good at a great many things but at the top of the list is giving good head.

'Of course,' I said.

'Then you know how to fluff,' said Nattie. 'So will you?'

After a deep breath, I was cornered and I said, 'yes'.

Nattie looked relieved, and turned to the crew and shouted, 'We're back on. Alexandra will fluff.'

The makeup was done, the cameras were ready and the first two girls walked on set. It started with two girls having coffee, but they were not wearing anything I would wear for a mid-morning coffee with a girlfriend unless you think sexy lingerie is the appropriate attire. The only lines in the film were spoken, and soon they were naked and kissing and that huge dildo I had had in my hands just an hour or so earlier was being put to good use.

Watching these two thin girls take such a huge dildo amazed me, and watching them kiss and fuck made me excited. I was sitting next to Nattie when I heard my name called.

'Alexandra!' I turned, and there was one of the male actors, naked and summoning me. 'I need you, please.'

I mouthed silently, 'Me?' He nodded.

I went over to him. 'Yes,' I said. It was odd standing fully dressed in front of a naked guy. 'Blow job please,' he said.

What is a girl to do? I had agreed to help. I sank to my knees and took his cock deep in my mouth. I had learnt how to deep throat and I took him to the hilt as I felt it get larger and larger.

'Ok, Mike. You're on,' Nattie said, and he withdrew from me, left me on my knees and went on set. For the next hour or so, it seemed I was permanently sucking on one or other of the actors' cocks. Sometimes I could taste the pussies of the girls they had just fucked.

Of course, with all the action on the set and all the BJs I was giving I was getting excited and wet, and the tensions were just building up; but there was no way I could get any release. My pussy was hot and needed to be fucked. I was watching them being satisfied and all I had done was take part in exaggerated foreplay of sucking on cock; I needed more, but that wasn't going to happen.

It was then I heard a noise behind me and a shout of 'Ouch!'

'What's happened?' I said, as I looked up at Mike, who I was sucking for the umpteenth time that morning.

'Looks like Honey has had an accident,' he said.

I looked around and Honey, one of the actors, was sitting holding her head.

'You ok?' asked Nattie.

'I feel giddy,' said Honey.

'Fuck,' said Nattie. 'What do we do now? We are supposed to have a three-girl, five guy finish.'

Suddenly all eyes seemed to be on me. I could see the look in their eyes.

'No, you don't. You do it, Nattie. You know what to do,' 'Too old,' she said. 'Come on Alexandra, after all, you have sucked every guy, and I can tell by your jeans you are excited.'

I looked down and saw the darker shade around my crotch. Again, what is a girl to do? Plus she was right, I had already become very intimate with all the guys and I was really horny. So, in for a penny, in for a pound, I thought.

I stripped and Mike led me onto the set, and soon I was oblivious to the camera in a mad twirl of sweaty bodies, huge cocks and sweet-tasting pussies. I came and I came again, and then one by one the guys also came, and like all the girls I was covered in sweat and cum. It was done. The scene had lasted over thirty minutes, and I lay exhausted. Nattie said, 'Go and have a shower.'

I showered, dressed and came back into the room. The others were already there, drinking tea and chatting.

'Is every shoot as eventful as this?' I said. 'You guys were really unlucky. Two girls not turning up and then Honey hitting her head.'

If ever there was a look of collective guilt, I saw it just then.

Nattie spoke. 'Alexandra. Damien told us this morning about your birthday adventures. Happy birthday, by the way.'

I nodded thanks.

'We were never meant to have fluffers. They only use them when there are big gang-bang scenes and they need to get multiple men through, a minute at a time. We were just letting you have some fun.' Her head sank a little with the confession.

'And Honey?' I turned to see her looking as fit as a fiddle. 'Are you okay Honey?' She nodded.

'Another set-up Alexandra. Sorry,' said Nattie. 'But you did have a good time?'

'Yes, I suppose I did. But don't ever do that to me again, Damien.' I mocked anger.

'Maybe we could invite all your friends round for a preview. Would you like that?'

'Aaaaahhhhhhhh!'

28. SEX TOY PARTY

This is a new business venture for me and I really want it to be successful. If it works, it could become a regular event. I have invited a number of my girlfriends to a party, to market and sell sex toys. I have been told that in the UK this is a really popular way of selling naughty toys to women; it sounds good to me. All I have to do is invite my girlfriends around to my house; give them a drink; show them the toys; demonstrate how they work, then they buy them and I take a commission.

Adam was also excited at the idea of all these women meeting together with lots of sexy toys; men are so predictable. I need this to be successful so I have a cunning plan which makes use of his naivety. Only women are invited, but I want to tease them and excite them, so I start the party with lots of drink and everyone gets a little bit tipsy. Then, as we agreed, I will send you a text saying '*it's all going well.*' That is the planned cue for you to arrive at the party; a man amid all those naughty women. But my plan will not allow you to ogle at the girls.

We are having a great time playing with dildos and other toys. One of the girls tries on a pair of sexy knickers, and as we all laugh, there is a moment of sudden quiet as there is a knock on the door.

I answer the door carefully and look at you as you start to walk in. I feign reluctance. 'Sorry darling, you can't come in now. This is a girls-only party. Isn't that right, girls?' I say, turning to my friends. They nod, but then I pretend to have an idea and say, 'Wait here. I want to chat with them.'

This is a good piece of acting and I have a huddle with the girls before I let you in. Now, you are the only man there and you are very good at acting surprised.

'If you want to stay,' I say, 'then it is just the right time because we need a man to help us demonstrate some of the men's toys.' There is a real surprise and a reluctance but you are finally persuaded by my girls who, by now, are almost pleading with you!

'Now, what shall we do first girls? What about these naughty pants with a strap for his cock?

'Yes!' is the chorus of approval.

You will need to change and you try and go into another room, but I and all of the other women, insist that you get naked right there in front of everyone. This was not in your plan and is something I saved up for you as a special treat. When we agreed on all this you thought that you would be able to sit there and just watch all us girls having a good time with all our toys. How wrong you were, and you'd better watch out as I might have some other surprises.

My darling, you should really learn to dance, because the striptease was embarrassing; but you did manage to get all your clothes off – finally – and then try on and model the naughty pants, the cock rings and clitoral stimulators. The girls go wild and I know that I will make really good sales. I could see that you liked what you were doing, with all those girls looking closely at your large cock. It got very large and stayed like that all the time.

We want to take a break from all the toys but I can't let you go now because, although everyone is a little tipsy, we want to party some more, and all the girls agree that you must stay and be a nude waiter for us! They grab at your clothes and hide them so that you have no choice and so you wander around the room, in the nude and very hard, serving drinks to everyone. That is making me very excited as all the girls admire you, and the cock I think of as mine!

But a full demonstration of a product is what sells, so I make you model more and sexier clothes, showing everyone how all the toys work. OMG, this is making me so excited that finally I also have to give a demonstration to everyone. I lie on the floor and show everyone how to masturbate with the pink Rabbit, which brings me to a screaming, shouting, shivering, quaking orgasm. Actually, I bought that for myself and call it my 'pink pussy friend'.

But there is one toy we haven't yet demonstrated – the strap-on – and I am not going to let you get away without that. You didn't expect it, we didn't talk about it and I am sure you didn't want it, but, my good boy, you bend over while all my guests are baying for me to fuck you up the arse.

Don't worry though, I won't embarrass you by making love to you in front of an audience. I am far too considerate. Hahaha!

29.   IN THE PARK

On a sunny day, I am reminded of the days on holiday when we managed to have sex on the beach without being caught. How many people were there around us? I didn't count because I was far too busy enjoying your sensuous touch, even though we were surrounded. Maybe someone saw, maybe someone took a private and quiet photo which they are lusting after now. We don't know and we don't care.

It is sunny and warm and today we are in a park having a walk, hand in hand; we buy ice cream and sit on a quiet park bench and watch the sun setting over the trees. There is something about ice cream that is very sexy; maybe it is the froth of ice around your lips as we share a kiss to lick it off each other. Finishing the ice cream does nothing to reduce our ardour, and as ever, we are both sexually excited.

The path where, like most people, we walk is over a hundred metres away. Will they see us? Will someone wander our way? That is the risk and the risk that excites us. You sit on the bench and I sit facing you, with your cock buried deep into my pussy, riding harder and harder until we come. What a mess on your trousers.

Will everyone know what has happened when they see the stain around your crotch?

30. FETISH CLUB

We have been planning this for many weeks and tonight we are going to a fetish party at a club in London; I am really excited as this is our first time! It is easy to make the decision and buy the tickets weeks in advance, but it is only when the day arrives that it becomes real. Reality is having the bath, looking out the clothes, getting in the car and parking just around the corner. Then the excitement is at its greatest. We are not there just to party, to be seen and to watch, our objective is somewhat more extreme; as we arrive, our excitement is matched with increasing apprehension.

The club is very full with both men and women. They are dressed in every sort of fetish clothing. There are leather and lycra, maids, doctors and nurses; the air is full of sexuality.

I am dressed in a short, black leather dress; it is cut low at both the front and back and I am not wearing either bra or panties, knowing that if I bend low anyone can see my pussy. Just that thought makes me excited and even wetter than I was in the taxi when I was thinking about what was going to happen. And you, my good boy? You are wearing only black working man's boots and a jockstrap, and the growing bulge that tells me that you are making the best of this experience. I wonder if it is me or the whole ambience of the night that is making you hard.

We watch the crowd; we have a drink and watch as a woman beats a man shackled to the wall. It is real, as we hear his screams as each blow hits and we see the red weals growing; then there is the overweight woman being led around on a lead with clamps on her nipples. Men are kneeling at the feet of women cleaning their boots to a bright shine with overworked tongues. Our courage is building and we are now ready to embark on our own plan.

It was not easy to find, but we do find that area that is not as dark as other corners; we take to the vacant mattress and our kissing becomes more intense. We hold each other close, as much to protect each other as in passion, and I drop to my knees and pull down your jockstrap and start to suck you. Who does this excite most? Me, because I have a cock in my mouth, or you because everyone can see your beautiful, large cock being worshipped by the most beautiful of all women?

I look around; a small crowd of both men and women have started to gather around and watch us. I stand, unzip and pull my dress above my head and step back so that you and the crowd can wonder at my perfect body.

I don't care which way we have sex, so long as we have sex in public. 69; then from behind; then on top; while all the time the crowd gets larger. By the time we finish over 100 people are watching us!

That was so exciting.

31. RAINBOW

The party had already started as Alexandra sat in her taxi. She didn't want to go, but then again, she didn't know that she was going to a party. Her boss had said there was a client who had phoned and asked for a meeting and that it had to be after normal working hours.

'Would she mind,' the client had said, 'going round to his flat, as he had other commitments?' It was very unusual, but they had been trying to get his account for four months now. Alexandra did not connect the arrival of that prospective client with an evening she and Adam had spent just a few days earlier.

Slightly drunk on a sexy night, they had both signed up for a very unusual offer.

Adam had also forgotten about the 'contract' they had both signed; but while Alexandra was still to be reminded, Adam had had his memory prompted an hour before when he was leaving for work, as usual. He had taken the train, as he usually did and was about to walk back to their flat when the car pulled up alongside him and the passenger had asked for directions. 'I live near there,' Adam had said.

'As you are going the same way, I can give you a lift. It would help me out as well.'

There was a passenger in the front seat and one more in the back. Adam got in the back, and as he did, the passenger had thrown a bag over his head and pinned him down, and his hands had been tied behind his back.

'Rainbow, Adam, Rainbow. Remember?' At first, he didn't and then it all came back to him.

'Rainbow? Fuck, Rainbow,' and he stopped resisting. It was in the contract.

All of that now seemed to have been a very long time ago, but in the here and now he had no real idea of time. His hands were still tied but now held high above his head, presumably suspended from some hook in the ceiling. His mouth was gagged, his eyes covered and he had been stripped down to his underpants. He did not know where he was, but he could hear voices: men and women. How many were here? He listened hard and settled on maybe six or seven. Was

Alexandra safe?

Since that night they hadn't talked any more about it. At first, he had fantasised about this evening, but nothing had happened, and he hadn't thought about it for months. What was going to happen?

Alexandra still didn't know. The taxi was close but she didn't know the precise location. She told her driver that she didn't know exactly where it was, and settled back in the seat cursing business. She had tried to call Adam but his phone was off. They were due to have a quiet dinner tonight but maybe he had been held up at work. He could have called her. Blast him.

She arrived, paid for the taxi and headed into the foyer of a modern building. What was the flat number? Okay, the eleventh floor, she thought; she headed to the lift, not noticing a young couple, maybe not too much older than her, also rushing for the lift before the doors closed.

'What floor?' Alexandra asked.

'Eleventh,' the woman replied.

'Must be a party,' Alexandra said, not knowing how true that was.

They arrived on the eleventh floor and the door opened. The woman stepped out, and politely the man let Alexandra go first. But as she stepped out, the woman in front turned to face her, and Alexandra saw her smile just as darkness fell into her world. The bag was pulled roughly onto her head. Alexandra kicked out but the woman in front held her hands as she was pushed back into the lift.

'Rainbow, Alexandra, Rainbow'.

Unlike Adam, Alexandra had thought about this more often and it both excited and frightened her. Often at work, she started to feel herself becoming moist and even wet at the prospect of hearing that word but then dismissed it as fantasy. It could never happen. It was far too outrageous a thing to happen, but then, here, today, it had. She remembered Rainbow much more quickly than Adam and had stopped kicking. Now she was scared.

Unable to see, she was held tight and heard the lift door close; again the lift moved; it stopped; then the doors opened and they walked. Alexandra couldn't work out whether they had gone up or down. She was led out and pushed down the corridor, not knowing which floor she was now on and knowing she could never find the same place again.

Had she been able to see, she would have noticed that the door of the flat was open before she was led in; there were four couples and odd singles, all in different stages of undress, with one woman already wearing no more than her bra and very brief panties; and there was, of course, a nearly naked and blindfolded Adam, arms high, suspended from the ceiling.

But otherwise, it was like any other small party. People were standing around, drinking and eating small canapés. They were talking and laughing. Generally, they paid no attention to Adam, except occasionally a passing woman and once a man reached down and grabbed or played briefly with his cock, keeping him hard.

As Alexandra was led in, initially they turned and took a mild interest, but by the time she was fully in the room they were all watching. Her hands had been tied, and like Adam, she was suspended by a rope tied to a hook in the ceiling. Wearing a blouse, bra, short skirt, panties and tights she was almost swinging, as the rope pulled her up to near tiptoes.

'This is your last chance,' a voice said. 'Is Rainbow go? Adam?'

'Yes,' it was a weak voice through the gag.

'Alexandra?' So they have her too, Adam thought. Alexandra wasn't sure if she should be relieved or upset to hear his voice.

'Yes.'

'Then let the party begin,' the voice said, as the party turned and resumed their conversations and laughing.

Alexandra was thinking about that night months earlier. They had been drinking champagne and celebrating her promotion at work. They had made love and were messing about on the computer. They had stumbled by accident across the Rainbow Group. Now she could also remember the website, word for word.

'We are a group of swinging couples who meet occasionally to share our bodies in an open and unselfconscious way, but even we like to spice up our parties. Are you an individual or couple who is looking for the ultimate adventure? If you sign this contract you agree, either individually or together, to be picked up off the street and used as our plaything at our party, and that means you consent to sex with either gender, to be used as we want, for whatever we want. All we guarantee is that pain is not part of it. To make it all the more exciting, you agree that this can happen at random, any time in the next six months. You will not know until you hear the word 'Rainbow' that it is us!'

For the first couple of weeks, every phone call Alexandra received meant she had to leave her office or homemade her think that it might be the Rainbow call, but with time the concern had diminished, and tonight it had not even occurred to her that it was the night. That new client! My God, they had been planning this for a long time.

'I think these need to come off,' the voice said, as her tights were removed by unseen hands.

'And these,' and her blouse and bra were taken. Now she, like Adam, was dressed only in panties. What was going to happen? Had her eyes not been covered, she would have been able to see a group of eight people standing around them.

They had decided that Alexandra was going to be dealt with first. From the same hook she had been tied to, they had now tied a swing, and she had been placed in it. She was lying on her back no more than a metre in the air. There was support under her shoulders and bottom. Her legs had been spread by ropes around her ankles which were pulled high and wide. Her head hung down. The effort of keeping it up was too much, and her long, fair hair almost touched the ground.

Now she was secure, she was left swinging while they turned their attention to Adam. He was laid on his back on a large table, spread-eagled, with his hands tied. The Rainbow Group stood back and admired their work.

One couple had lost interest in their guests of honour, but they knew their turn would come. They had started to kiss and undress each other. Her breasts sagged slightly as he took off her bra. He cupped her breast and sucked on a nipple. She sank to her knees, and while doing so, removed his trousers and pants and took his cock in her mouth. They weren't hidden in a bedroom but were there in the middle of the room, as others walked around them.

Alexandra was relieved that the fullness of her embarrassment was saved by her panties, but this was to be short-lived.

'Now, what can we do with Alexandra while she is still wearing these knickers?' the voice said. Not much, she thought, with my legs like this they will never come off.

She felt a hand on her breast, one caressing her thigh and another running down her leg. At least three people, she thought, were interested in her body, and then another was running a hand over her pussy through her panties. She was getting wetter and wetter with all the attention. Her panties were pulled aside and a finger caressed her clit and slowly started to penetrate her.

Suddenly the feel of the cold steel of the scissors made her twitch. 'I think these should come off'. She felt the steel draw down her belly, then pull and cut at the material of her panties, which loosened before dropping to the floor. A hand drew a line from her breasts before arriving at her now fully exposed and throbbing pussy, before first one finger and then two were pushed inside her. With the hood still over her head, she couldn't see the flash after flash of cameras, recording every minute of her humiliation.

She tried to collect her emotions. She was not naturally promiscuous, and since she had started dating Adam there had not been anyone else – well unless you count the actors on the porn film set; but here she was consenting because she had said yes to Rainbow, about to have sex with multiple unknown men and women. She should be frightened, she should feel angry and resentful, she should feel invaded but she felt excited; all her senses were in overdrive and she was highly aroused.

Her head was yanked up, the hood was pulled tight and a hole made above her mouth. It was then that she felt the first cock start to thrust deep into her pussy and then another down her throat. What should she concentrate on? Neither, she thought – they will know what to do. In both, the thrusting got stronger. She started to gag, just as she started to feel the tingling sensation in her thighs and the contractions begin in her pussy.

Meanwhile, Adam was being sucked hard while lying on the table. He had assumed it was by a woman, it never occurred to him that it was a guy; which it was. Already astride him, a woman was getting ready to sit on his face. His hood had been pulled back to expose his mouth. Naked and squatting, she lowered herself onto his mouth and gratefully received his tongue.

Alexandra had just had her first orgasm of the evening. She was fucked in the pussy and ass. She had taken more than one cock in her mouth; she had licked pussy and taken more than one strap-on. Everyone there had taken her, and some in more than one way. She had lost count of the orgasms and her clit was tender – she shook at the slightest touch. She had swallowed cum from more than one man and was left swinging in a contented haze.

Adam was also being fucked; first by a woman with a huge strap-on and then by two of the men. A woman had sucked him dry and he had taken a cock in his mouth for the first time.

Just as Alexandra was relaxing, she felt one, then two fingers plunge deep into her pussy, and push harder and harder and faster and faster. They were reaching a G-spot she never even knew about. The tension was rising; the heat in her pussy increasing; the tingling around her body growing. Her back arched, the fingers were moving faster and faster, and then she came in a way she had never come before. It embraced her whole body which shivered and shook but she also felt a new sensation as her pussy convulsed and contracted and she felt liquid juices squirting with force across the room. She was weak, she was tender to touch, and she screamed the most delicious scream of joy.

While the Rainbow Group returned to drinks and bites, Alexandra and Adam were left to relax and recuperate. The party moved on and there were random couplings; two men with one woman; then three with one woman who had cocks in her ass and her pussy and her mouth. Two women were playing with one man, slowly teasing him and nearly making him come, but always stopping just in time. Some were just naked, seated at the bar, drinking and talking about nothing.

The party was ending and Alexandra and Adam were both trying to take in what had happened. They were untied – still blindfolded – and dressed. They were led down the corridor to the lift and the door closed. They held hands as the lift moved. Then they heard the door open, but nothing happened. As it started to close again, Adam stuck out his foot to stop it. Tentatively, he lifted his hood. Only Alexandra was there. He lifted her hood and kissed her.

They walked out, hailed a cab and said nothing on the way home.

32. NATURIST BREAK

Where and how an idea develops is not always easy to pin down, but this one had been nagging at Alexandra for many months. Maybe it started when she was browsing through holiday brochures and came across one including access to a naturist beach. The thought of being naked among lots of other people was exciting, although she knew that being excited and horny was not the real reason that most people chose naturists holidays; for her it was.

Alexandra wanted to feel the excitement; she wanted others to be looking at her with lust on their mind and she revelled in the thought of being the centre of sexual exhilaration.

This year's holiday plans were made (not including the naturist beach), but the thought had not left her. So when idle browsing of the internet had highlighted a nearby naturist spa which clearly allowed for very permissive behaviour, the thoughts resurfaced. She only hesitated to talk about it to Adam because she was sure that he would reject the idea immediately, and then she would be forced to go by herself. Then what would happen if she met someone else?

Then it was clear. She was going to go whatever so better to enlist his support. Alexandra had decided it was much better to recruit him.

'You mean naked?' he said.

'I am sure it is optional,' she said. 'You will be able to use a towel.'

Adam nodded tentatively, still sceptical.

Plans were made to go in just over a week, and as the day approached, even Alexandra was becoming a little more concerned. She wasn't sure she would be brave enough and might, at the last minute, run away screaming.

When the day arrived it was warm and sunny, and Alexandra smiled to herself as she watched Adam pack a small bag with swimming trunks and a towel. His expectations were very clear; he was not going to be undressed. Well, we will see, she thought; but to make sure he stayed confident, she made sure he watched as she also packed a bikini and a silk sarong. After all, she thought, they could hardly queue in the restaurant in the nude?

In the car, driving there, they both avoided any direct conversation and talked about anything else, each putting up the front that this was normal. The GPS gave them directions, and as they pulled into a car park Alexandra saw Adam's surprise. It was not empty and deserted but full of many other cars.

'There must be hundreds of people here,' he said. 'I thought it would be empty.'

Alexandra shrugged. She had thought, and maybe even hoped, the same.

Collecting their bags, they walked to the main building, paid their entrance fee and were ready to head towards the changing room. Adam was looking around for the men's room and finally, he went to ask at reception.

'There is just a single, communal room,' the receptionist said, and pointed in its direction; Adam was totally distracted by a naked couple walking past them, heading off in some direction or other. Alexandra and Adam looked at each other and knew there was now no alternative; gripping each other firmly by the hand, they headed off. It was Alexandra who poked her head cautiously around the door and then pulled Adam in after her.

Other than being single-gender, it was like any other gym changing room with lockers; but for Adam, it was thankfully empty. They stripped down and Alexandra watched as Adam pulled on his swimming trunks and stood with a towel on his shoulders. Alexandra was naked but felt the need to wear her sarong. They walked to the door where they saw the notice: NO CLOTHES PAST THIS POINT. They looked at each other and both knew what the other felt: I want to go home! But Alexandra had been planning this fantasy for a long time and was not going to give up now.

'We will just have to do as they say,' she said. Then she walked back to her locker, took off the sarong and turned back to Adam. 'Come on, you need to get those off.'

He looked at her. She had a beautiful body and was standing naked in front of him, her breasts firm and not drooping at all, long and slender legs and a firm, flat tummy. He knew that there was a potential problem looming: he would soon have an erection.

'Do it, Adam. Please don't let me down.'

He found resolve, pulled down his shorts while quickly wrapping the towel around his waist (there was only so far he would go) and threw the shorts to Alexandra; and that was how they walked, holding each other's hand to provide comfort and reassurance, into the core of the club.

'Where first?' he said, averting his eyes from all the other brazenly naked guests.

'I want to try the hot tub first.'

'Ok,' he said nervously, and, following the signs, they walked in that direction, passing many other naked visitors on the way. Wearing just a towel, for the first time, Adam felt self-conscious and overdressed. Alexandra was exhilarated. She was naked and as she walked she felt released and empowered. She knew that she had a wonderful body and felt that everyone looked at her as she passed them.

She felt a tingle of sexual excitement as they found the tub. It was large and there were already half a dozen people in there: four men and two women. The couples were sitting close together.

As she slipped into the water she smiled, as Adam tried to minimise the time between losing his towel and being covered by the bubbling water.

'Hi. I am Alexandra and this is Adam,' she said to the others. Adam sat close to her as they all chatted. She found out that there was only one true couple and all the others were singles, two of whom had struck up a very recent close relationship. Alexandra watched as first, they kissed intimately, then it was clear that under the water hands were exploring. It excited her and she let her hand move onto Adam's thigh and then his cock, which she felt grow under her massage. She looked at his face and saw that, with her guidance, he was finally starting to relax.

'Darling,' he said, 'we are here for a long time. Please, not too fast!'

She smiled as the conversation with the others continued, but now his hand was firmly on her pussy while his fingers desperately tried to penetrate her from an impossible position.

'Let's go and explore the rest of the place,' she said.

'I would love to,' Adam replied, 'but you will have to stop doing what you are doing. I can't go right now.'

She smiled, stopped her massage and then ten minutes later she got out. As she did so, she took his towel with hers and said, 'come on'.

'Give me my towel, please darling?'

'No. You don't need it now and you can't stay in there all day. Let's go and get a drink,' and she started walking.

He now had no choice and self-consciously pulled himself out of the tub and walked towards her.

'Now that isn't too bad, is it?' Alexandra said, smiling and walking that bit ahead of him so that he had to follow. He didn't know if he should try and cover his cock with his hands as he walked but decided that would draw even greater attention to him. So he strode behind her, sure his face was crimson with embarrassment.

Over the day their confidence increased and they sun-bathed together and even had a naked drink in the restaurant before walking around the gardens.

'Adam,' Alexandra said, 'do you love me?'

'Of course,' he said, 'but why do you ask me now?'

'Because except in the tub you've hardly touched me all day and we haven't gone into any of the playrooms.'

'Darling,' he said, 'that's because I am scared that I might get an erection in public and I don't think that would be appreciated by the other people.'

She looked at him and smiled. 'It's okay to have an erection in the right parts of the complex. Come on, let's go and explore what else they have here.'

So they did.

They followed a sign to the 'PLAY ROOM' and went inside. The lights were dimmed and there were sofas and even a bed. In the room were couples and even a threesome, with two men and a woman. This was the first time that either of them had seen or watched another couple having sex, and for a moment they stood in awe.

Later they realised that they had both had the same thought: in porn, the women are all beautiful; the men all have a six-pack and a cock a mile long, but here they were normal people. There were sagging breasts, beer bellies, too much hair in places it shouldn't be, and small cocks.

They sat close together on a sofa and soon were kissing passionately as hands explored each other. Alexandra was wet with desire and Adam was hard from the expert touch of both Alexandra's hands and mouth; but when it came to sex, both found it intimidating in front of other people.

'Let's see if we can find a quieter place,' Alexandra said, 'where we can be more private.'

They stood up and left, and as Alexandra looked at Adam, she smiled. He was walking around in public with a large erection, only concerned about finding a place where they could make love.

'Let's go and see what the sauna is like?' she said.

It was a large sauna and already another couple were there, but by now they were used to being naked around other people, especially as they were entwined in each other and not worried about new visitors.

Alexandra and Adam sat on a lower, less hot bench and immediately resumed at the point they had left off in the playroom. He cupped her breasts and played with her nipples, or he massaged her back, which was already sweaty with the heat. Alexandra turned and sat on his lap facing him.

'I love you,' she said, as slowly she sat on his cock, riding him and kissing him at the same time. They were both hot and the sweat was already streaming down their bodies. It was slow sex as she pushed herself up so that the tip of his cock nearly came out, before sitting down so hard that he penetrated her deeply. The rhythm was regular and they both smiled. Then Adam could feel her pussy becoming tighter on him, pulling him closer; the pace increased and the smile transformed as she started a long, low regular moan, before exploding into a loud scream as they came together.

She sank back into his arms.

'That was beautiful,' a voice said, and they realised that the other couple had been watching them.

'Thank you,' was all Alexandra could think of saying.

They left the sauna and returned to the changing room. 'We need a shower. Do they have them here?' Adam asked and Alexandra went to explore.

'Come here,' Alexandra said, and pointed Adam towards a large open – and again communal – shower; so they showered together. They washed each other and at one point Adam was even on his knees in front of Alexandra, licking at her pussy, with the excuse that he wanted to make sure it was properly clean!

Alexandra

VI. A LITTLE BIT OF GITA IN MY LIFE

Five years on and I was now Doctor Alexandra S—, PhD. It was as a 28-year-old that I returned to Kyiv. The 2009 version of Kyiv was very different from the one I had left. It was freer, easier and there was no sign of the problems which were about to come and which we face today.

I had planned to spend only two years in London, but this got stretched. It was a wonderful time and I regret none of it, especially those years with Adam.

I always need to travel, I need an escape. This was made easier as my modelling took me to many exotic places, but none of them was home. My home is Ukraine and Kyiv, so even though I went to London as often as I could, I used to return to Kyiv to see old friends, visit favourite places and speak my own language.

My life was moving forward. I was now fully qualified and I had my doctorate, so there were no more degrees that I wanted or needed to take. My modelling was going really well, but more importantly, I could start to build a new career as a professional psychologist.

From all you have read, it may seem to you that I have flitted around from academia to modelling and never done what you might call a proper day's work in my life.

Well, for a time in an office was my life. With a doctorate completed, I thought that I should get out into the real world, but for a time I had to take an office job while I established a psychology business.

To start with, I had to take a string of secretarial jobs – most of which bored me totally. Because it was a 'proper job' (9 am to 5 pm, four weeks holiday, etc.) I had to cut down on my modelling, and that hurt me a great deal – not just financially, but also because I enjoyed it. Unfortunately, I had to work in an office to make sure I had enough money to live.

I will own up and say that it was not always fun, and I find the office environment a claustrophobic place to sit from early morning into the evening. They are boring places and I can understand why there are office romances and all the jokes about sex in the stationery cupboard.

I always delivered the tasks set for me, but as you might have guessed it was an environment perfectly suited to a dreamer. I could sit at my desk, process my work and dream my fantasies – all at the same time. I rarely enjoyed the work, but if I had to be there I was going to make the best of it. Yes, you guessed it. That is the recipe for many of my dreams.

33.   UNDER THE DESK

It was Valentine's Day and Alexandra was sad. Well, she wasn't sad generally, but she knew who she loved and she wasn't sure that he loved her. In fact, she wasn't even sure he had ever looked lovingly at her. Despite that, she went to work with her usual happy heart because at least she spent most of every day with James; he was her boss. He was running his own business and obviously had given himself the largest office. It had its own bathroom, so he didn't have to come out even to go to the toilet. Maybe, she thought, he had the largest... no! When she thought like that it was impossible to carry on working as she felt the moisture in her pussy.

However, there was some benefit to going to work. If she couldn't have her boss, she could at least have some fun. Although it was an open-plan office, Alexandra's desk was slightly hidden from the rest of the staff, so she had some privacy. It had started a couple of months ago when she had found a website where models received money just for chatting on their webcams to members. Well, it wasn't only chatting, as many of the models stripped and played with themselves for all to watch.

Of course, Alexandra couldn't strip at work and at first, she just chatted to men. At times there were hundreds in her chatroom watching her, and they loved that she was at work and could spin the cam and show them all her co-workers. If only her colleagues knew she was having naughty and sexy conversations on her webcam with men from all around the world and that they were part of the star attraction. Soon every lunchtime she was a regular cammer. She loved the raunchy chat. She loved the lewd suggestions. She loved strangers she couldn't see, telling her they wanted to fuck her; and then one day she couldn't resist it anymore. She wore a tight jumper with a low-cut top to work. She had chosen it carefully that morning, knowing that she wanted to excite her viewers, and so it happened.

She had just wanted to show the jumper and show off the shape of her breasts, but then the excitement got too much: she cupped a breast and pulled it out of her jumper and showed it to the two hundred and fifty-two people by then in her online chatroom.

With all those men watching her, the exhilaration was electric;

then she was excited by the money they gave, but even better was the excitement at the thought – and the very slight risk – that someone in the office would catch her. She loved that risk.

From then on, it had been easy. She wore shorter dresses so she could easily pull them up to show flimsy panties, then one day she had taken off her panties and shown everyone her wet and engorged pussy. She daren't touch it as she was sure that she would come, and with her screams, she would have the whole office running to her to see what was wrong.

Camming had become a habit and she had become more daring, hoping none of her colleagues had noticed; but all the time she was hoping that her boss, James, would find her and she would be the one for him. She wanted him to take her, but she felt that he had never even been close to seeing her in that way. She had even fantasised that he was sitting alone in his office, slowly playing with his cock while watching her cam show.

Today, Valentine's Day, she had decided that she would not cam. It was his day and she would not spoil herself for anyone else. Her skirt was short as usual, but her blouse was more demure.

He was going to be in the office all day. There was a team meeting in the morning and then a client meeting in the afternoon, and every time they met she had tried to look at him lovingly, but he didn't seem to see. When it came to lunchtime he just opened his door and walked past her desk. She had even posted him an anonymous Valentine's card; she smiled when it arrived in the morning post and simply added it to all of his other mail, but there was no comment from him, not even a knowing smile.

'Hi Alexandra, just going to lunch. I'm meeting Bob at the restaurant and then we're back here with his team for the meeting,' and with that, he was gone.

Alexandra had her sandwich and as normal, then went into his office to make sure it was tidy for the meeting. She cleaned coffee cups out and then the rolled up balls of paper on the floor – more discarded ideas – crawling under his desk on her hands and knees to collect them all. There, in the dark space under his desk, she suddenly felt comforted and calm. It was a dark space and it was his space and she sat there cross-legged with closed eyes and thought of him. As she did, her hand reached down to her pussy which she suddenly realised was starting to become moist. Just thinking of him made her excited.

Protected by the vanity screen, she stretched her legs so she could take off her panties, unzipped her skirt and removed it, putting both behind her. She unbuttoned her blouse and removed her bra, which was also discarded. This was exciting and so much better than any cam show.

She returned to sitting cross-legged and her naked bottom was warmed by the carpeted floor; she was feeling very horny and excited as she slowly massaged her clit. Her eyes were closed and she was dreaming of James making love to her. She was in a world of her own, but it was soon disturbed. In her dreams he was naked and had just swept her up in his arms to take her off to bed; but in the real world, he was there, with her, back in his office.

'Bob – take a seat while I see if I can get Alexandra to rustle up some coffee,' he said. He was back and Alexandra froze. Any noise of getting dressed would draw attention. Please God, she thought, I hope they use the couch and coffee table for their meeting!

'Sorry Bob, there's no sign of her. You will have to wait for your coffee. Now, what were you saying about Alexandra? I must hear this before the others arrive.'

Alexandra wanted to hear but it was not easy, crouched as she was under his desk. At least he was on the other side – sitting on the desk, she thought, with Bob on the sofa.

'It was Brad,' he said, 'and if I have this right, it was from this friend of a friend and he recognised my office. Apparently, he watches your Alexandra strip for them all at lunchtime on a cam show.'

'Well, said James, 'at least it's during the lunch hour and not in office time. But it is serious. Carry on. What does she do? I'm not sure I believe it.

Alexandra just sat listening as she and her boss heard a full description of her camming.

'But there's more,' Bob was saying. 'When she talks to these guys, she says that she fancies her boss – yes, you – like hell, and is hoping and waiting for him to make a move on her.'

There was silence and then James spoke, 'I will have to speak to her about this, but about making a move on her – you know, Bob, I would if I could. She's pretty hot, but how can I make a move on my secretary?'

Alexandra was as red as a tomato, but also excited. Here she was, nearly naked, hearing that he also liked her. But if he found her now then all that would change in an instant. Damn, damn, damn.

'I just hope no one in my office is watching her,' James said, and Alexandra thought 'oops'. That had occurred to her as a possibility, but if anyone really was hooked on her shows, that would really add to her embarrassment.

Now she heard other voices and the meeting was clearly about to start. How long was it going to last? She couldn't remember. An hour? Please let it be less. Please let it be over quickly.

'Gentlemen, let's use my desk,' James said, we can lay out the maps better there.'

No, please not the desk, thought Alexandra, but she heard him walk around.

'Please be seated,' he said, pulling out his seat and sitting down. As he rolled his seat towards his desk, his feet touched Alexandra's leg. He stopped. He looked under his desk and saw Alexandra bare-breasted, no skirt, no pants; a pussy looking straight up at him. Alexandra looked at him as he peered at her. Arms out, she shrugged, smiled and winked.

'Problem James?' said Bob.

What would he say? she wondered.

'No problem, Bob. The carpet is just a bit crumpled and stopped my chair. All sorted now,' he said, as he pulled the chair closer to the desk with his feet resting on Alexandra's lap.

What would she do? Well, she might as well have some fun. It couldn't get any worse. She was bound to be fired now. So she undid his shoelaces and took off his shoes and started to massage his feet. He didn't resist as she heard him carry on with the meeting. She was still excited and she took off a sock and pushed his foot onto her now dripping pussy. Slowly he understood and his toes started to touch and tease her. She held his foot in her hand and guided him and coaxed him to make her enjoyment all the greater.

She felt so horny and reached up to discover a large and twitching bump in his trousers. She rubbed his cock and felt it get larger and larger.

Keep going. She turned herself quietly so her head was now nearly in his lap and she rubbed him with both hands.

Keep going. He was still talking and the meeting was progressing.

Keep going, she thought. She found his belt and loosened it. She undid the top of his trousers and unzipped him. She reached inside his pants and pulled out his cock, which met all her expectations. She licked down the shaft, took his balls in her mouth and finally lipped the tip of his cock before taking him deep into her mouth. She didn't know where she had learnt this skill, but she could take all of him deep down her throat. She worked hard at his cock and could sense him getting larger in her mouth.

'You ok, James?' Bob said, 'You look a little tense.'

'Actually, Bob, I don't feel too good. I think we are nearly done anyway. Does everyone agree? Do you mind if I don't see you out? I just need to get a little moment alone.'

Although Alexandra heard everyone move and doors opening it didn't stop her on her mission. She may be finished at the office but she wanted to taste his cum before she left for the last time; as she heard the door close, James came in a hot salty gush down her throat, spilling out and down her chin and breasts.

He sank back into the chair and didn't say anything at first.

'So,' he said, 'that was not what I expected from this meeting.' He was lying back in his chair.

'I think I need a shower. Come here.'

Alexandra crept out on her hands and knees.

'Why didn't you tell me?' he said, looking down at her.

'Tell you what? I am so sorry, I didn't think you would be back so early.'

'No, I meant you tell me what you thought about me. Let's go and have a shower. I need one and I can see you do as well.

He led her into the bathroom and took off her blouse. She was now naked and still in the office. He undressed and led her to the shower. Warm water cascaded around them. They kissed deeply and he held her close.

'You won't be able to carry on working here, you know?' he said.

He is going to fire me and kick me out, she thought.

'But—' she had started to say, as he put his finger to her lips.

'You know the rules of the firm. We don't allow married couples to work here. Happy Valentine's Day, my darling Alexandra, my little kitten.'

34. IN MY OFFICE

It is early evening and you have arrived at my office to collect me and take us home. As usual, you walk straight into my office. It is late and I am alone as most of my colleagues have gone home, but one or two say they may be coming back after visiting clients. We don't know where my boss is.

Even at the end of the day I am looking as sexy as ever, and as always you make me excited; we greet each other with a kiss, but there is a little more intensity because you don't know that I have been watching naughty videos during the afternoon and I am feeling very horny.

We talk about locking the office but we can't because others may still come back, but that is not a hindrance to what we have in mind. We clean all the papers off my desk and make love on it, we have sex on the sofa and we have sex in the main office, running around naked like young children.

Do we have sex in my boss's office? Now that's another story!

35.   THE WORKMAN

Alexandra was in the office. It was lunchtime and she had meant to go out with her colleagues but, as ever, she was working too hard and they couldn't wait. So, there she was, they had gone and she was alone. She made herself a coffee and was thinking about what to do next. More work, she thought, and it is my lunchtime.

She looked through the window where at least there was something interesting to see. A young man who had been working on repairs in the office in the morning was lying on the grass relaxing in the sun, using his shirt as a pillow. Alexandra thought he looked rather sexy; a state made even greater by her own aroused feelings; she had spent the morning trying to decide which of the half-naked, bikini-clad models' photographs should be put in the magazine. Sometimes when the right mood took her, she imagined it was her who was the model, and after the shoot, the photographer had taken her to the changing room and... But then the phone would ring or there would be a call for help and the trance would be broken; both Alexandra and her thoughts had to move on.

As she gazed out of the window, her repairman stood and put on his shirt, doing up only a couple of the buttons. As she watched him, unobserved, she felt the first heat of excitement. How could she attract his attention? The task was taken away from her as he looked up and smiled, and she smiled back. She was wearing a short skirt and a very sexy blouse, and as she stood up to move to the window, her skirt rose up and showed her pretty but tiny and transparent knickers. Ooops. She had wanted to flirt but maybe not that much. He saw and she saw he had seen.

Why not, she thought? I have the time and he is dishy... so, why not? She stood at the window and pulled the blouse tight across her breasts and her nipples were hard and outlined. He watched. She undid the top two buttons on her blouse and her breasts were nearly exposed. She could see that he was getting excited, every bit as much as she was.

She wanted to hold him, so she motioned to him to come to the door. He nodded. Where would they go to have sex? Maybe they would go into the stationery cupboard, or maybe more riskily in the open on her desk, or maybe on the director's desk. Yes, that would be fun. Every time the director called her in afterwards she would see a stain on the desk to remind her of her repairman.

She went to the door to meet her lunchtime lover but there was a problem, a big problem. He was repairing the main locks, and as all her colleagues had left they had slammed the door, and now it wouldn't open. She was locked in and he was locked out. All that was there was a large hole where a new lock was to be fitted.

'They will be back soon. What can we do?'

'It will take me an hour to fix.'

There was both urgency and despair in their voices. Both had reached a point where there was no return without a long afternoon of deep frustrations.

'I want your cock so badly,' she said, and then as she looked forlornly at the door, through the hole a cock appeared. At first, she reached to touch it, and as she did it grew harder and fatter, and as it grew she knelt down and took it all in her mouth. She could hear his moan on the other side of the door, but as she sucked harder and deeper, she wanted so much more. So she pulled up her skirt and took off her panties, then turned with her back to the door; then she slowly pushed the cock into her pussy. She rocked backwards and forwards and back again, and felt him grow and fill her. It was heaven. There she was, fucking in the office. This was so much better than lunch and all the time he was getting larger and harder until, with a scream, she came with an orgasmic climax.

Over that year or so of office work, I was soon promoted and I moved on from pure secretarial work to a management role. I learnt some special skills and was a junior account manager and designer in a company where I had a very misogynistic male boss.

I needed strategies to establish myself as a good worker and individual. Maybe my chosen route was just a little out of the ordinary, but so many women really just don't understand the power they have over men.

Alexandra

36. THE MISOGYNIST

'Alexandra: get in here – now.' That was how James has always spoken to me. He is my boss, but more than that, he is my married boss. He is head of graphic design and I am one of the team. James is one of the world's beautiful people; on the outside at least. He is handsome and tall. He can be engaging and charming when needed, but mostly he sees his staff as slaves, to be used and consumed to further his own career.

I had always thought when I was recruited to work for him that maybe part of the reason was my looks and not just my skills as a designer. Without blowing my own trumpet, I am also beautiful: clear skin, slim, long blonde hair and beautiful white teeth; but I am also very talented at my job.

My suspicions were right, and with time, I had come to resent being recruited purely as an ornament for him to show off as a trophy to clients. We had been in presentations with clients and he always made me fetch the coffee and run errands so he could show I always did his beckoning. 'Alexandra will book a taxi for you,' or 'Alexandra, be an angel and get us all some sandwiches.' I resented it because I am good at my job and not just a good-looking woman, although reluctantly I also recognised that when we went together to clients I could see we made a *celebrity couple* and that his looks and my beauty did charm work prospects.

There was also an animal charm and sometimes, though rarely, he would also spare some of that charm for me. Annoyingly, when he did, I felt a weakness at the knees and a deep sense of uncertainty about my feelings. So, this time when I heard him shout for me across the office, I wasn't sure which James to expect. I gathered up a pad and pencil and saw the look of the others, my co-workers, both wishing me well and pleased it wasn't them called in for the probable reprimand. Because often it was a scolding and a chastisement. I couldn't think of any mistake I had made or where I had gone wrong, but sometimes that didn't matter.

'Alexandra, where the fuck are you?' he shouted, and I hurried as fast as I could in my slightly too high-heeled shoes, while also straightening my pin-striped, pencil-cut skirt.

'About time,' he said, getting up from his desk and pointing for me to sit on the sofa by the coffee table. He watched, smiling, as I sat down, attempting to be elegant. The low sofa nearly swallowed me as I made contact, and my legs lifted slightly off the ground. He watched and smirked. Blast you, I thought. You do this on purpose, don't you? Just to watch women make fools of themselves trying to retain some dignity. But still, I smiled through the latest of his indulgences.

He got straight to the point.

'As you know, we have a joint client and staff seminar in six weeks. It's a three-day residential event: staff only on day one, joined by clients on days two and three. Here is the agenda and I want you to arrange it all. It must be your top priority for the next few weeks. My wife can't make it so I want you to host it with me. You look nice enough. There will be a lot of work to be done at the event, so make sure you have a room close to mine. I need you nearby. Ok? Thanks.'

He gave me a wad of papers as a sign that I was clearly dismissed, and returned to his desk. I hadn't said a word. You look nice enough: the bastard! And that dig about rooms being close together. Do you think I don't know what you're trying on? I'll show you, you bastard.

Of course, the next six weeks were hell. Too much to do and every insult he could muster was thrown in my direction. But as we closed in on the date, all was in hand.

'Alexandra, get in here. Now.' His voice echoed around the office and with my normal defensiveness, I wondered again what had gone wrong.

'Well done,' he said, 'you've done a good job and you will be the perfect hostess at the dinner, so I have a present for you.'

This was unusual and totally out of character; first a compliment and now a present. James was known to be mean and wouldn't spend a penny on anything that was thought unnecessary, although he did believe that his clothes and expensive face treatments were essential spends. I was standing there, just looking at him.

'So,' I said.

'Hunt,' he said. Look around. Your present is here.' Now he was playing games. I didn't know what to do. 'Go on, look for it. Look for your present.'

'James, I don't have time to play games. Just give me whatever it is.'

'Of course not,' he said. 'Presents always need to be accompanied by a fanfare.'

There was a choice and so tentatively I looked on his desk. I didn't know what I was looking for, which made the task more difficult. Was it a letter or maybe even a bonus cheque? I looked at him as I moved papers around.

'Nope. Very cold,' he said, as I moved around the office. I looked on chairs and under chairs and he followed me around smiling.

'There is nowhere else,' I said.

'Oh yes, there is. Show some initiative.'

I glanced in the direction of the clothes closet; I hadn't looked in there. I looked back at James for reassurance and there was a nod of approval. I opened the door and there, hanging inside, was the most beautiful, long evening dress, cut slim and very tight; the shoulders were bare except for a thin strap, and it had a deep, plunging neckline.

'For me?' I asked, with a certain amount of incredulity. 'Will it fit me?'

'Well, it is not for me and I am assured that it will,' he said, and I wondered how he could be so sure. 'There were meant to be three parts to the present but on reflection, I decided there need only be two.' Even in his generosity, he could be mean.

'Now see if you can find the second present,' he said. 'Maybe I should make it easier. Try the top drawer at my desk.'

So I looked, and there was a string of pearls. Not too long nor too short. It was just perfect.

'James, why have you done this? I was just doing my job. I suppose you will want them back after the event?'

He laughed.

'No, you can keep them. Aren't you interested in the third

present?'

At this time I was on the cusp of a decision. I had a choice. I could go down the sexual harassment route or I could remind myself he hadn't actually touched me, just given me two rather beautiful presents. I decided. I would play his game. 'Okay. What is the third present, which you haven't bought?'

'I was also going to buy you some lingerie to wear with the dress, but as I looked at it I decided it is cut so tight that it is a dress best worn without any underwear. Don't you agree?'

It hadn't yet occurred to me what lingerie to wear with that dress. It was cut very tight. 'I agree,' I said, with an air of indifference.

'Good,' he said, 'so will you do me the honour of making sure you don't wear anything underneath?' And with that, I was again dismissed. Maybe I had made the wrong decision.

This was a side of James I had never seen before: generous, but still with the same abruptness; lecherous and dismissive, but I knew he would never find out if I was or wasn't wearing any underwear. So what the hell.

I took the dress home that night and tried it on. It hugged my figure tighter than a glove. I wouldn't be able to eat anything for days before, as any little bump would show. It was tight until below the knee and then opened out with wide ruffles. It was beautiful, and wearing it I looked as beautiful as I ever had; despite all my reservations, silently I thanked him.

The gala dinner was on the second night, and despite my promise to him, I had brought with me a tiny G-string. As I showered I started to wonder what purpose the string actually served. What false modesty was I covering that the dress didn't? I dressed without any lingerie; my only covering seemingly the pearls shaped around my neck. I tried to walk. My longest stride, at best, was no more than a foot and half; I prayed there wouldn't be a fire alarm, as surely I wouldn't get out without ripping off my dress. With that thought, I wished I had worn even that little G-string. Isn't that what mothers always warn you about?

I walked slowly to James' room and knocked on the door. Wearing a dinner suit, he looked as handsome as I had ever seen him; even men can have their eye turned by a good-looking man. I looked at the wedding ring on his finger to remind myself he was married, because at that moment I could well have melted into his arms.

'You look ravishing, Alexandra. If we didn't have to go to dinner I might just be tempted to ravish you right now.'

'You might think so,' I said, 'but you wouldn't be successful.'

'We will never know.' He smiled and said, 'let's go,' and on his arm, I went with him to the ballroom. Of course, all the staff and some of the clients knew who I was, but to other guests, he just introduced me as Alexandra.

Not Alexandra one of my design team, nor Alexandra who organised it all. It was always just Alexandra. At dinner, because of the dress, I could eat very little; there was wine but I drank little, for fear of needing the toilet and having to get out of the dress; and when we danced I was so restricted I could only dance the slow and intimate dances.

Across the table, James looked at me and said, 'Did you keep the promise, Alexandra?' and I just nodded. Of course, a client asked which promise. James said, 'Are you going to tell him, Alexandra?'

'It was a promise between us James,' I said.

'You can share it if you want to, Alexandra,' he said, smiling contentedly, knowing the embarrassment he was causing, and the guest asked me again as I started to turn red.

'You'd better tell him, Alexandra. Part of the company ethos is openness and honesty. You should answer him,' he said, laughing slightly louder. By now many eyes around the table were looking at me and all were waiting for my answer.

'Yes, James. I kept my promise,' I said, hoping that my answer would finish it all and cut the conversation short, but all eyes were on me and I knew I hadn't succeeded. James looked at me. Why was he doing this?

All around me I heard, 'What was the promise?' There was nowhere I could retreat.

'I promised James that I would not wear any underwear with this dress. I am naked other than what you see.' There, I had said it, and

I looked downwards to avert any eye contact. If you can hear silence, that was the moment. The women looked at me, almost mouthing 'you slut', while the men all tried to discern the line of a breast, the bulge of a nipple or a protruding pelvic bone; or so I thought.

Now, you may find this difficult to believe, but oddly, it brought me closer to understanding James. He had humiliated me in public but he had done it to show that this most beautiful of women was his. She did what he wanted. His woman was not only clever but also a sexual and sensuous woman. Perversely, it was the biggest compliment he could have given me.

The evening drifted towards its end, and all in all, I had enjoyed myself. My revelation had made me the centre of all the men's attention, and despite what had happened, some even had the courtesy to talk to me intelligently and not assume I was just a dumb blonde. Maybe James thought he had broken me, and even though I had arranged everything I had become a trophy for him to show off; but he was wrong. I had sorted out all three days perfectly. I wasn't a trophy. The contradictions just kept on growing. I knew I still had my self-confidence, and my dignity and I was more in control than him. In time, and I wasn't sure when he would also understand that.

As we headed up to the rooms I heard James asking me, 'come and have a nightcap, Alexandra.' It was an instruction, not a question, and still unable to walk easily I followed him towards his room.

'Did you enjoy this evening?' he asked. I nodded an acknowledgement as I tried to sit on yet another low sofa while he stood there watching me.

His arrogance was unmoved; I know he thought he had broken me and turned me into a sexual being but I was going to resist. I didn't like his attitude but on the other hand as I thought about it, and him, I was becoming excited at the thought of seeing the evening through to a finale that we both knew now was almost inevitable. I enjoyed him believing that I was at the whim of his power. I enjoyed toying with him. It was time now to turn the tables and use the power that I now possessed.

'Look, James,' I said, 'don't give me any of that twaddle about your wife doesn't understand you. If you want me, if you want sex with me, then there is a price you have to pay.'

He moved to the drinks cabinet, pausing only momentarily from pouring his brandy, and asked, 'is the price high?'

'If you want a mistress then I will be that mistress and I won't expect you to leave your wife or anything like that. I will decide when the affair is finished and if you treat me well as your mistress I will never ask for more. But while I am your mistress, if I ever find out there is someone else then I will destroy you. Do you understand? And you will buy me presents. I like clothes and I like jewellery. So far you have shown you have good taste.'

And while I spoke I held out my hand so he could help me stand. I stood, I turned and let him pull up my hair so he could undo the long zip on my dress. The dress didn't fall to the ground as he hoped, as I held it close to my breasts with only the long curve of my naked back visible to him.

'And at the office, you will treat me with respect. You will never shout for me and you will promote me only – and I mean only – when I deserve it. Do you understand?'

I looked at him and could see the thought of sex was capturing him. I know that every man is at his most vulnerable and likely to make any promise when the thought of sex with a beautiful girl is so close. Whatever men think about us being the weaker sex, they are so wrong.

'Do you understand and will you keep this promise just as I have kept mine?' I knew there was no need to say that to remind him of my promise because I held all the cards in this poker game. He put his glass down and looked at me.

'I had plans for this evening, but this has far exceeded my deepest desire. This is what I have wanted ever since you first walked into the office. I agree to all your terms and I will keep my promise.'

'Would you like to see what is under the dress?' I asked, knowing full well the answer. He nodded.

I slipped the shoulder strap off and my dress fell to the floor; I stood there naked in front of him. He walked towards me and took me in his arms and carried me to the bed.

37. SHOPPING FOR SHOES

Finally, the office life was all too much for me, so one day I gave it all up and for a few months lived off my savings as I tried to work out what to do with my life.

I know shopping for women is always life-changing but this time it really was. I met Liliya who was to become my best friend. Liliya is wild, even by my standards, and it was with her that I later shared many of my most exciting adventures. This was the first time we met.

━━━━━━━━━━━━━━━━━━━━

It was summer in Kyiv, lazily warm and Alexandra was lying on the black silk sheets of her large bed. Sunlight was streaming through the French windows, casting flickering shadows of the cherry tree just outside her room.

As ever, or so it seemed, she was in a playful mood. Why do others treat life so seriously, she thought, that today should be a time to bring a little joy to the world. She chose her new short, red dress. Today, she thought, no underwear – the day is too beautiful and too warm; today she wanted to feel free.

She bathed, dried, dressed and left her flat. Walking through the busy shopping streets, she felt the eyes of everyone on her. She grew in the confidence her beauty gave her. At each shop she stopped and looked through the windows, not seeing the dresses and shoes, but looking for who was inside. She was looking for one person in particular: a specific woman. She wanted to find a woman of beauty; a woman who might also share her love of life and her passion for freedom and expression.

There she was. It was a shoe shop with beautiful shoes and a beautiful assistant. Like Alexandra, she was tall and had a statuesque quality, and seemed aloof. She was above the rest of the world and in control of all that was her own empire.

Alexandra entered and slowly walked around inspecting the shoes, but these were not her main interest – this assistant was. Looking directly at her, she said, 'I would like to try these on. And these,' she said, holding two shoes from different pairs. She went to sit on a chair and wait, watching for the assistant to return from the stockroom at the back.

It was a simple chair, one of many in line, and Alexandra had chosen a central one. As she sat, her dress rode up slightly, and she made no attempt to tug it back down, leaving more of her long legs exposed. The assistant returned and knelt in front of Alexandra, the box of shoes at the ready to help her try them on. As Alexandra stretched out her leg and pointed her foot to receive the shoe, naturally her legs parted slightly.

Her foot rested gently in the assistant's lap and, looking straight into her eyes, she asked 'what is your name?'

'Liliya.'

'Thank you, Liliya, can you help and put the shoe on my foot please?'

While this was, of course, common practice, there was a momentary look of surprise as Liliya tried to fit the shoe. She wasn't concentrating because her eyes were elsewhere: much higher up Alexandra's leg. As she knelt in front of Alexandra, she looked up and saw the beautiful shaved pussy now so visible, so enticing and so welcoming.

Alexandra's legs parted a little more to make sure that Liliya had a perfect view, and Liliya smiled and slowly persuaded the shoe onto the foot.

'I don't think they will suit me, Liliya,' Alexandra said. 'What do you think?'

Liliya had not let go of Alexandra's foot, and if anything, her grip was now much more on her calf.

'Most definitely not,' she replied, still smiling and returning the stare.

'Liliya, I am going to lunch. Will you join me?'

Liliya stood alongside Alexandra, linked arms and said, 'let's go.'

38. PAINTED IN KYIV

Alexandra and Liliya laughed and flirted over a light lunch and Alexandra said, 'come with me,' an invitation which Liliya accepted. So it was that they walked arm-in-arm to Viktoria's studio.

'Join me for the afternoon,' Alexandra had said. 'I think you will enjoy it. Viktoria is going to paint me.'

'Why not?' Liliya said, 'this will be far better than working in the shop. I'm sure they won't miss me and I definitely won't miss them.'

Viktoria's was a typical artist's studio. Painted and half-painted canvases were everywhere and the floor was covered in a rainbow streak of spilt paints.

'Are you sure you want to do this, Alexandra?' Viktoria asked. 'You may get into trouble.'

'Of course,' she said, 'the world deserves to see my beauty. Do you agree with me Liliya?'

Not really understanding the conversation, all Liliya could do was nod.

'Ok, let's do it!' said Viktoria, with a hint of a smile. 'Get undressed, then.'

Liliya sat in a chair and watched as Alexandra undressed. She couldn't take her eyes off her. She was tall; her breasts were pert and didn't need a bra. She was slim and she was beautiful, and her pussy was every bit as enticing as it was in the shop.

Viktoria looked at Alexandra and said, 'A T-shirt and hot pants. I think that's what we agreed?'

'Yes,' said Alexandra.

Liliya couldn't believe what happened next. The paints were not applied to any canvas, but directly onto Alexandra's skin. Alexandra was the canvass. Naked, but apparently dressed, as the T-shirt and hot pants were painted onto her body.

Liliya watched, and then when Viktoria had finished, she studied Alexandra. At a first glance she looked dressed, but a closer look showed the pert nipples and the gentle lines of her pussy lips.

'What do you think Liliya? Do you like this picture?' asked Alexandra. 'All I need now is my shoes and we can leave.'

'Leave?' asked Liliya, 'what do you mean, leave?'

'Why, you and I are going for a walk and maybe some soothing afternoon tea. Viktoria will catch up with us later.'

If Alexandra felt a little bit nervous, which she did, Liliya was in a worse state. 'You can't go out like that,' she said. 'You are nude. Who knows what will happen.'

'But that's the point, Liliya. We need to find out what will happen. Now, come on – let's go.'

Alexandra was feeling far less confident than she sounded and the first steps were tentative and nervous. First, Liliya peeped around the door to see if anyone was on the street, and in a quiet moment, they both stepped onto the pavement.

Initial nervousness soon turned into confidence and they headed into the main shopping centre. For a couple of hours Alexandra, naked except for a thin layer of paint, and Liliya walked around Kyiv looking in shops, laughing and behaving like all the other shoppers. Alexandra noticed how few people turned to look at her. To the casual observer (and most shoppers are casual observers), to all intents and purposes, she was dressed, but Alexandra knew she was naked in public; a feeling which exhilarated her. A few thought they saw something different in the statuesque pair; most thought Alexandra's clothes too tight and skimpy and some who took a second look saw through the camouflage; they were the ones that came round for a second look or even to take a sneaky photograph on their cameras.

Whatever the reaction of other people, no one was as excited as Liliya, who was deriving genuine sexual excitement from walking around in public with a naked friend.

Their confidence was at a peak of excitement, but Alexandra wanted more. In the middle of the shopping centre, she stopped to look at Liliya and turned to face her. They were standing close together and Liliya was waiting for Alexandra to speak because clearly, she had something on her mind, but Alexandra said nothing and just pulled her close; immediately Liliya knew what was about to happen. Their heads tilted and their lips met in a passionate and deep kiss. More people looked at them now and more saw how little

Alexandra had on. Liliya was heady and unsteady on her feet, both through the suddenness and intensity of the kiss, and the touch of nakedness as her hands held Alexandra's waist. She hadn't noticed that Viktoria had caught up with them and was circling the embracing couple with her camera, catching the carnal desire playing out in front of her.

The attention of a photographer and the lesbian kiss started to draw the beginning of a crowd around them. This meant greater intensity in the study of each woman, with a greater realisation that at least one of the women was nude. That thought excited Alexandra.

They parted and repeated the kiss a few more times, but eventually, the day had to end. The three laughing and smiling girls interlocked their arms, with Alexandra in the middle, and strode back to Viktoria's studio.

'Wow, that was so cool,' Alexandra said, looking at Liliya, 'will you wash me? Help take this paint off me?'

Liliya stood in front of Alexandra and slowly stepped out of her own clothes, dropping them clumsily on the floor. Alexandra reached out and took Liliya's hand, and lead her to the shower.

The water brushed their bodies and Liliya took the sponge and slowly washed away the layers of paint; first the T-shirt and finally the hot pants. She faced Alexandra and pulled her close as the sponge slowly and sensuously circled her back; as their breasts pushed close together, their lips again closed in on each other in a passionate kiss. Their bodies entwined as the water vainly tried to push them apart.

Free of the office job, I could return to my academic interests and modelling. I went back to the university to become a research fellow in my favourite subject and a part-time lecturer to undergraduates. I made sure that they all stayed awake – I didn't want any young men (or women for that matter) starting to daydream fantasies as I was lecturing!

I was beginning to collect a portfolio of case studies from many different women who were the basis of my research. I would meet them, understand their background, undertake some basic psychological tests and then document their fantasies.

I now had the perfect lifestyle: work I loved and the chance to travel again with my modelling.

Quite often over the last few years as a model, I have had to work in Moscow. I have worked at the Moscow Fashion Show and I have also had specific photoshoots (mainly sexy lingerie), but this time I was there collecting case studies.

I like Moscow. I like the architecture and the clubs are great, although the weather is, at best, variable, I hate that the two main airports are so far apart and I hate the busy, dangerous ring road, but I like the Russian people. And their leaders? I think here we should pass on my political views.

Anyway, there was a six-day trip to be organised with work spread sparsely over the visit, leaving a great deal of free time. I left all the local arrangements to Gita who had once been a co-researcher in Kyiv before she moved to Moscow.

I was in a good mood after one of my last calls with Gita to finalise the arrangements. We had talked through all the administrative details and she was managing my diary, arranging specifics with all of the women I was planning to meet.

We also talked about all the different types of fantasy and I asked her how many she thought she covered with her fantasies, and even how many she had put into practice. She had asked the same of me.

It was in this context, and maybe rather foolishly, that I had thrown in the idea that we should try and tick off as many of the fantasy categories as we could in the short period of my visit. I knew she fully understood, and Gita was sure that she could make some arrangements. That was probably my big mistake because I had forgotten how diligent and focused Gita can be.

'If I do,' she said, 'you know that sometimes I will tell you what is going to happen and sometimes you will only find out when it is happening. My research shows that a lack of foreknowledge, a total surprise, adds to the excitement.'

'Sure,' I said.

I agreed, thinking it would be an interesting challenge and wondered how many categories she would get us through in such a short time.

I was not left disappointed.

39. WELCOME TO MOSCOW

Packing and getting to the airport had been vexing and even before the plane had rolled onto the runway, Alexandra had taken the chance for a moment to relax with a glass of champagne. It was only as the plane took off for Moscow, on schedule, that she started to think about her job and the task ahead.

The plane touched down and Alexandra was excited about all that lay ahead of her. She had her passport stamped, collected her luggage and then headed into the airport lounge, where Gita was supposed to be waiting for her. She looked around but Gita was nowhere to be seen. There was, however, a young man holding up a sign with the name *Alexandra* written on it. In smaller letters was *Gita*. It must be for her.

Alexandra introduced herself and found that Gita had sent the car. He was kind. He carried her luggage and led her towards the road, where a large 4x4 with darkened windows pulled up. Alexandra looked at the car and thought that Gita had gone overboard and hoped that she wasn't going to have to pay for this taxi!

Free of her luggage, Alexandra reached to open the back door; she grasped the handle, only to find that the door was already partly open. She thought she could see other people inside, but before she had a chance to properly gather her senses, she was pushed from behind straight into the car. Alexandra stumbled and was crawling about, confused, on the carpeted floor when her hands were grasped tight, her legs pinned to the floor, a crude cloth roughly stuffed into her mouth and a hood thrown over her head. She tried to scream but no audible sound came out of her throat. She thrashed around but her limbs were being tied and soon she couldn't move.

Why her? What had she done? Alexandra was terrified and thought that Gita must also have been abducted. Was she still alright, was she even alive? Alexandra tried to listen to what was happening. She could hear their voices but was totally unsure she would be able to recognise them later when the police arrested them, as surely they would.

She was confident they would be arrested and someone must

have seen what happened at the airport. She didn't know what to do but the ordeal was about to become far worse. As the car pulled away, she was still tied and unable to shout or move, and she felt her clothes being cut off. Piece by piece she was becoming naked. She thought she heard at least three voices, but now they weren't speaking: they were laughing. She was being humiliated and she was frightened. They drove and drove, and after an unknown time, they finally stopped.

Alexandra's legs were untied, she was pulled out of the car, and she was half-pulled / half-walked forward. The ground felt hard on her bare feet, so she wasn't in the countryside, but if she was on the pavement were others watching her? Would they make good witnesses to her plight? Surely someone would notice a naked and bound woman being marched along a road? After a time it didn't matter because she was inside a building, which from the echo of the voices, was a large and cavernous place. From the sounds, it seemed like there were many people there, but there were no clues as to how many.

She now was like a puppet: not happy, but with no choice but to let whatever was going to happen to her, happen. Her arms were taken, tied and pulled wide. The same happened to her legs, so she was secured in a standing position and spread wide. There had been no sexual contact and despite all her attempts to quell all such thoughts, the sexuality of what was happening did cause a stirring in her pussy. If her pussy was starting to become wet, her mouth was dry, and not made easier by the gag that was still in place. She felt a body close and it reached to her face and pulled at the hood.

At first, when it was removed she had to close her eyes to try and shield them from a strong light shining straight at her, but as her sight returned, she saw where she was. She was in a large room, probably in a warehouse, with banks of seats in front of her; on the seats were maybe sixty, seventy or even eighty people. They were mainly men, but there were women as well, and in front of them all was Alexandra: tied, spread and naked; the centre of their attention and seated in the middle looking at her intently was Gita, who stood up and slowly walked forward.

She whispered in Alexandra's ear, 'welcome to Moscow. I thought I should make it as exciting an arrival as possible. I hope, on reflection, you will find it exciting. This is phase one. You can say no to stop it, or we could move on to phase two if you want. Do you want to know more?'

Alexandra nodded while trying to find words. Gita saw her problem and gently removed the gag. Alexandra didn't know what words she could say. Did she want to shout at Gita? She didn't know. She looked at the audience and their anticipation, and now that the real physical threat had been removed, her excitement was building. What could phase two be?

'What is phase two, Gita? Will I be safe?'

Gita nodded. 'Of course, you will be safe, but if you say *yes,* then for the next two hours you will not close your legs or your mouth; your arse and your pussy will have to take everything that is put in them. The agreement now cannot be revoked and no shout of *stop* or *no more* will be heard. Do you understand?'

Alexandra did not know if she understood and looked at all those in front of her. They were drinking, but not so much to be a rowdy crowd, and they were being served by naked women carrying trays of shots and beer. She was here for fantasies and one of the great fantasies is forced sex. Sex without permission, but controlled in some manner. She was not being asked to consent to any one person's sexual advance, but to anything from this group.

'Have you been tied here, Gita? Do you know what it is like?' Gita nodded and asked, 'Do you agree?'

Alexandra was still thinking as she nodded and said, 'Yes.'

Gita returned to her seat and said to the audience, 'She agrees.'

With that, nothing much happened. There was no stampede towards Alexandra who was still strung up. Slowly one man walked toward her. He placed a hand on her breast and slowly ran it down her belly to finger her clit which sent a shiver through the whole of her body. Then more men and some women moved towards her, and soon there were hands all over her body.

Over the next two hours, she was tied and retied in different positions. Not for one moment was she free to move away or resist any advance. She vowed to try and count the number of times that she sucked on a cock, was penetrated in the pussy or arse, tasted the saltiness of cum running copiously down her face, or licked a pussy, but she was soon so overcome by the orgasms that came and went that counting was impossible.

Finally, everyone was spent and Alexandra was left limp and wrapped in a towelling robe, with her hair matted and wet with streaks of semen. Gita was sitting next to her.

'Welcome to Moscow,' she said.

40. SELLING MYSELF

Finally, back in Alexandra's hotel, Gita and Alexandra sat in the coffee shop. Gita had driven her there after *the adventure,* as she liked to call it.

First Alexandra had had a shower, and Gita had sat talking to her while sitting on the toilet seat. They had been friends in Kyiv, but Alexandra saw that Gita had developed and become much more open now. There was something very natural in the way that Gita sat in the bathroom chatting while Alexandra was naked in the shower, but Gita had just spent two hours watching Alexandra naked, being fucked and fingered. Why should she now feel embarrassed watching her shower?

'Which bit did you like best?' Gita asked.

'I still need to take it all in. I was petrified when I was abducted because I didn't know what was happening, and I was worried for you as well. When I knew what was happening in the room, I was excited by seeing all those people looking at me. Then as it started I just couldn't stop coming, and it was made so much better by being tied and not being able to say *no.* Although sometime in the next week I will get my revenge on you, Gita. You need to expect the unexpected!'

'I'll look forward to that.'

Alexandra spent the following morning in the lounge of a large international hotel, interviewing one of her research subjects. It was not one of her most dynamic interviews, but she appreciated the openness of anyone telling her their deeper sexual fantasies. It may be natural to Alexandra, it was her job, but it did not come easily to everyone. She was now waiting for Gita in the hotel bar. She was seated at a low table reading papers and a research journal, unaware of what was happening around her.

What was happening was that most of the handful of men sitting at the bar were watching her very closely. Alexandra had dressed much as she did most days, a simple jumper – not too tight – stockings and a short skirt. What she hadn't realised was that as she sat in the low chair, her skirt had risen up and she was showing a great deal of thigh between her skirt and stocking tops. One of the men at the bar finally plucked up the courage to walk toward her and talk. He stood above her looking down. 'How much?' he asked.

'I'm sorry. I don't understand you,' she replied.

'You look very sexy,' he said, 'I assume you are selling?'

Alexandra looked at him quizzically, and then she understood. She looked down at her short skirt and long legs showing all the flesh; her whole demeanour could be seen as provocative and he clearly thought she was a prostitute. For a moment she dwelt on the thought and sad assumption that all men seem to think that sex can be bought, but worse that any woman dressed sexily was advertising herself for sale. On a different day, she would have given him a lecture on feminism and men's attitudes, but she was here intending to live as many of the fantasies she could. This was not an opportunity to be missed, but still, she needed time to reconcile it all.

'How much can you afford?' she asked. Better, she thought, to play along and maximise the benefit.

He looked at her. Clearly, he had never had to negotiate for sex so openly before. 'Three hundred and fifty dollars.' It was more a question than a statement.

'You have a room here?'

'Yes.'

'I will think about it,' Alexandra said, 'I am on my lunch hour now. Ask again in thirty minutes,' and she turned back to her papers. He looked at her and then at his watch, and turned back to the bar.

His attempt to pick her up was noted by the others. They also noted that while he hadn't done a deal, he hadn't been rejected either, and by the look at his watch, he had been rebuffed only for a short time and not forever. That encouraged them to think that they might also have a chance. Four more men approached her, and to each, she said almost the same. She told each of them what the last had offered. One said he intended to pay nothing, but because he was such a good lover she should go with him for free. She laughed openly and dismissively at that. There were now four bidders, and by the end of the half-hour she had raised the offer to six hundred dollars; an offer she accepted. Sadly, she thought it was the first man who was the most handsome, and Alexandra thought he deserved to win for the bravery of his initial approach.

The winner was a businessman in his mid-forties. As they took the lift to a higher floor in the hotel, he started to tell her his story about being away from home and being unloved by his wife. Alexandra stopped him.

'I won't tell you anything about me and I don't need to know anything about you. We will be strangers to each other. I am sure that will be more exciting.' This was all new to her and she was thinking as fast as she could as she executed her plan. She sensed his nervousness and she knew she was in the position of control; a place she understood very well. It's an odd paradox, she thought, that these men buy a woman, buy sex and then the nerves take over and they become the lead rather than the leader. Then she also remembered the stories of all the rapes and assaults on women. Not all men were gentle and concerned for her welfare and she was grateful she had chosen an encounter with someone who looked as nervous as he did.

He opened the room door and showed her in, and they stood there just looking at each other before he ran around tidying up the usual detritus of a used hotel room.

'I suppose you will want to be paid first?' he said.

'Of course,' she said, grateful that at least one of them was being business-like. He handed her a wad of notes which, self-consciously, she counted.

'Thank you,' she said, as she stuffed them into her handbag. Suddenly he jumped forward, put his hands around her waist and planted a big kiss on her lips with his tongue exploring deep into her mouth. Alexandra was at a loss. It wasn't a very attractive experience but she had been paid a lot of money. She pushed him gently away. She knew what to do. Reaching down, she put her hand on his cock. She could feel it growing inside his trousers, '

You paid to fuck me. You paid for me to suck you. You paid to lick my pussy. But I am sorry, not to kiss me. There is intimate and then there is really intimate. Only my boyfriend kisses me. I do hope you understand?' and she pulled one of her sexy little girl's faces.

'Of course,' he said. 'You have a very lucky boyfriend. Does he know what you do?'

'Stranger, let's stay strangers,' Alexandra answered.

He nodded and said, 'let's have sex,' and with that, he started to undress. Alexandra took a deep breath. There was no going back now, and she watched him undress while she also stripped. He was no Greek god, he was just a normal man with a slight belly. As he lay on the bed getting excited, Alexandra saw that he was normal in every aspect. He looked at Alexandra, who was standing beside him.

'Turn around. Let me see you,' he said, and Alexandra obliged, turning to have her body inspected. She was proud of her body. It was firm and her breasts were pert, but she did not like being inspected to make sure she was up to scratch; inspected to make sure she was worth six hundred dollars.

'Very, very pretty,' he said. 'Now come here.' Summoning every ounce of her sexiness, Alexandra slipped onto the bed to lie beside him. He was not a very good lover. He was unimaginative, and awkward with the condoms. He took her clumsily from behind, licked her pussy roughly and wanted a sixty-niner before lying on top of her, pumping hard until he came. Alexandra had learnt some of the rules of this game and as he came, she faked a screaming wild orgasm; it concerned him enough to worry that people in other rooms might hear.

'Don't worry,' she said, 'this is what bedrooms are for. They will understand.'

After his climax, she lay beside him for a moment, as if in post-coital bliss. But this was not a time to dwell on the past with a lover and she got out of bed, went to the bathroom while gathering her clothes, washed and dressed. He was still lying on the bed.

'You were fantastic,' he said, smiling.

'Thank you,' she replied, 'so were you,' lying.

She left him content in bed as she took the lift back to the bar.

'Where have you been?' Gita asked.

'It's a story to tell,' Alexandra replied, 'but let's go and eat somewhere else. I don't think I should stay here,' knowing that two of the fantasies were already fulfilled.

Alexandra

41. WHAT AM I BID FOR GITA?

'So, what have you been doing?' Gita asked as they pushed past shoppers on the pavement.

'Let's get a drink and I will tell you. You won't believe it.'

Gita didn't. 'That is outrageous,' she said, 'now tell me all. Did it meet your fantasy's needs?'

They were now in a coffee shop, sipping on cappuccinos. Gita laughed as Alexandra had a ring of frothy milk around her lips. 'It looks as though you didn't clean all the cum away! Now tell me.'

'It wasn't as exciting as I thought it would be.' Alexandra said. 'The sex was average and did not turn me on, but I will tell you what was surprising, it was the control I had over him to make his fantasies come true. For a moment a fat old man believed he had won the heart of a beautiful young girl. I enjoyed much more the barter beforehand, with all the men trying to buy me. That is when I felt most excited. But you will understand it all better later. I have a plan for you.'

Gita perked up. 'You have a plan?'

'I do, my friend. Be at the hotel, all spick and span at ten tonight and you will have a treat.'

'I can't wait,' said Gita.

'You may not think so later,' Alexandra said, with a grin.

Gita and Alexandra left the hotel at ten, with Gita desperately trying to get more information out of Alexandra, who refused to say a thing. She had been doing her research on the sexual underworld of Moscow and was even a little disappointed that Gita hadn't come up with this idea. It sounded exciting and it was time to get in some retaliation.

They took a taxi and arrived at the door of a club featuring a range of events, but Alexandra didn't allow Gita a chance to dawdle and read the notices. She paid for both of them, pointing out she now had lots of money after her lunchtime adventure.

'You know the rules, Gita; they are just the same as yours. Just say *yes* and trust me. Now, stay here and don't talk to anyone. I want this to be a real surprise for you. I will go and see the organisers.'

Gita nodded and watched as Alexandra pushed deep into the club, to return five minutes later.

'Come with me,' she said, leading Gita by the hand into the club. Gita looked around. It was still early and only half full. There was a dance floor, loud music, a bar and a small raised area or stage. On the stage were ten floor-to-ceiling poles, and chained to each of the first four was a woman, and on the fifth, a man. All were naked and gagged. None looked happy, but then again none looked sad – just concerned.

'What is this?' Gita asked.

'You will find out soon enough, my friend, because shortly you will be one of those.'

'What?'

'Yes, now strip and I will hand you over.'

Gita looked at her friend but knew there was no arguing with her. After what she had done when Alexandra had first landed in Moscow, there was no way to say *no*. So on the dance floor, she started to undress.

'Not here, Gita. There,' Alexandra said, pointing at the stage.' She saw the look on Gita's face. 'And be sexy. I will get a better price.'

'You're selling me?'

'Of course. Didn't I tell you? This is a slave auction. Oops, I forgot. Sorry. When you are sold you will be their slave and will have to do everything your owner says. Now go, and don't let me down. It took a lot of organising to get you on here.'

Slowly Gita did as she was told. She climbed the few steps to the stage and undressed, throwing her clothes to Alexandra, who stood and watched with a self-satisfied look. Many others watched too, and when she had finished and was naked, a man came, took her arm and led her to the poles. There she was tethered, her arms high in the air, alongside the others, who watched her with a sense of pity.

Over the next hour, the club filled to breaking point, and more were tied to the poles. Finally, there were nine other slaves ready to be sold: six women and four men altogether. Gita searched out for Alexandra among the crowd, but couldn't see her as she had gone to the bar. Men and women came onto the stage to inspect and study the slaves. At first, Gita couldn't bring herself to look into their eyes, keeping her head bowed; but later, as the ire rose inside her, she stared straight back with an intense and threatening look. Maybe that will put them off, she thought. She overheard a conversation.

'The auction starts in ten minutes.' Then, looking at Gita and weighing up her breasts, 'this one looks like a filly worth mounting.' Then, not for the first time that evening, the man put his hand on her pussy and started to push a finger inside her. Gita recoiled and tried to move away. "Oh yes, this one will buck and give a good ride.' Gita wanted to tell him where to keep his fingers, but the gag stopped her.

The MC was on the stage and the first of the women were taken off the pole and made to walk up and down along the stage, like a catwalk model.

'This is Alysia,' the MC said. 'She is a full pain slut and will take a severe beating. Now, what do I hear for her?

Gita couldn't take it all in as the bids came from the audience. It seemed that a price had been struck and Alysia was handed to another woman who had come on the stage. While the auction continued, Gita watched as the girl – still tied – was marched towards the door and chased out with a whip and a scream. Another woman had been sold. A man was now being sold. Again, he was marched up and down the stage. A woman came from the audience and used her hand to make him hard. It seemed that his size was the key to a better price. He was bought by the woman.

More women and more men were sold. The second man was described as bisexual and was bought by a group of three men dressed in boots, leather chaps, no pants, and leather waistcoats. Gita was sure his night would be painful. The next woman was described as loving and sexy and not to be used for hard play, but only soft excitement. Gita hoped that she would be described similarly. She noted that women didn't raise much of a price.

There was no one left other than Gita. Ah, she thought, Alexandra has set me up to feel the excitement, not to be sold; but her hopes were quashed when she was taken down from her ties and told to parade – which sullenly she did.

She heard the description. 'She will only take mild pain but is available for full service. Apparently, she is a very good cock-sucker but also an expert with a pussy. Likes bondage and can be fully restrained. Needs to be returned to central Moscow when done with. Now, what am I bid?'

Gita couldn't believe it. Earlier Alexandra had sold herself, and as a result, had all that money in her purse; now Gita was being sold and she wouldn't even see the money – she supposed. The bidding increased, and finally, the man said, 'Are we all done? Good. Sold to the couple over by the bar.'

A man and a woman came to the stage as Gita watched. They handed over a wad of roubles and walked towards Gita.

'Turn around,' and Gita could think of nothing else she could do but obey. Her wrists were handcuffed behind her back.

'Let's go,' the woman said, and she led Gita towards the door of the club. Gita suddenly realised they were leaving and said, 'I don't have my clothes.'

'You won't need those,' the woman replied, and kept pushing Gita onwards and out onto the street. They walked along the pavement, with passers-by stopping and staring at the naked woman with her hands cuffed behind her back.

Meanwhile, Alexandra had a sudden pang of conscience as she stood on the stage and took the auction money – less 20% for the club, of course – from the auctioneer.

'I do hope she is safe?' she said.

'Don't worry. They take girls regularly and we know where they live. All the girls come back smiling.'

That cheered Alexandra as she collected her coat and checked that she still had all of Gita's clothes in her bag. She took a taxi back to her hotel, had a quick nightcap, went to her room and went to bed and sleep.

It was around five in the morning, as the sun was just coming up, that there was a knock on the door. Deep in her dreams, at first Alexandra didn't hear it, but she got to the door as the knocking resumed for the third time.

She opened the door and there was Gita, still naked.

'Can I come in?' she said.

Gita was standing at the door with one arm across her breasts and the other across her pussy, trying desperately to maintain some modesty, which once in the room she gave in to. Alexandra went to the bathroom and brought back the towelling robe which she placed around Gita. For a moment they hugged and held each other.

'How did you get back? Why are you still naked?'

Gita looked at her. 'Because you took my clothes. So when they drove me here and left me outside, I had to walk into the reception and ask them which was your room, then I took a lift. I don't think anyone else saw me.'

Alexandra was making her a cup of tea. 'Well,' she said, 'it is my turn to ask you: how was it? What happened?'

Gita sipped at the tea and stirred in extra sugar. 'I can't take you through it all. There is so much to tell. I was embarrassed at first when I was nude on the stage, but I got to enjoy it. I got excited as the auction was taking place – all those people who actually wanted me. It is good to be wanted. I got scared when the couple came to get me, then when they marched me out of the club naked I was petrified.'

'You walked out naked!' Alexandra exclaimed. 'Yes. They handcuffed me and we walked down the street to their car. It must have been 400 hundred metres and we passed lots of people who stared at me. They made me walk in front of them. I decided just to be brave and walk with my head held high. We travelled in their car out of the city. I sat in the back and they didn't say a word to me. I had watched that first woman was being whipped as she left and I thought they were going to hurt me, but there was no way out. I had no clothes! They marched me into the house, and to my horror, they had visitors there. It was a dinner party and they were all dressed up in their best clothes. and I was their naked waitress.'

Alexandra was engrossed in the story. 'Carry on,' she said.

'I served the food. They had a chef cooking in the kitchen and I got all sorts of lewd comments from him as I came for plates of food.

I thought I might have problems as he kept smacking my bottom when I was loaded with all the plates. When they started eating I had to crawl under the table. It was all part of a game they had devised.'

'Do tell me more,' Alexandra said. 'I want to hear it all.'

'It was a large dinner table, very wide, with a large white table cloth hiding me, and they had had special seats made. The seat they sat on wasn't a complete square but more like a U shape. I had to go under the table and, one by one, lick a pussy or suck a cock; each for no more than a minute before moving on. Their game was not to show any reaction, and they had to guess who I was sucking at any particular moment.'

'But why the odd-shaped chairs?'

'So that I could get close to them without them having to move around and give the game away. I did this for maybe twenty minutes while they ate. I was told to move randomly from one to the other. I really enjoyed that because as they kept score I wanted to see who would lose. At the end of the course, when they added up the tally, a woman had lost. I knew she would because she was so wet when I licked her that I went back to her more often and she almost came. I heard her gasp once as I sucked on her clit and they all laughed.'

'What happened? She was the loser?'

'Yes, she lost. I was made to stand and watch, as slowly she was made to totally undress, and then they all sat down to the next course of food and it all started again. But this time I was not allowed to lick her. I did see her try and masturbate once but they stopped her. The next time, a man lost, and the same thing happened. He stripped and had to sit through cheese with his naked cock twitching and wanting so much to be touched – but I wasn't allowed to.'

'They couldn't have been eating all the time, surely? So after that, they sent you home?'

'No, I wish. There was a next stage. They had finished the food and I was made to stand again and watch as they put up a sling from a hook in the ceiling.'

'A sling? What's that?'

'Mmm, let me try and describe it. Well, you sit in it and it holds you with support under your bottom, your back and each leg, and you can swing back and forward. I was put in it and then blindfolded, but the way it was set up I couldn't get out. I was swinging there, a metre or so off the floor, and I discovered that it kept my legs spread wide. Then they just sort of used me.'

Alexandra looked at her, imagining what she meant, and unsure if she should ask Gita to expand on the detail of *use her,* not wanting to break the spell of her imagination. She had to ask. She needed detail.

'What do you mean *used me*?' Alexandra asked.

'You want every sordid detail, don't you?' Gita laughed. 'Ok, well, with me just swinging there, lying back, they could take me any way they wanted. I felt cock in my arse and pussy and a dildo, so I suppose at least one of the girls had a strap-on. And of course, there were all sorts of things in my mouth.'

'What do you mean *all sorts of things*?'

Gita looked at her. 'I mean there was a lot of cock and pussy in my mouth. I don't how long it lasted, but while I was in the sling I was being fucked continuously. After a time I thought it best to let them deal with my pussy and arse while I concentrated on sucking well on whatever I had to. I just let the orgasms come, one after the other. They seemed to like that. They liked watching me squirm and try and get away, but every time I started to orgasm, someone would start to lick my clit to keep me going. It was both heaven and hell, being forced to orgasm over and over again.

'I can imagine it all now, but how did you get back here?'

'When they had finished I was covered in cum. Of course, I couldn't wipe it off because my hands and arms were still locked into the sling. One of the guys got dressed and put handcuffs on me and led me down to the car which was still parked outside the house. He told me not to worry because he was taking me back to Moscow, and asked where I wanted him to take me. I said your hotel and we just drove in silence. When we got here he undid the cuffs and said, 'we're here'; then he said goodbye and pushed me out. There I was, standing naked on the pavement, thankful that it was early morning with hardly anyone around. So I walked in and you know the rest.'

'Are we still friends?' Alexandra asked. 'I mean, you don't hate me for what I did?'

Gita looked at her before answering. 'If I hadn't first arranged your welcome I might well be angry. If I had been whipped and beaten I would have hated you, but luckily it was sexy and exciting. But I do think we should get some control into this: it could have gone horribly wrong.' Alexandra had thought the same. 'Let's get some sleep and we can plan tomorrow later. It's nearly tomorrow already.'

42. LIVE ON STAGE

While Alexandra was again working, this time listening and taking notes about a case, she had become so engrossed in Olga's story she hadn't noticed the ebb and flow of customers into the coffee shop. It was only when she went to the counter to reorder that she realised that there was an entirely different group of people there from when she first arrived. She sat down again opposite Olga.

'How does it feel to talk about this now?' she asked.

'Wonderful,' Olga replied, 'you don't know how frustrating it is to have the most wonderful tale and not be able to tell it to anyone. I mean, who could I talk to?'

Alexandra nodded knowingly. She felt the same. There had been many women and men in her life. Some had been very close and others more distant, but there had never been one person who she could really talk to about her fantasies.

She wondered if any couple could ever be so open and trusting in each other to be able to say out loud what was deep in their heart. She reflected. That was not quite true. Of course, couples talked about their fears, hopes and aspirations. They expressed their love in many ways, but somehow it seems they couldn't bring it upon themselves to talk about sex with quite the same openness.

She could understand why Olga had not been able to tell her husband about this fantasy. If she had been open they could have gone to the club together. What would have happened then, she wondered? Would she have still gone on the stage and performed for an audience? If she had, would her husband have objected? Probably.

There was certainly enough in her experience to make monogamy exciting and adventurous. For a moment, however, she remembered the Rainbow party with Adam and felt an immediate pang of guilt. There she had been in a relationship but had allowed herself to be used. She could have said no, but she hadn't.

She soon managed to rationalise it and her thoughts now eased the pain. Hers was not serial swinging – not going every weekend to a swinging party and never being satisfied with the sex with their own partner, but she saw all the flaws in her argument. That was the purpose and power of fantasy: it allowed the excitement to go beyond the confines of the couple's relationship and embrace other adventures, without the need to actually have sex with third parties.

She was pleased that she was not in a relationship now, so she didn't have to explain her behaviour to anyone else.

On the other hand, if both parties were happy to see their partner with someone else, then was it for her to object? No, of course, it wasn't, and she was happy she didn't have to draw a moral conclusion, just accept that she didn't really understand.

For the same reason, she couldn't understand men who wanted to be cuckolded, but again that was their concern. She was about to raise this issue when Olga said, 'would you like me to tell you the rest of the story, and the end?'

'Of course, I want to hear everything.'

Olga was just about to start when the waitress arrived at their table with the new coffees and placed them gently on the table. She looked at Alexandra and said, 'I'm sure we have met. I've seen you somewhere before. I just can't place it.'

They looked at each other. Alexandra spoke. 'I don't think so. This is my first visit to Moscow for a couple of years and I only arrived a few nights ago, from Kyiv.'

The waitress looked at her some more. 'Oh, now I remember you. I saw you at the show just after you had flown in. You won't remember me specifically, you were far too occupied with other people. Did you enjoy it?' She smiled and Alexandra tried to avoid looking very embarrassed.

'Oh yes,' Alexandra said, 'the show. It was very good. I had a wonderful time, thank you.'

'I am pleased. It was so special being able to get so close and intimate with the performers. I mean, you could almost touch them.' The waitress was smiling. Clearly, thought Alexandra, she had been one of the audience, and had maybe stroked her breasts or rubbed her clit. Maybe Alexandra had even licked her pussy.

'I agree,' said Alexandra, 'and I am sure the performers appreciated the intimacy of the venue. Thank you.' The waitress returned to her duties and Alexandra tried to compose herself.

She wondered if Olga had the same feelings as her. Olga had already told Alexandra how she had gone alone to a club with male strippers and been picked from the audience to join them on stage – well, it wasn't quite so simple but that was the outcome. Wearing small pants which showed just how large he was, the stripper had come off the stage and started walking around the audience, taunting and teasing the women. He had dwelt longer with Olga than with most and when she put her hand on his crotch, he took her by the hand and led her towards the stage. Olga knew what was happening and resisted – but not too much because deep down she wanted to be taken.

To the wolf-whistles, cat-calls and screams of the audience, she had danced on stage; first, he pulled her jumper over her head, then her bra and skirt were removed, leaving her wearing just her knickers. For a moment she hesitated. Would she allow herself to be totally stripped? But he was experienced at this and didn't give her the time to think; suddenly there she was – naked and being displayed to the audience.

At that moment she was so horny she wanted to have sex in front of everyone on the stage; but he stopped, said thank you, and she was returned to her place. Alexandra asked if he was still wearing his underwear, and was surprised that Olga almost couldn't remember, she was so engrossed in her 'performance'.

'Oh, didn't I say? He had taken those off quite early and he was walking around with this huge cock sticking out in front of him.'

'Where were we?' Alexandra asked. 'Ah yes, you were going to tell me what happened next. Sorry about that interruption.'

'Well, after I had been picked out of the audience and brought onto the stage where I was naked, I couldn't really just get dressed and go back and sit in the audience, it just didn't feel right. So I gathered up all my clothes and followed this girl backstage into the dressing rooms. I think I've seen too many films and I assumed that every performer would have their own room, but of course, they didn't. It was one big changing room for all the men and women.

There were naked men and women all over the place, and they didn't care about their nakedness. It all seemed so refreshing and natural. There was a couple who were about to go on stage and the man was, well, he wasn't hard, and he said to no one in particular, 'someone come and give me a hand.'

'And you made him hard?' Alexandra asked.

'Oh no, not me. But one of the girls went up to him and got on her knees and just gave him a blow job until he was hard, then he put on the robe and went on stage and she returned to her makeup. It just seemed all so natural.'

'So, what did you do?'

'I talked to the girls and explained why I was there. I mean, that thing I was telling you, about wanting to watch a couple making love in front of me? I explained that I thought it would be more exciting if it was in a public show. But I felt their stage show was too orchestrated, so even though they had fucked it hadn't quite fulfilled my fantasy – I needed something more intimate. They were very kind and said they understood and said how brave I was to get on stage. They asked me why I had done it, and I had to say I couldn't explain. So we were just talking and the couple – the man and the woman from before – came back. Of course, he was still as hard as he was when he had walked out because he hadn't come on stage, presumably because there were more shows that night.'

'Of course,' said Alexandra, although she was thinking that there were many men she knew who get hard again quite quickly.

Olga took a sip of coffee but Alexandra couldn't wait to hear the rest of the story and said, 'And?'

'Well, the girl I was talking to – and you have to remember that we were all still nude – went up to another of the male performers and started to caress him. I mean, she ran her hands all over his body, which was pretty hot, and started to play with his cock; then they started having sex right there in front of me, and the others seemed to take no notice! It wasn't like the sex on the stage, it had more emotion and feeling. Possibly, that was because it was right in front of me. Then, as they paused momentarily, the girl turned to me and said, 'come closer, come here, Olga.'

Of course, I did and I was within touching distance as they moved into a doggy position. He was standing behind her as she leant forward. His cock was hard and just on the edge of her vagina and she said, 'guide him into me, Olga.'

At first, I didn't understand, but he took my hand and placed it on his cock, and I held him and moved his cock towards and into her pussy. I have to say that at that moment I was dripping wet with excitement.

'Rub my clit,' she said, so while he was pushing in and out, in I massaged her clit until she was on the edge of coming. I could see her stomach tense and her thighs twitch and her pussy tightening around his cock, and as she came he reached out and grabbed one of my tits, then put his hand on my pussy, sticking his fingers inside me; I came just as she came.

He pulled out of her and I'm sure I saw, inches away, the thick white cum ooze slowly out of her pussy. Maybe it was just her pussy juices. Alexandra, it was wonderful and so exciting.'

As she had been telling her story, Alexandra wished that they were in a private place so that she could touch herself, because she had become over-excited with all she had heard.

'That is some story,' she said, and for the moment all her considerations about any guilt that Olga might have felt were pushed far away in her thoughts. 'Can I use this story in my studies?' she asked Olga.

'Of course,' Olga replied, 'so long as you don't use my real name. I want my story to be heard to show other women that it is possible to fulfil fantasies.'

"Thank you, Olga. There are many other questions I need to ask about how you felt afterwards and all the emotions you had, but it is a wonderful and uplifting story.'

Alexandra asked all her questions and they parted, promising to stay close in future years. She sat in her taxi excited and wanting to tell Gita all about the story she had just heard. She read through her notes, thinking that Olga was a brave and very modern woman.

Through all she heard, Alexandra had become very excited, and for the first time in a few hours wondered what Gita had planned for the evening. She needed both the physical and mental release of something special.

(I have done as she asked and Olga is not her real name.)

43. AN OPEN DOOR

Gita and Alexandra met in the hotel bar. It was early evening and, almost word for word, Alexandra retold Olga's story to Gita who was both excited and impressed.

'What a story,' she said,' but I think we might have another great story tonight. You up for it?'

'Of course,' Alexandra replied. 'You going to tell me what it is?'

'No.'

'Oh, please just tell me that I am not going to be tied up and exhibited and fucked again. It's going to be something different, isn't it?' Alexandra asked.

'Yes,' said Gita, 'we're just waiting for a text message.' Just as she was saying this, her phone buzzed. She looked at the message and replied with a whir of fingers and thumbs. 'Right,' she said, 'it's on. We need to be going now. Drink up.'

They hailed a taxi and all the way Alexandra quizzed Gita on what was planned, but she revealed nothing. The taxi pulled up outside a smart block of flats; they paid and walked into the lobby. There was a concierge who stopped them and asked where they were going.

'Flat 1205,' Gita said.

'I will need to phone and check,' he said.

'That won't be any good,' Gita said. 'He is ill and can't get out of bed. That is why we are here; to cook him a meal and take care of him.' The concierge took no notice, rang and there was no answer.

'I am sorry,' he said, 'I can't let you through.' Gita shrugged and taking Alexandra's arm they turned and left.

'Well, it looks as though that idea has run its course,' Alexandra said to Gita as they walked away.

'We thought that might happen, but it was best to attack from the front first. I was told we can get in through the garage. Come with me.' With Alexandra chasing behind Gita, they walked down a spiral car ramp into the underground garage, headed to the left and there was a door which had been jammed open.

'You're supposed to have a key pass but he said it was always open. Here we go.' They pushed at the door and it opened and they came out by the lift. They took a deep breath as the lift passed the ground floor, hoping it wouldn't open, as they didn't want to have to again explain to the concierge how they had got past him. On the twelfth floor, they found flat five.

'Ready Alexandra? Here is tonight's fun. You go first,' Gita said, as Alexandra went to ring the doorbell.

'No. It will be unlocked.' Alexandra looked at her friend and turned the door handle; she pushed at the door, which opened as had been promised. As she looked inside, she turned to ask Gita, 'have you been here before?'

'No,' was the curt answer.

Alexandra looked into a modern flat with large lounge windows facing onto the city, now lit by neon in the night sky. The first thing that struck her as odd was that most of the furniture had been pushed to the edge of the room. That was apart from a low, rectangular, pine coffee table, lit brightly by a spotlight in the centre of the room. But it was what was set out on the table that immediately excited her, and she looked at Gita with a huge smile across her face.

Gita put a finger to her lips, signifying silence. They tiptoed into the room and Gita picked up the long horsewhip that was lying on the floor. With a *whoosh* that surprised even Alexandra, she swung it and hit the limp cock, causing a jump and yelp from the naked man, who was lying, tied tightly, on the table.

Alexandra surveyed the scene. He was lying on his back. His legs were spread wide, his knees were bent so that his feet were nearly on the floor, and his ankles were tied to the table legs. At the other end of the table, his wrists were also tied to the table legs. He couldn't move. He was masked and had a gag in his mouth and he was wired up to an iPod so that he couldn't hear.

'Who tied him?' Alexandra asked. 'Are they still here?'

'He tied himself,' said Gita. 'If we hadn't managed to get in he would be here for a long time.'

'I don't believe you,' Alexandra said, as she checked the knots. They were tight and he was immobile other than his head, which turned to try and make out who was there. 'Do you know him, Gita?'

'No. I have never met him. It was all arranged through an

intermediary and text messages.'

'So, we could be anyone. Wow, what a thrill-seeker this one is. What can we do with him?'

'Anything we want, I suppose,' Gita said. 'Let me check his blindfold. I want to make sure he can't see us. That is his rule. He must never know who has come into his flat and used him. Have you seen all these toys here? I suppose we can use them all?'

The surprise of the naked man had blinded Alexandra to everything else that had been laid out. There were large and even larger dildos, all presumably for his arse; lubricant; candles and matches; whips and paddles; and lots more rope.

She really didn't know what to do next, but she knew she wasn't going to ask him. Meanwhile, Gita still had the whip in her hand and was gently rubbing its end on his cock, which twitched and grew larger. It was nearly erect as again she swung hard, catching it halfway down the shaft. Again his body jumped but he couldn't release his ties. Alexandra saw that there was a mark forming where it had hit.

'You take one of these as well and we can stand either side,' Gita said. It was taking Alexandra a moment longer than Gita to get into this, but soon she was there. They counted up to twenty as blows struck his thighs and cock with near-perfect symmetry. The redness was getting worse.

Gita looked at the candles and Alexandra nodded. They took one each and lit them. Starting at his stomach they dripped the hot molten wax onto his body. The pain seemed not too bad, although as each drip fell and landed on his bare skin, it caused a squeak through the gag; but he knew, and they knew, that soon it would become much worse. They dripped the wax on him and each drip moved nearer to his cock. As it hit his pubes the pain must have increased and may be made even worse as the wax was now hitting the rawness of an area which had been shaved bare and recently whipped.

Gita held up her hand to stop Alexandra. 'I know what we will do,' she said, and she picked up a length of thin rope, brought the ends together and wrapped a loop of rope over his cock, tied it tight at the base, wrapped the ends around his balls and tied some more.

As the blood pumped into his cock and was unable to leave, they saw it grow larger, pulling the foreskin back and tight. The end of his cock was now fully exposed.

Gita relit the candle and started again to drip the wax. With each drip on his cock, the wave of pain caused his body to arch and the spasms increased. If it was real pain or just anticipation neither of them knew, but as the hot wax finally landed on the exposed end of his cock, he jumped and pulled hard on his ropes; if it hadn't been for the gag, he would almost certainly have screamed, attracting the attention of all the neighbours. This caused the girls to smile but certainly not to stop, as drip-by-drip they tipped their wax onto his cock until it was covered like a roughly-made candle; while all the time he tried – and failed – to scream.

'Maybe you should undo the rope around his cock,' Gita said. 'We don't want it to fall off. What should we try next?'

They looked around. It was not possible to use all the toys while he was on his back.

'We need to get him standing up,' Alexandra said, so they untied his hands so he could sit up, then they retied them behind his back. After untying his legs, they made him stand. He was wobbly, while they led him towards a dining table that had been pushed to the side of the room. Alexandra looked at the dildos. Why not choose the largest, she thought; after all, this is not foreplay.

'Are we going to lube his arse before we stick it in?' Gita asked.

'Well, I'm not doing it,' Alexandra replied. They compromised and lubed the end of the extraordinarily large dildo before twisting and screwing it deep inside him. It was not only large in girth but also long. They managed, after some time and effort, to push it all in. They looked at each other with a real sense of satisfaction; a task well done. They didn't really know what to do next.

'Stay there and don't move,' Gita shouted at him. He nodded.

She took Alexandra by the arm and pulled her towards the kitchen. Finally out of earshot, she said, 'what do we do next?' I have never been in this situation before. Do you want to fuck him or suck him or anything like that?'

Alexandra shook her head. 'No way, but are you having a good time Gita?'

'Too right I am. You?'

Alexandra smiled. 'Very much, thank you. I think we should smack him on the arse a bit and tie some of those things to his balls and then we need to find a grand finale. I have an idea for that.'

'Sounds great,' said Gita, and they returned to find their bound and naked man just where they left him, his chest lying on the table, his bottom facing them.

'Stand up and turn around,' Gita said, and Alexandra attached weights to his balls which pulled them downwards; as she finished, she slapped his cock which sent wax flying and the weights swinging like a pendulum. He did not like that.

'Now turn around,' she said, and she pushed his chest back onto the table. They chose a paddle and a whip and beat his arse and the tops of his thighs, leaving more marks of deep redness as the blood tried to heal the throbbing wounds. They worked perfectly together in silence, enjoying the experience of control over a man. As he moved, twisted and hopped around to avoid each new blow, the dildo slipped silently out and onto the floor. The girls looked at each other and Alexandra winked at Gita.

She walked to where all the toys were laid out and picked up a pair of light latex gloves. She put them on, put lube on her fingers and started to ram her fist into the now gaping hole of his arse. It was not easy at first, but with a push, she found her hand deep inside him. He wanted this. He allowed it and had prepared for it, but maybe he had not expected two such committed attendants.

'We are nearly finished with you,' Gita said, as Alexandra nodded and threw the glove on the floor. 'We have one last test for you, but first, we want to make sure you are fully satisfied before we leave.' She knew that he was hoping for them to do something sexual for him. Gita undid his hands and said, 'now masturbate for us. We want to see you come. We want you to wank into this glass,' and she carefully placed a wine glass in his hand.

They sat on the sofa while his hand moved his cock backwards and forwards again, spreading the now cold candle wax around the room. It was an effort for him – he was slow in coming and the women started to become bored – but finally, there was a gush of white cum oozing from his cock and into the wine glass. He stood, still masked and blind, holding the glass out in front of him. Gita looked at it while Alexandra took off his gag.

'Drink it. What makes you think we want it?' Obediently he raised the glass to his lips, tipped it up, and poured the contents into his mouth.

'Good boy,' Alexandra said, 'now, you have a choice of three things to finish your challenge. Do you want to hear them?' He nodded and Gita was also keen to see what Alexandra had in mind.

She carried on. 'First, you could stand there with your legs apart and we will each take five big kicks at your balls – as hard as we can – and if you scream or resist we will do it all again; five more times each. Would you like that?'

He shook his head and said, 'no'.

She continued. 'Then, in that case, we will take you downstairs with us, dressed just as you are now, and we will take you with us onto the street, tie you to a lamppost, take off your blindfold and then call the newspaper. Would you like that? I am sure your colleagues at work will find it amusing, especially with all your scars and marks. Would you like that?'

He hesitated. Alexandra thought that maybe he would like it, but could not risk it. After all, he probably had a good job. The flat was not cheap. Then he said, 'no'.

'In that case, you have rejected the first two of my three options; so it has to be the third.'

'If I don't like the third, can't I go back to the first two?' he asked.

'Of course not,' Alexandra said. 'You have already rejected those, you stupid boy. Put your hands behind your back,' and with that, she fitted on his now limp cock a chastity device that she had found among the toys. She padlocked the cage around his cock. He knew what was happening and it was all made a lot easier as his cock had shrunk away to nothing.

Alexandra and Gita put on their coats as he remained upright.

'We are going now. Do not take off your mask for five minutes after we have gone.'

'Will you tell me where the key for the chastity device is, or will I have to search?' he asked, rather plaintively.

'Oh, didn't I tell you?' Alexandra said, 'I will keep the key and post it back to you sometime soon. But don't expect it for at least a month. I am very busy for the next few weeks. I hope you can trust the post here not to lose it?'

He thought about saying something but there was silence. There was no way he could object or chase them. They left and took the lift down to the basement, walked out and hailed a taxi.

'Wow,' said Alexandra, 'that was great. I was so wet.'

'Can you imagine what he is thinking now? He got all he wanted and then you walk away with the key. He will be petrified. You can't get those things off without the key. What if he has a date with a girlfriend tomorrow?'

'Then he has a lot of explaining to do,' Alexandra replied.

'Will you send it back tomorrow?' Gita said.

'No, of course not. I will send it back in about six weeks. I will post it from Kyiv. That will give him even more excitement than anything we did. It isn't even midnight. Any idea what we can do next?'

'I'm sure I can think of something,' Gita replied. 'I think we did quite well. Agreed, Alexandra?'

44. WORKING NAKED

Birthdays, as you have read before, are the source of many of my adventures. This one proved to be no different and it doesn't need much more explanation.

I have always had the urge to be nude in public. I have been to topless beaches and nudist beaches but none of those experiences really did it for me because all the other people there were also topless or naked. I didn't feel the excitement I was coming to crave. It wasn't the true exhibitionism which I wanted. I used to think about getting into my car without my clothes, driving to the shops and wandering around the supermarket naked; but of course, I couldn't because although I don't know the law I am sure I would get arrested.

I used to search the internet for videos and pictures of women nude in public places, and every time I found one I would watch and watch again, then go and find my toys and make myself come hard. It became an obsession which I knew once more I had to turn into a reality. There was only one way I could think of, and that was to become a model for one of the websites I used to watch.

It was my birthday and I needed another set of challenges; this seemed to be just right. I filled in the application form, which included having to send a nude picture of myself. That caused me a problem. I had never sent anyone a nude picture of myself, but then I thought if I'm having doubts now, how will I manage the challenge I have set myself? So I stripped, stood in front of the mirror, pouted and posed, took several photographs, sent them off and started waiting very impatiently each day to see if there was an email in reply. Finally, it came. I was accepted, consent forms were signed, and arrangements were made.

My day was to be a summer day in Prague – an all-expenses-paid trip and a modelling fee, but I think I would have paid them, had they asked. I was at a point in my life when this just seemed like a great thing to do.

They had a scenario arranged and they were to tell me on the day. It was an evening shoot and I spent the day in a state of panic and anticipation. They came for me in a car and I was taken to an open-air beer hall in a public market. On the way, they explained what was going to happen.

I and two other girls were going to serve beer to the customers who were there for a normal night out – they were not actors – but a game was being played at the same time. As we gave the customers their beer, they had to choose one of three different coloured stones. Each colour represented one of the waitresses, but we didn't know which girl was which colour. As the stones were collected they were counted, and whichever waitress had the most, had to take off an item of clothing. Then we would carry on serving, but because they wouldn't tell us which was our colour, we never knew who was next.

We started fully dressed in a nice skirt, blouse and even a school tie, which we seemed to lose very quickly. They said, though, that the shoot was planned to last about two hours – this was going to be a very slow striptease.

I asked what would happen if I didn't collect most of the right colour that night, would that be the end of the shoot for me? They said there would be another shoot the next day, and if I lost tonight I would be used then. Being used is exactly what I thought it was.

It was a warm evening, there were beer tables outside and there must have been hundreds of people there, mainly men but many women too; all there just for a drink and a night out. Think of it as an open-air pub.

At first, it was easy. As we raced out serving the beer and collecting tokens, we all quickly lost ties and shoes; then I saw that one of the girls, Kristen I think, had taken off her blouse. Panic set in; this might be me soon. I didn't have to wait long, I got my instruction: blouse off. That was two of us now without a blouse.

I can't say if it was rigged or not, but soon I was out there in a crowd without my skirt, in just my bra and panties. I kept saying to myself it was just like wearing a bikini but I knew that it wasn't. It was nearly ten at night and here I was in a town in the Czech Republic, in a frilly G-string and bra, serving beer; but worse, the other girls still had their skirts on, and surely it would take a great many tokens for them to catch up?

Time seemed to go slowly. When we started serving beer I don't think any of the customers knew what was happening, but the penny had dropped, and every time we came out there were cat-calls and wolf-whistles. Of course, I was taking the opportunity to have a few drinks as well, so my inhibitions were lowered. A few more forays into the crowd, and when I got back to the bar the dreaded message came: bra off.

Oh, I forgot to say that of course there was a film crew and photographer from the site following us around, because all the time this was all being caught on camera.

So I stood there at the bar entrance and looked at the teeming hordes of people across at the beer tables. I thought of running but I reminded myself of the excitement I was feeling and the contract I had signed. As my bra came off there was a shout of hooray from the crowd, and the orders for beer increased. 'Come here, no – come here,' they shouted.

If they could have seen properly in the dark they would have seen that they weren't the only ones getting excited. The wet patch on my panties must have been a huge stain. On one hand, I hoped that I would lose and that one of the other girls would get the task of serving nude, but I thought if not today then it will be tomorrow. I was winning, and because of that, I was getting naked. That was how it was. I was only one pair of pants short of being nude and the other girls still had bras on; one girl even still had her skirt as well.

I went into the crowd wearing just my panties. I sat on customers' laps and let them touch my breasts. The excitement was driving me wild. I have to say, if someone had come up to me just then and offered to fuck me I would have said yes, but that didn't happen.

The other girls were still serving beer and, like me, collecting the coloured pebbles. Then we were all back at the bar entrance and the organiser gave them their clothes.

'You two can get dressed,' she said, 'we have a winner.' I looked at them and they didn't look too disappointed. They took their shirts and blouses and I just stood there waiting for my clothes.

None came.

'I need your knickers now,' the organiser said to me. I looked at the other girls dressing.

'Here? Now?' I think I said, and she said, 'Yes'.

I had no choice. I took a shot of something for courage. I am not sure what it was but it burnt as it went down my throat. The others were dressed and I was the only nearly naked person there. But this is what I wanted. I didn't want to share my moment. I hooked my panties with my thumbs, and without bending my knees I pulled them to the floor. I was naked and in public.

I took a tray of beers as I headed into the crowd and I hoped no one could see the moisture running down the inside of my thigh. To me, it felt like a stream. My pussy was hot and I am sure if anyone had touched me at that moment I would have come straight away.

At the behest of the film crew, I pushed my way into the most crowded area. Men and even women pushed themselves against me, and I was fondled and touched. Again, I'm not sure if it was rigged by the camera crew, but I was told to go into another of the busy areas.

My route ahead was blocked and as I tried to turn to go back I realised I was surrounded; that was when I first felt a hand from behind reach out; a finger touched my clit and then went deep into me. Surrounded by people and still holding a heavy tray I couldn't move and I just swayed and melted as I was touched, stroked, manhandled and fingered. As I said, it was too much for me. I was on heat. I put the beers down and turned and leaned back against the table, then started to touch myself.

Someone must have cleared the table, as I was pushed back onto it and lay there with legs wide apart, masturbating. Once or twice I looked around. There must have been fifty, sixty or maybe more men just watching me. I saw the flash of cameras as everyone was recording their own memories. I didn't mind, I was in another world.

Soon the men could take no more and there were cocks all around me. Some fucked me. Some men held my ankles while others fucked my ass and there were, of course, cocks stuffed down my throat. I should have minded. This wasn't part of the deal, but I was so hot then I could have gone on all night.

Most seemed to come on my face, and eventually, I had to walk back to the bar. The film crew followed me as I felt the cum drip down my face because I was told not to wipe it off while they were still filming.

My fantasy had become a reality, and I was still on a high all through the night.

I didn't work the next day but I did do another public nudity show six months later with the same crew. Every once in a while, when the urge becomes really strong, I phone them and they arrange a shoot. It really is the best thing since sex was invented. Mmmm.

VII.VASYLKO: WELL BORN

As well as working at the university I often travelled around continental Europe for my modelling shoots, so I count myself well-travelled and broad-minded. Also, I am now able to speak Ukrainian, Russian (both learnt as a child), English and some very poor German.

With my doctorate, I consider myself intelligent, and as a successful model I know I am beautiful. It is a potent mix and I will own up and say that these two thoughts have fuelled my self-confidence, although to be honest, it was probably never really under any threat.

Like most women, I want to be romanced, and many of my dreams are soft and romantic. An ideal dream is to be somewhere in the countryside, walking with a lover barefoot among green, fresh grass. We would be holding hands, and maybe if our cottage or house is not too close to others, then we could even undress, shed our clothes and walk naked. It would be so nice not to be bound by any limits and to feel only total freedom. How good it would be to enjoy the freshness of the air, the smell of flowers and nature permeating every cell of my body.

Or maybe I would like to wear tiny shorts and a loose top, of course without a bra. I think that on a warm summer day that would be the best way to have a rest far from the rush in the city. I imagine my lover and myself sitting outside drinking fruit juice, eating homemade bread, local cheeses, and freshly picked fruits, and just having a perfect time together; only him and me.

There are a few more fantasies like this recorded in these pages, but the best source is those magazines scattered around doctor's waiting rooms all over the world!

Even in a short relationship, it is worth the effort it takes to understand each other, both intellectually and physically. It takes time to discover what each likes. We have our fantasies and sometimes there they should stay: in our minds and the realms of imagination. Some will always remain fantasies, never to be fulfilled, but still fuelling our wonderful life together. However, sometimes we can live out our fantasies!

I had had two long-term lovers – Mikhail and Adam – but both relationships had ended. Many times I have asked myself if that is a fault in me and my personality and I have reached the simple conclusion that until then I hadn't yet found the right man. On the other hand that didn't mean I felt the need to save myself for 'him' whoever he is. But then it changed.

Just like any woman I want to find that perfect man and build that perfect relationship. Now that I am into my thirties I hope I have finally found that man, and he has brought out my romantic side without diminishing any of my naughty thoughts.

45.   HOW TO TREAT WOMEN

Tall, beautiful and confident, she was in control of herself and her life. Men turned as she walked through the town and followed her. She knew and was relaxed. She wasn't upset by the stares and she almost encouraged them.

Her dresses were short and her shoes high, stretching her long legs beyond every man's dreams. She sat sipping coffee and reading, her eyes relaxed behind large dark glasses, not worrying about who was watching her. Men moved restlessly in their chairs as they aimed for a better view. Female companions fumed as their husband's and boyfriend's attention was drawn away.

At home, she prepared for her evening. In her room, she stepped out of her clothes and admired herself in the full-length mirror. Not one fault. Not one blemish. She was the queen of all she surveyed. As she showered she knew that she could have any man; and any man, after they had spent a night together, would tell all of his friends she was the best night he had ever had.

But few had the opportunity to tell. She was in charge, she decided and she didn't often decide on anyone.

Tonight she was with friends in a bar. Her clothes were not provocative, she was already an 'agent provocateur'; she was magnetic and needed no further allure.

He was older than her. Significantly older and sitting at the bar with, even Alexandra had to admit, was a beautiful girl, maybe marginally older than herself but no less beautiful. They moved to the restaurant and Alexandra noticed how carefully he attended to her in a way she had rarely experienced with the men in her life, who always focussed on her body, eager for sex, eager for conquest, eager to brag.

Alexandra watched them. Who was he and she wondered why she hadn't seen him before? As they left Alexandra started to think that all the men she had met weren't men. They were boys.

46.   A LESSON IS LEARNT

Sometimes nothing goes as planned. It was raining and Alexandra was getting wet. She didn't have an umbrella and she was trying to catch the eye of any taxi driver. There, suddenly, was an empty cab, its light glowing. She raised a hand, and as it slowed, she relaxed. At last: a haven from the rain; but then, from nowhere, she heard a wolf-whistle and the cab pulled up short, and he stepped from the building almost straight into the dryness of the car. Alexandra's shoulder slumped as she resigned herself to a further drenching but the cab pulled up and the door opened just a little.

'I am awfully sorry but I think I hijacked your cab. Please get in and we will take you wherever.' As she slid into the taxi she realised it was him, the man from the restaurant.

If she had ever thought of a plan for when she met him she would be dressed to kill with high heels and a plunging neckline. They would be at dinner and then they would dance close and slowly, with her body pushed close to him, but here she was with her hair limp and her makeup smudged. She stopped in her thoughts. She had formed a plan to meet him which meant she had wanted to meet him. She had never been with a man quite so old but now she wanted him.

'Where shall we take you?' he asked. She gave her home address.

'Isn't it out of your way?' she asked.

'I'm in no hurry. I have done all I need for the day. Now I know where you live. As I stole your cab you will let me make amends and take you to dinner tonight. Shall I send my driver around at seven?'

Passively she nodded, and at dinner, he showed all the attentiveness she had witnessed that first evening.

'The problem with people today,' he said, sipping at a glass of Pouilly Fume 'is that they don't understand the lessons learnt by us in the late 60s and 70s. You all assume that 'free love' was promiscuous sex with no emotion. You are all quite wrong, and that is why you all have such a pessimistic view about sex. You know,' he said, leaning forward and looking straight into her eyes, 'you can still make love to a stranger and not have sex.'

She felt the magic of his eyes as they looked deeply into hers and suddenly, for the first time in her life, she wanted this man. Not any man, this man.

'I don't understand. Is that true?' she asked. 'Will you show me?'

'Of course,' he said, 'how could I ever turn down such a genuine plea from one so beautiful, but not tonight if that is what you were hoping. Tonight you will go home and tuck yourself up in your beautiful bed. I will be with you tomorrow at eight.'

Alexandra was both tense and excited all day. She didn't know why. She didn't know him, and here she was about to have sex with him, or as he said, make love. Was there a difference? She doubted it.

At eight he arrived wearing a loose shirt and baggy linen trousers, a throwback to an earlier age, carrying a large bag and a bottle of champagne.

'I think this is still chilled but maybe you could put it in the fridge for a few moments?' he said. 'And do you have a serving plate? I took the liberty to bring some sushi. I knew you would be confused about what was going to happen. I really do hope you don't mind? I really like those jeans but can you change into something a little looser and relaxed?

Alexandra stood still for a moment. Nothing had happened like this before. Previously she always knew. Previously the game was played with her rules. There is always so much to learn, she thought, as she took the champagne.

Returning, she saw him lighting candles in the lounge.

'Now some champagne and maybe some sushi? You see, sex needs to be part of an emotional relationship and not just physical. Making love is a holistic experience and that is what you will experience. Now, stand here opposite me.'

There was music playing quietly and the candles were throwing a soft light.

'Put this silk scarf on and cover your eyes. Don't be afraid. I am doing the same.'

They were standing close and she could smell his perfume. The silk felt soft around her eyes and although she should be worried by the blindfold she only felt relaxed and happy.

'We spend too much time,' he said, 'forgetting we have five senses and not using them all. We are far too dominated by what we see. We are too impressed by outward beauty, but by removing our sight we will now have to use our other senses. We will connect at deeper levels. We will see the beauty within. We will use our hands to see each other anew.'

Alexandra felt an electric sensation as first she felt the touch of his hand on her head and then slowly running through her hair. His hand was outlining her face as a blind man might 'see' her. She did likewise, feeling the strength of his character through his face; she felt a powerful neck while his hands reached down to her shoulders.

The touch was slow and so careful that Alexandra thought she already felt she knew him well. The perfumes of the candles were intoxicating and she felt light-headed. The music was hypnotic.

Slowly she unbuttoned his shirt which fell silently to the floor, to rest alongside hers; she outlined every muscle and curve on his body. They were naked, still standing, still facing each other, feeling and touching and knowing. With some hidden force, not a push or a word, she realised she was lying on the floor and he was kissing her; first, her breasts, taking her already erect nipples slowly in his mouth.

She wanted him inside her. There was a heat that ran right through her body. She needed him as she had never needed anyone. She wanted to feel him. She wanted him to be deep inside her. She wanted them to be as one, and slowly, with consent and passion, they started to make love. She felt her orgasm grow until it had enveloped her whole body. She felt him grow inside her. A scream and her back arched as she pulled him in deeper and deeper and felt the warmth of his body. They lay close together, her head on his chest, feeling his heart as it beat out a rhythm of love. The clock had moved forward more than two hours. Two hours of making love.

'I must go,' he said, 'but now you have started to understand how making love is so different from sex. You have so much to learn my lapushka, Alexandra. You have so much to enjoy. Never stop. These boys are not for you.'

It was during that experience I thought about a relationship with an older man. I couldn't forget his words: 'these boys are not for you.'

I had always wanted to be on the catwalk in Paris, London or Moscow, but I am not tall enough, so I have been restricted to being a photographic model, where I specialise in lingerie and swimwear. You may well have seen me in a magazine or on a billboard, but to be honest, that is more likely if you have been to Kyiv or Moscow, which is where most of my work is shown.

My work as a model gave me a new and different perspective on my academic work. I would spend days barely dressed, often being shot in public places with crowds gathering around us. I could see in the men's eyes their attitude towards me, and I needed a riposte. I needed to find ways to look sexy for the camera and not show what I really felt about all the leering men. The easiest way was to revert to my imagination, and my way was to have sexy, sometimes romantic thoughts that allowed me to drift into my own, occasionally very naughty, fantasies. Then I could feel sexy and wanton, the look the photographer was normally looking for; those sexy looks you see in the photographs are real!

Often I would be feeling really horny and excited as the shoot moved on. I might be thinking about the photographer, a lover or sometimes (but rarely) someone in the crowd. I would imagine all the different ways we would have sex together. I had become so good at building these fantasies, not just in front of the camera but also even as I was walking around a shop, that I would often feel myself becoming wet and excited from my thoughts; but I am getting ahead of myself.

Alexandra

47. MODELLING BY THE SEA SHORE

Alexandra works as a photo model for cosmetics, lingerie and swimwear. She is thin, has long, slim legs, her breasts are full and beautifully rounded, and her blonde hair frames a stunningly pretty and sculpted face. Her looks are to be envied, but not for the first time today, she is both reflective and frustrated.

Reflective because it is now three years since she left her long-term lover who had gambled one too many times and wagered their love away. Since then there has been no one in her life. She misses love and she misses being in love; she misses intimate hugs and kisses; but most of all, she misses not having someone in her life. Alexandra is not just a person of strong emotions, she is also a person who needs all the physical aspects of love.

Because she is young and pretty there have always been many suitors and opportunities. Like bees around a honey pot, young and older men are always offering themselves to her, but although she needs sex, she is not the type of person who gives her body easily to any man just to satisfy her desires. She calls it respect. So, since him, there has been no sex, and that is why today Alexandra is feeling frustrated.

In the meantime she distracts herself by flirting outrageously, knowing full well the effect she is having; it amuses her but it is never really satisfying. Wherever she goes she knows that both men and women turn their heads to see her.

The women are jealous of her toned body and her good looks; they all want to be her, knowing then they could have any man they wanted. The men dream of afternoons and mornings in her arms; discovering her naked and ready for hot and sexy nights. And while their heads turn, their trousers stretch with the thought of her rounded lips covering their body with kisses.

Alexandra phoned her sister Anna and complained. 'Why can't I find a man who will take care of me?' she said. 'He doesn't have to be a prince or a hero, just a man who loves me for being a woman who will love him as no other man has ever been loved.'

Alexandra shrugged as she heard her sister say very little. There was no reasonable answer.

Today's schedule was much like any other on a modelling assignment: swimwear on a beach on the Black Sea coast. The weather was warm and so, thankfully, was the sea. She pouted and posed as the photographer prowled around her, and his assistant moved reflectors to either sharpen or dull the light. There had already been two clothes changes and the final change was into a silver leopard-skin bikini, cut low on her breasts with a small G-string. Around them, an inquisitive crowd had formed and Alexandra could see the same old collection of sad voyeurs and would-be suitors. Her professionalism told her to keep smiling and focus on her work but her heart was heavy.

At least, she thought, she could look forward to the evening when she could take control and again flirt extravagantly and maybe even in the process break another heart; but the evening wouldn't last long. To catch the best light the shoot started again early in the morning so she couldn't be late for bed. She looked around at all those watching her. They must all think it was such a glamorous life. If only they knew.

The sun was setting; her photographer shouted 'wrap' and the day was done. Alexandra headed back to her room. Standing, sitting, squatting and posing for the camera is much harder work than most people think, so now she needed a relaxing bath. As she lay there she looked down at her body as the water washed around her. Why am I only seen as a body, she thought? I also have a loving heart.

She sighed. But if I am just a body then I shouldn't let them down. I should at least have some fun and flirt and drive all those men wild.

She dried patting herself gently with the large, white, fluffy hotel towel, wrapped it around her and sat at the mirror to put on her makeup. What should it be tonight? Natural tones or the powerful red lips of a temptress? Temptress, she thought. Tonight I will be the temptress.

The towel dropped to the floor and she walked naked to the wardrobe. What would she wear? Maybe the tight white T-shirt and short denim shorts. Then they could all see her nipples through the cloth and the frayed shorts just seemed to force eyes to her pussy.

She could sit at the bar; her legs slightly apart and then suggestively take the straw of her drink and play around with it on her lips. But who would be there? Who would the 'they' be? Deep in her heart, she knew. They would be the same normal collection of sad hopefuls.

Or maybe this, she thought, as she looked at a dress in the wardrobe. Yes, this was what she would wear. The evening was still warm and it was perfect. In patterned pink it was not so much a dress as a flowing skirt with straps that barely covered her breasts and scooped down, revealing a bare back, so low that it seemed half her bottom was on display. She took the dress out and held it in front of her as she turned and twirled in front of the mirror. The skirt was tight at the top and opened out to a full dress at her ankles. Cool, light, flowing, sexy and sultry. Perfect.

Putting the dress back on the hanger she sought out her jewellery. She liked her jewellery and she liked the sparkle and the extra excitement she always felt when she thought about her gold and silver. She chose the long gold earrings with the light blue stone, then two rings on the middle finger of her left hand; she wondered wistfully if one day they may be replaced by a wedding ring; a new ring, placed there by a new lover. Which necklace? She rummaged through the selection in the box in front of her while she dreamed, and looked at her hand She chose the gold chain and the Coptic cross to match her earrings.

Time to take the dress off the hanger and put it on; it felt cool and sexy. She looked in the mirror and knew she was beautiful and special. Again she turned and twirled and saw the line of her breasts. It is odd, she thought. If she wore nothing it could never be half as sexy and provocative as when she was scantily dressed and half covered. She knew when she walked every man would be looking at her, seeing the line of her body, seeing the shape of her breasts, and each would hope that a bit of material would slip so they could see more. What fools men are!

Every woman would look first at her and then closely examine her own man as he looked at Alexandra; and at that moment, jealousy would quickly turn to hatred. Tough luck, she thought, but she knew that that night those women would benefit as their men made love to them, the passion in their loins driven by the excitement and desire Alexandra had generated. So what if these men thought of Alexandra with each thrust into their wives and girlfriends? So what if both were thinking of her to fuel their imaginations, even though none would guess that there would still be no sex for Alexandra?

It was warm and she could hear the sound of the waves gently lapping onto the sand as she headed down to the barista bar with its straw roof, rustic tables and chairs, where couples chatted over a cocktail or early dinner. It was typical of a seaside holiday resort. There were small groups of men standing around with beers or vodkas in hand. There were fewer groups of women but each group was eyeing the other in the ritual dance of social foreplay.

It was into this milieu that Alexandra walked, heading straight to the bar. Conversations stopped, eyes turned and men were brought back to their task by their partners.

'Champagne,' she said, rather quietly. It was said as if she was talking to someone sitting next to her. It wasn't an instruction but still, the barman jumped up, ignoring others who had been waiting longer. As she sat at the bar, her back straight, she glanced into the mirror behind the bar to judge her impact on the room and smiled. It was just as she had imagined. She saw the single men, still in groups, trying not to look her way but always falling to temptation, while the vicious arrows of jealousy were being shot into her sultry, naked back by women.

It was then, in the mirror, that she saw him.

He was in many ways ordinary. He wasn't especially tall and maybe just slightly overweight. It was hard to tell his age but he was older than her. His clothes were casual: a simple white shirt, baggy, light-coloured linen trousers and open sandals. He was at a table where he had a clear sight of her but he just kept reading the newspaper and occasionally writing on a pad of paper on the table. She checked on him again and he never once looked at her. He must be gay because no straight man could ignore her, but then a couple joined him briefly. They shared a glass of wine and clearly, he flirted with the woman, but that it is what a gay man would do anyway, she thought. Alexandra saw the smile as he made his companion laugh; he touched her shoulder and whispered in her ear as they both looked at the man. There was a twinkle in his eye. Maybe he wasn't gay, but still, he didn't look at Alexandra.

She called for another glass of champagne. This time her voice was louder. She wanted him to hear but still, he was unmoved. This was a challenge to Alexandra but not one that could be addressed tonight. Tonight was an early-to-bed night. There was always another day.

The next shoot started early, at six, with the good sun. There were again three changes of swimwear and she was finishing with a simple red bikini with both skimpy top and bottoms. They were nearly done and it was still only eight o'clock. She was beginning to think of how hungry she had become when a waiter from the hotel walked toward her with a note.

'Join me for breakfast in the sun lounge? Vasylko.'

At least it was a question and not an instruction, but who on earth was Vasylko? It wasn't a name she knew and although she had no inclination to join anyone for breakfast she would at least find out as she passed the restaurant on the way back to her room. Maybe it was an old friend with a new nickname. With the sun the temperature rose and wearing her large silver mirror sunglasses and a flimsy kaftan wrap she headed back towards the hotel to check the lounge and discover more about Vasylko.

The man from last night, the one who hadn't noticed her, was alone at a table. Instinct pulled her towards him and she stood over him, hopefully looking as angry as she felt.

'Why do you think you can just invite me to breakfast?' Alexandra was surprised by her own strident approach. It wasn't planned. 'Because it's breakfast time because you have been working and must be hungry, but most importantly...'

He hesitated and took a sip from a glass of sparkling orange juice.

'And most importantly,' she asked, feeling irritated by his intervention in her life.

'And most importantly,' he said, 'most importantly because it's sunny. Now would you like a Bucks Fizz? I know you like champagne. You shouted it so loud last night that they probably heard you in Kyiv and you can only have such beautiful skin by drinking fresh orange juice.'

While Alexandra tried to balance the continuing anger, inflamed with the mild insult about how she had ordered her champagne last night – she had to agree that she was loud – or flattered by his compliment, he had called the waiter and ordered breakfast for her.

'I am having smoked salmon and scrambled eggs with a little white toast,' he said to the waiter, 'and my guest is having the same?'

He looked at Alexandra and said, 'is that good for you?'

She smiled, that was exactly what she would have ordered, and her anger was dissolving as quickly as it had risen. She sat down next to him and was about to nod her agreement to breakfast, when already he was replying for her, without waiting for her answer. 'Of course, you would,' he said. She was confused. Had he ordered for her without waiting for her answer or had he just responded very quickly to her nod?

As they talked quickly it didn't seem to matter. The conversation hovered over trivial topics but he was amusing her; he was clever, undoubtedly, but never patronising; he was talking with her and not at her. There was a tingle in her heart and a sudden uncertainty and frailty in her normally rock-solid personae; suddenly she felt very self-conscious, wearing only her bikini and a nearly transparent beach dress.

She had spent most of the last three days being photographed wearing very little and watched by a crowd of leering men. In the evenings and lounging around the pool, she had dressed provocatively to incite unrest and jealousy, but that was for all men and not just one man. Although they had just met, already she felt protected by him and she wanted to be stimulating only for him and not everyone else.

However, he remained unflustered, and except for the occasional glance, he did not look at her body. She was so used to men talking at her breasts that she almost found it disconcerting. He was looking into her eyes. He was asking questions about music, her family, her favourite films and even politics. He was treating her as a person and he made her feel relaxed and comfortable. She had an immediate and compelling need to open herself up to him. She took off her sunglasses. She wanted him to see her eyes. She wanted him to see into her soul.

Alexandra hadn't noticed that they had sat and talked for over two hours, nor that other guests had been and gone, but he broke the spell.

'I have to work today,' he said. 'Would you like dinner tonight?'

'Yes I would,' Alexandra said. 'What do you do?'

'I help dreams become a reality.' He smiled. It was a soft, engaging but teasing smile and Alexandra wanted to see it more often. 'We will meet here at eight?' he said.

He stood, she stood, he put his hands on her shoulders and pulled her closer. He kissed her gently on each cheek, then left, and she was sitting alone.

Alexandra spent the day on her own, sunbathing on the beach, fending off requests to share a drink or play some beach game, and all the while she thought of Vasylko. Okay, he wasn't the most handsome man, and he wasn't the youngest, but he had a simplicity, openness and humour that attracted her. No, that wasn't right; he didn't just attract her, she was already infatuated with him and she couldn't wait until eight o'clock.

Throughout the day, time moved slowly. She was bathed and ready to dress long before seven. What would she wear? It had to be stylish, and simple but maybe a little impish and provocative. There was no need for stockings or tights as it was too hot, and that helped with the choice of simple flat shoes. Then simple gold stud earrings and a matching gold chain were the accessories of choice. She put these on and looked in the mirror; shoes, earrings and a necklace. If I turned up like this then even he would have to look at me! I guess I need to wear something more.

Finally, she had decided. It was a short skirt of a soft material that flowed as she walked. It finished well above her knees and then a plain white blouse of voile that was just a little transparent. Now, what lingerie? Of course, she should wear a bra as otherwise, he could see her breasts, but to wear a bra would spoil the look of the blouse.

It had been a very long time since she had dressed to please any one person specifically; more often she dressed only to provoke a reaction. Normally she did not care but this time she did. This time she wanted it to be perfect. She wanted him to see her as a person and not just a body but also she wanted him to be excited by her; the decision not to wear a bra was made.

She looked again in the mirror at her naked self. If no bra, she thought, then I can choose any panties; but which? Was it the plethora of choices that meant it was all so difficult or was it that Alexandra wanted to make the right sexy decision to complement and excite her playful and interesting self? She narrowed the choice down to two. Either it was the very, very small G-string or nothing. The thought of the freedom of being without lingerie excited her, so that was her choice.

Last night she wasn't wearing lingerie but there was a difference between last night and tonight. Last night she dressed for herself and she dressed for her fantasies. Tonight she was dressing for Vasylko's fantasies. Her fantasies were becoming realities, just as he said.

Alexandra found it hard not to be early and she sat in her room watching the clock tick towards eight o'clock until finally it was all too much and she was in the restaurant three minutes early. He was not there, and forsaking her normal place at the bar she sat at a table. He was not yet late and she reconciled herself to waiting.

She didn't have to wait long, but it did something very odd to her; being by herself she was nervous, and now she wasn't looking at how people looked at her. She was only worried about how she looked for him. There was a vulnerability which rounded her personality and softened her complexion, so she looked even more beautiful.

She saw him walk towards the restaurant, stop and talk to a couple and then a woman. He saw her and waved, but still finished the conversation which seemed to last forever; then he walked straight to Alexandra's table.

He kissed her on the cheek, sat down and called the waiter. 'Champagne please, for both of us. How are you? Did you have a good day?' and he talked to her as if they had been together all their lives.

Alexandra felt relaxed and laughed, held his hand across the table and didn't once look to see what other people were doing, because she was with her man. Had her sister asked her she would never have described the man that sat opposite as the one for her but that, she thought, is fate and love; Cupid must have the most unusual sense of humour.

Although dinner was finished, there were still so many words unspoken, and when the music from the DJ slowed, they danced a little. He had simply said, 'I like this tune,' stood and taken her hand as she joined him. As he held her close, the heat in her body was rising, and as they danced he whispered, 'do you want to go for a walk before we turn in for bed?'

Whose bed, she thought and for a moment happiness was replaced by fear as she considered that this might just be another – very clever – seduction.

'Yes, Vasylko. I would like that,' she said, and they left hand in hand to walk down the beach. Alexandra put her arm around his waist and he put his around her shoulders. They walked and talked and then he said, 'Look at the stars. You know, they are so far away they may already have died. We need to live while we can. Life is for living.'

Alexandra stopped and turned towards him, and first, their eyes locked and then their lips. At first, it was a tentative touching of lips, then it became more frenetic as their tongues searched for each other. Alexandra pulled away and kissed and bit at his neck before their mouths re-engaged. They pulled each other closer, both wanting to become as one. Alexandra started undoing her own blouse as she wanted him to kiss her breast and then her nipples; Vasylko reached to gently cup a breast.

She pulled him closer, wanting to feel him getting excited and hard, knowing that this would start to release all the pent-up passion that she had kept hidden for years. Vasylko understood and pulled at his own shirt, which was soon open and cast away. They pulled each other close and for the first time enjoyed the feeling of flesh on flesh, then the pace increased and became almost frantic as the passion in Alexandra, so long hidden, was finally released.

They dropped to the sand, tore at their clothes and undressed each other. They were just a stone's throw down the beach from the restaurant and in the distance she could still hear the soft and slow sound of the music, but the fear of being found or seen was no restraint. It was not exhibitionism but a pure, unbridled passion for each other.

Soon Alexandra felt him deep inside her. She felt each thrust not as an intrusion or violation, but as a release. The frustrations of the years ebbed away as deep inside her the heat of an orgasm built. He slowed and looked in her eyes, and as they met she saw love. He pushed harder and faster and with each thrust, her passion rose. The heady mixture of pain and joy was sending Alexandra into another world, as she felt the sweet warmth as he came, then relaxed back onto her body.

'Where have you been all my life, Alexandra?'

'Waiting for you, and now we have found each other I will never let you go.'

'I love you.'

48.   HAREM

My relationship with Vasylko flourished and soon my dreams became very romantic. Soft and beautiful fantasies are wonderful and very comforting. Vasylko was always able to find the right words to tell me how much he loved me.

The Sultan had a problem. He had four beautiful wives. Each night he made love to one of them, but he enjoyed them all. One day, his father told the Court of the Land that when he died the new Sultan would rule, but he had to choose just one wife; that wife would then bear his children. He knew he would have to make a decision, and the Sultan sat and thought. How would he choose? In their own way, each was special and pampered him in special ways, so he decided to set them all a test. He called his wives together and sat them around him.

He looked at his harem. They were all dressed similarly: a silken head dress that covered flowing hair; a tiny bra which showed their nipples standing erect because each thought they were to be summoned to his room; silken trousers which ballooned out at the leg but were belted tight at the waist; and panties of such sheer voile that each was always exposed. He looked at his wives and his manhood rose as he looked at the place where he would enter them. Each of his wives was moist with anticipation.

'My wives, I must choose but one of you,' he said, 'and to make that choice there will be tests. I want a wife who is strong and a wife who is beautiful. I want a wife who is clever and a wife that can make my manhood stand strong. I will make my final choice in six weeks. The first test will be a test of strength.'

So, the first test of strength was set for a week later. Wife number One stood in a circle marked out with a rope. She stood with her hands on her hips and legs apart, wearing just a bra and panties. She called wife number Two in with her. She was no match, One was much stronger. She slapped Two, she punched her and when Two said, 'no more', One took the rope and tied her hands behind her back and stripped her bare. Two stood aside, naked and exposed. The same fate befell number Three.

One turned to Four and said, 'Come here. It's your turn to show how weak you are,' but Four said, 'I know I am weak. I will pray and ask my God for strength one day,' and One let her be.

One wanted to show her strength, so she took the two tied wives and threw them on the floor. She sat on the face of the first and said, 'use your tongue and make me come as if I was the Sultan.' She wanted to show the Sultan how strong she was, and Two did as she was told, for she could not move away.

Then she took Three and lay her on her belly; then, taking a stick, she used it in Three's rear passage until it was deep inside. As she pushed, Three screamed, but One did not stop. She turned to the Sultan and said, 'You see, Master, I am the strongest of them all.'

And the Sultan said, 'I see'.

A week later, it was the test of beauty. The wives were prepared with hair washed and combed and makeup on their faces. They stood in front of the Sultan. He looked at each.

One was strong, but the strength had lined her face. Two was beautiful: her eyes were clear and the makeup made her mouth look large and inviting for the Sultan's manhood. Three was less skilled, and her makeup was smudged and not as beautiful as Two.

The Sultan looked at Four. Her hair shined and was long, but she had no makeup. The Sultan looked at her and said, 'You have no makeup Four. Why?'

Four looked at him and said, 'God can see my beauty and my beauty is in my soul.'

And Two said, 'You see, Master, I am the most beautiful of all,' and the Sultan said, 'I see'.

Then the Sultan wanted to see who was the cleverest, and the test was set for the following week. He set each of his wives a puzzle. One looked at the puzzle and stared, but could not make the pieces whole. Two stared as well and didn't know what to do. Three took the pieces and soon the puzzle was complete. She looked at the problems One and Two were having and smiled.

Four sat and didn't move. All the pieces were as the Sultan had put them down in front of her. The Sultan turned to Four and said, 'Can't you even start the puzzle? And Four said, 'Not only can I start the puzzle but I can finish the puzzle. My cleverness is known to my God because he gave it to me.'

And Three said, ''You see, Master, I am the most clever of all.'

And the Sultan said, 'I see'.

And the Sultan said, your next test will be to see who can make my manhood strongest. On the day I call you, let it be known that I will have exercised my manhood four times before you arrive.

On the first day, One arrived in the Sultan's chamber. She wanted to show her strength, so she took some rope and tied the Sultan's wrists to the bed, then she took off all the Sultan's clothes and tied his ankles to the bed, with his legs spread wide. She stood above him and slowly undressed. But his manhood did not move. She stroked it, kissed it, sucked it and beat it, but it would not move.

A week later, Two arrived in his chamber. She wanted to show her beauty. She sat the Sultan in his chair and stood before him. The music played and she danced for him the dance of seven veils. As each veil was removed she looked to see if the Sultan's manhood moved. She danced all the veils until there were no more, then she sat on the Sultan's lap, but his manhood never moved.

A further week later, Three arrived in the Sultan's chamber. She wanted to show how clever she was. She sat the Sultan at a table and gave him some cards. She said, 'We will cut the cards and whoever has the lowest numbered card has to remove a piece of clothing.' The Sultan said, 'I see.'

To show how clever she was, she had arranged the cards so that she always lost and soon she was naked. The Sultan sat and watched, but still, his manhood didn't move.

Finally, a week later, Four arrived in the Sultan's chamber. The Sultan was depressed. None of his wives had made his manhood move and Four was weak, she was not the prettiest and she showed that she was not the cleverest either.

She wore nothing other than a simple sheer veil. It was draped over her head and reached the floor. Through the veil, the Sultan could see the fine lines of her face, her small and beautiful breasts, the mound of her secret passage and her long, toned legs.

She stood in front of the Sultan. She stood still and did not move and did not say anything. The Sultan looked at her and looked some more. 'Come here,' he said at last. 'I want to touch you.'

'No,' she said. 'We have made love many times but if I am to be your wife then I must be your wife as if I was a virgin. You cannot touch me again until we are married.'

The Sultan was getting angry. 'Come here,' he said. 'No,' she said, saying just as she had said before.

The Sultan got angrier. 'Come here,' he said. 'No,' she said, saying just as she had said before. He reached out, but she was just out of reach as she stepped back at a pace.

The Sultan looked at her and smiled, as he felt his manhood rise.

'You are strong because you said no when your Sultan ordered you. You are beautiful because you know where the heart of all beauty lies. You are clever because you tempted and yet took it away before I could taste the fruit, and' he said, 'you made my manhood rise. You will be my wife. And no longer will you be called Four. I shall call you Alexandra, for Alexandra means courageous and one who lives by their principles and inner self.

So Alexandra became the Sultan's wife and bore him three children, and she had three handmaidens who washed her and clothed her and combed her hair. And they were called One, Two and Three.

49.   A LETTER FROM VASYLKO

My dearest Alexa,

I can think of nothing other than *'eating you'*. I can only think about eating you in each and every way.

- I will lay you on the bed and drip chocolate on you, then eat every last bit from your body.
- I want to nibble on your neck and ears while running my hands through your silken hair.
- I want you naked and leaning against a wall while I kneel in front of you. I will pour oil over your breasts and caress them while I eat your pussy.
- While on the bed I will cover your pussy with cream and eat strawberries from your pussy.
- I want to wake in the morning with you next to me, and the first thing we do is kiss; I want to cover your whole body with kisses and nibble on your toes.
- I will make sushi and place it all over your body. I will use you as my naked plate and I will eat each one by kissing it off you.

All my love,
Vasylko

Alexandra

50.   HONEYMOON DREAMS

My relationship with Vasylko was developing and my more romantic feelings were often to the fore, and like every woman I thought about a wedding day and I had some very romantic ideas. Well, maybe it wasn't the wedding that I thought about most, but the honeymoon.

The wedding was in the afternoon and was at first for other people: parents, sisters and friends; but slowly and unseen it had become more. It was their chance to say to the world 'we are now one, we have made a commitment to each other, for our friends to witness'.

He had written his own words to say to her at that special moment. He said:

Forever I will love you and cherish you.

Without condition, I give you my body, soul and heart. I promise to love you and only you. You are the Alpha and Omega of my life: it's beginning and its ending.

I will look after and protect you for all time, without end. I will forever be by your side.

I will be a companion to you, and will forever be your best friend. I will be your faithful partner. Where you go I will go, and where you stay I will stay. Your people will be my people. I will never disappear.

I rejoice in the strength we have united as one.

I have a passion for life and I promise you a life of passion.

I now ask these friends to carry our message to all others and bear witness to my promises to you. I give you this ring as a symbol of my commitment.

The wedding breakfast and party lasted till late. The flight to the Indian Ocean island was early. Alexandra and her new husband had wanted to be together. They had been casting those glances that said

'I want to be alone with you all evening' but to no avail.

Tired, they sat on the plane, in love. Early morning, and as the doors opened they felt a hot breeze drift down the plane. They cleared customs, and with their luggage, soon were in a jeep driving along beach roads separated from the sea by only white sands free of all people.

Their cottage was on the beach and they were alone at last. All the build-up had been tiring and, finally alone, they lay together naked on the bed and fell asleep in each other's arms.

Now I could tell you about every night that followed and I could tell you how Alexandra had planned each night to be different and special for her new husband – and one day I will tell you what she did; how she moved from wild hippy to slutty temptress, from dominatrix to loving wife, but those I will save for later. For now, I will tell you only about that first night they spent together.

Dinner had been delivered to their cottage by the hotel; waiters had set a table on the veranda and the food, under huge silver domes, was left for them. She had teased him as they ate, by playing with the food. At one time she slowly undid the buttons on her blouse to show the line of her breast; then, when nearly all had been undone, she leant forward and he saw that her nipples were erect and hardened after teasing with a cube of ice from her drink.

As dinner finished without too much being said, they got up and started walking to the beach. Both were barefoot and the marks in the sand were close as they walked with his hand around her waist. Often they stopped, faced each other and kissed.

It was during one of these moments that the passion and love they felt for each other grew so strong that the few items of clothing they were wearing were discarded. First Alexandra had opened her blouse so she could feel both the warm breeze and him close; his shirt was already open; her flowing skirt was undone by him and dropped to the sand to reveal – to his surprise – a naked Alexandra because she had no underwear on. His clothes were similarly abandoned.

Now, you may have thought that at this moment I would be telling you how they sank to their knees on the sand and made love there and then. How she felt him deep inside her after he had first kissed her lips and then breasts, before using his tongue to bring her to dizzy exciting heights. Well, to be honest, it was eventually like that, but not before they had walked naked along the beach. They had no thought that someone else may be walking there. It wasn't that they were exhibitionists wanting to be seen, it was just that they were in love and only had eyes for each other. The rest of the world didn't exist. They were as one, and the world at that moment only contained them.

So on this day, they were in love and no one else mattered. They walked naked along the beach at the edge of the sea, and with the rhythm of low waves washing onto the beach they held each other, and for the first time as husband and wife, they made love.

Alexandra

51. THE TAXI DRIVER

Alexandra had been to a party at the university and was happy and excited about life. She was wearing a little Father Christmas dress, red boots and tiny red panties, and as ever, she looked very, very sexy.

It had been a great party; there had been lots of laughter with colleagues and just enough drink to raise the spirit. It was a shame that the party had come to an end and it was finally time to go home.

She pulled on her coat, said her goodbyes and left to get the taxi which had been booked. It was cold outside and the snow flurries were in the air; Alexandra was frozen. She saw the car and hoped that the heater was on as she jumped onto the back seat. Reflected in his rear-view mirror she could see that the driver's eyes were soft and even sexy, and that made her feel safe as the taxi pulled away and she relaxed. Through the streets; stopping at occasional traffic lights; weaving past pedestrians staggering back from similar events; she felt both at peace and sexy, wanting to be home with her husband.

After all the alcohol she had drunk she was settling back into the seat to nap when she realised: she had left her purse in the office at the university. Panic ensued. They were now well into the journey and she really didn't want to go back to the office again, but what was the alternative?

'Driver,' she said, 'I have left my purse in the office. I am sorry I have no money.'

'Do you want to go back and collect it?' he said.

Alexandra thought again. No, she didn't want to go back. It was cold and she was now warm. 'Not really,' she said, 'is there anything else I have that I could use to pay you?'

She felt the car pull over to the side of the road and stop. The driver looked around at her. She liked the look on his face. He was handsome, kind and very sexy.

'I am not sure what you mean,' he said, 'but I think I should just get you home and you can owe me the money. I am a married man,' and with that, he turned to look ahead again and the car pulled away.

By now the thought was fixed in Alexandra's mind. 'Do you

mind if I have the backlight on?' she asked. She wanted him to be able to see her. 'No, Miss,' he said.

She sat in the back and she caught his eye and smiled. She knew she had his attention when he moved the rear-view mirror to see her better; slowly she undid the top buttons of her dress, put her hand inside and massaged one of her breasts. He was watching in the mirror as she pulled her breast out from the bra and played with her nipple. She could imagine what it would be doing to him. She knew he would be getting hard, she knew he would be getting excited. Would he change his mind?

He kept driving, but she noticed he was driving more slowly. Was it to prolong the journey or was it that he was unable to concentrate? Alexandra was amused. She liked the power she had over men. She pulled her skirt up high so that the little panties were clearly visible. She knew he was watching as he adjusted the mirror down further. She pulled her panties to one side and started to play with her pussy. Her eyes were closed but she knew other eyes were clearly on her.

'Are you sure there is nothing I can do to pay you for this trip,' she asked?

'No, Miss. I think we should just get you back to your home,' he said.

Again she smiled. 'It is very hot in here,' she said, wanting to attract his attention, 'I think I should take these off,' and she pulled her panties down past her ankles, reached over to the front seat and gave them to him. "Maybe this will do for part payment?' she said.

Quietly he put them in his pocket and looked back in his mirror to see her sitting back in the seat with her legs spread wide, playing with her pussy and clit.

'I think Miss that you shouldn't do too much more of that,' he said.

'Why?'

'Because you should save some of that for your husband.'

'But I think he would enjoy this if he knew,' Alexandra said, as she pushed at least two fingers deep into her pussy.

They drove on, and as they drove Alexandra carried on enjoying herself. They pulled up at her home.

'I think we are home, Miss,' he said.

'I think we are,' Alexandra said.

'I hope you are still in the mood to look after your husband?' he said.

'Oh, I am sure that he will be very excited and very hard and want to make wild love to me as soon as I get through the door,' Alexandra said.

'I am sure he will be,' said the driver. 'Would you like me to come in with you and tell him all that you did on this journey?'

Alexandra thought about that but not for very long, then she said, 'For fuck's sake, Vasylko, please just park the car, come inside and fuck me. I'm fed up with you as my taxi driver. Come and be my lover again. Please come and fuck me hard.'

Alexandra

52. STRAWBERRIES

I imagine a summer's day – well, it has to be summer for strawberries to be in season – and I dream that I am still in bed and you have brought me a tray of breakfast with some coffee and fruit. I love these early moments of a new day while I am still half awake and the first person I see is you.

I have propped myself up against the pillow as you sit on the edge of the bed, and we are talking and laughing as we eat and start another new day together. Of course, I am naked under the bedsheets as we never wear anything like pyjamas. In your eyes, I can see all the love you have for me and I know that as I sit here you are captivated by my eyes, lips, silky hair and of course my breasts.

I have coffee in one hand and a croissant in the other and I like the way you take a strawberry, take off the green stem and feed me. It is a loving and sweet gesture. We enjoyed it so much that you do it again, but this time you hold it between your lips and I lean forward and take a bite as we kiss.

This makes us both very playful and the next time you squeeze some of the strawberry juice onto my breasts so that you can lick it off, and that starts to make me excited. I can always get horny in the mornings.

I slide down to lie on the bed and pull the duvet away. With the invitation of my naked body, you squeeze the juice onto my tummy while starting to massage my pussy and clit and licking the sweet juices off my midriff. I'm not sure who's enjoying that the most.

Then next, you take the strawberry and start to rub it on my pussy, making the creamy white juices start to flow. Do they taste sweet together? Again you cover a strawberry with my juices but this time you let me taste how sweet it is and I want more, which you give. You chose the sweetest and ripest fruit and tentatively push it halfway into my pussy before sucking the juices from it.

Are you licking the strawberry? Are you licking my pussy? Or are you licking my clit? It doesn't matter because all my senses are being stimulated and driven to new and powerful heights.

Alexandra

53.   SO TIRED AND SUSHI

It has been a busy week at work, always too much to do and I am tired; but as I come through the door you are pleased to see me, even though we have only been apart for a few hours. We kiss and you hold me tight and can see the tiredness in my eyes.

'Why don't you have a bath and I will bring you some wine?' you say, knowing that I need to relax. I do love that you are so loving and careful towards me and to this suggestion, there is very little resistance. I kick off my shoes, throw my jacket on a chair and plod away wearily. I add just a little bit too much bubble bath and I can hear the cork being taken from a bottle. I lie in the warm water and look forward to that. Lost in a mass of bubbles with only my head visible, my eyes are closed.

'Can I talk, darling,' you whisper?

'Why so quiet?' I say.

'I was scared of even saying a word. I didn't want to make you jump. Here's your wine,' which I take and smile. 'When you have finished and dried will you wear the nearly transparent kaftan I love so much?'

'Please Vasylko, not tonight. I am so tired.'

'I understand.'

I love the relaxation of a bath and I hope that while I am resting here you will make some small sushi with smoked salmon; share a glass of wine; pull the curtains and light all the scented candles, and of course choose the music carefully – wistful and ethereal is the selection I would like.

I wonder what I will wear and maybe I will do as he wants because I feel so much better now. I will not disappoint him and I will stand in the doorway with the light behind me and he will see my silhouette through the diaphanous material. I will wear a loving smile; sit next to him on the sofa; rest my head on his lap; stretch out and let him stroke my hair and feed me sushi and allow the weary day to be slowly washed away.

Alexandra

VIII. MY MUM

In the dedication, I said that my parents know what I do and are wonderfully supportive, and I have shared all of my fantasies with my Mum, Iryna.

We are best friends and I share everything with her. She knows all about my relationships and my fantasies. We even go shopping together for sex toys!

I loved going home to see her and my dad, and we would sit at home in Lviv with a cup of tea or coffee and I would tell her about my work.

Mum and I like to relax together enjoying the simple ways of our time with each other as company. Yesterday my Mum and I celebrated Mother's Day by spending time together going out to eat pizza. I haven't eaten so much pizza for a very long time and was amused to watch as she drank beer. We go to the sauna together and there is no embarrassment as we sit naked in the sauna, talking about everything from the mundane to stories about my latest lover – and yes, she does want to know if he has a big cock and knows how to use it! My mother is just like one of my girlfriends.

We talk about a gre–at many things, including my work and the latest fantasies I have heard. She is interested and not at all judgemental. Actually, we are like two close friends and I am lucky to have such a mother. So if this book is dedicated to anyone, it is to them: my wonderful parents.

My Mum is really interested in my work and I remember well the day when she said that she also wanted to share her fantasies with me. She wanted to be one of my case studies. At first, I was reluctant, trying to find professional reasons why she couldn't, but I relented. It was a strange experience interviewing my mother and treating her just like anyone else. But we sat in the kitchen, this time with the tape recorder on the table and my pad of paper perched beside a coffee cup.

We had always been very open with each other, but it still took a moment of adjustment to hear my mother being so explicit about her fantasies. My mum and dad were married in their twenties and have been together and in love the whole time. My mum had never been unfaithful. And you know what she said to me?

'It's all because I have these wonderful fantasies which I share with your dad. He loves hearing all my naughty stories!' Things like that have brought us even closer together.

I know better than most people from all my work as a psychologist that our relationships with our mother and father are hugely important to how we develop in our later lives. All I can say is that both have been wonderfully supportive and loving; a daughter could never want for more.

I told my mother what I was planning to do with this book and she pleaded with me to include her fantasies. I tried to explain it was a book of my fantasies but she wouldn't have it!

It is as a thank you to her for all she has done for me all my life that I have allowed her fantasies to be included and this section are all hers.

54. TEENAGE AFFAIR

As I rediscovered myself I remembered a time with a friend when we were away on holiday. She and I were teenagers and roughly the same age. We were in the hotel bedroom and I remember each night I lay in the bed next to hers listening as she masturbated. I remember it left me feeling very horny. I never dared to do it myself but it stirred racy dreams about a day when I would also have sex with her.

I am not sure I know now what I meant by having sex with her. I didn't actually know. I was too naive. Over time the feelings reduced and my memories of that holiday diminished, but one day three things came together to change all that.

First, the desires I had were reawakened by a small affair I had when I cheated on my husband. Since then I have had many random experiences, and had I been younger or single, you might even have called me, rather disparagingly, a slut. Secondly, I had an online buddy called Sam. I told him everything and he always challenged me with direct questions. It was through his questioning that I realised exactly what I wanted to do, and finally, it all came together when I was again on holiday, staying with that teenage friend.

I had been at her home, deep in the countryside, for two days, leaving my husband working back in Kyiv. Zoya, my friend, was married and she had just come in from dropping the kids at school while I was still in bed wearing nothing but a T-shirt and a duvet.

I was chatting to Sam online and telling him about that original holiday with Zoya.

'Do you want to fuck her?' he asked. As always, he was direct.

'Not sure,' I typed, 'maybe.'

'Liar. You do. Otherwise, why are you sitting there, still in bed with no pants on, waiting for her to come home? Be honest with yourself.'

Our conversation continued in this vein when Zoya walked in and sat on the edge of the bed. I had already told her about Sam and it seemed natural that she just started to read our conversation.

'Zoya's joined us,' I typed.

'Nice. Hi Zoya. Truth or dare?' Sam said.

'Truth,' she had me type. She didn't have to join us, but as I told you, Sam was direct and sometimes crazy.

'Truth,' he typed, 'Do you want to lick Iryna's pussy?' I can still see the words now. I looked at Zoya and shrugged as if I didn't know where it came from.

'Why do you ask that?' she typed?

'Truth!'

'I often think I would,' she typed.

'Then ask Iryna to pull down the duvet. She has no knickers on.'

'How do you know she wants to show me?' Zoya typed, taking over the keyboard while my pussy was getting oh so wet. I was desperate for her to say yes and ask to see my pussy, and then maybe touch it.

'Why do you think she has stayed in bed in nothing but a T-shirt and duvet waiting for you to come home?' he typed.

He was orchestrating the events and manipulating her.

'This is getting dangerous,' Zoya typed.

'Why dangerous?' he typed. 'Wars are dangerous. Love and peace are good.'

'I am married,' Zoya said.

'If your husband was there, do you think he would want to watch you and Iryna get it on?' he asked.

Zoya looked at me, smiled and typed 'probably.'

'Then do what you have both been thinking about for twenty years. Are you still dressed Zoya?' Sam answered.

'Yes,' she said.

'Then Iryna, you should reach out and undo the buttons on her dress and let it fall to the floor.' I looked at Zoya.

'Would you like me to help you undress?' I said, and she nodded.

'And?' said Sam.

'My dress is on the floor,' Zoya typed.

'Pull back the duvet,' Sam typed.

'Goodbye Sam,' Zoya typed, 'we have things to do.'

Zoya pulled back the duvet and looked at my pussy. I took off my T-shirt and she reached out and cupped my breasts. She leant forward and kissed my nipple. I just lay back on the bed and watched as Zoya took off her bra and panties. Here we were, two forty-somethings about to have sex, and about to re-live a moment from more than twenty-five years ago.

The sex was beautiful. I still fuck men but I have a special place for Zoya. We have so many years to catch up on and we started on that over the holiday.

Alexandra

55. TRAIN DREAMS

There are some basic urges in life which cannot be resisted: the need to eat; the need to sleep; and increasingly for me, the need for sex. The urges I now feel are the same as those I had when I was a teenager and in my early twenties. Then, as now, I dream about sex. I look at men as they stand around in the office and wonder about the size of their cock. I imagine them taking me, having me, using me and simply fucking me.

In fact, I'm not sure if these urges are not stronger now. When I was that teenager they were all wrapped in candyfloss and thoughts of love. Then, each man was a potential husband, father and homemaker. But now the urges are no more than lust. I have the husband, my two daughters and I have the child – well, he is more a man now, at eighteen – and I have the home.

My husband's attention to me is not diminished. Not for us; a kiss on the cheek as he leaves for work, a quick cuddle in bed and infrequent sex. When we were younger we would have sex all around the house. Then I became pregnant. Now I am also a mother and for a time while my children were younger mothering was more important. Sex was a lower concern as tiredness and my priorities changed.

Now Nikolay, my son, is heading away soon to university, and I have started working part-time, so all those deep-rooted urges have returned and, as I said, are now even stronger.

I work three days a week as a secretary and I have to travel on the underground train to Kyiv. It is always crowded and people are squashed in like sardines in a tin. At first, it was me just being practical; it is summer and hot, and generally, everyone was wearing fewer and lighter clothes, but I started to get a kick from slightly exposing myself.

Even though I'm now in my forties, although I say so myself I still have a great body: long slim legs and great boobs. They don't sag and I have even been accused of having a boob job (which I haven't), they are so good.

I was at work the first time the urge to be adventurous came and so I went to the bathroom, took off my bra and stuffed it in my bag.

I was wearing a loose blouse and I undid one more button, and as we all stood close together on the train I knew that the man facing me was looking straight down at my tits and maybe even catching sight of my nipples. I tried to be nonchalant but the excitement was building up deep in my pussy, and when I got home I ripped off my clothes and lay on the bed touching myself until I came.

I now started to look forward to my trips on the underground.

Once I changed as I left the office and wore a really tight blouse, again with no bra, and with the excitement, my nipples were hard and shone through like calling beacons to all those around me. Then I became more adventurous and I dressed differently. I wore higher heels, shorter skirts and tighter, more revealing tops; and on the subway, I would stand closer and face-to-face with fellow male travellers.

Once, when the train was very busy and we were all packed tight in there, I was face-to-face with a man; he couldn't have been more than twenty-five, and my crotch was being pushed into his. He was looking at my tits, and as the train lurched across old rails he grabbed my ass to keep us both – and the rest of the carriage – still standing. His hand stayed just a little longer than it should. I looked at him, smiled and said, 'thanks'.

'My pleasure,' he said and winked.

I couldn't wait to be on that train, to be crowded and pushed around. My daring increased until one day at lunchtime I abandoned my panties in the desk drawer. I could almost feel the moisture on the inside of my legs as I walked around. I thought that on the train all my fellow commuters would smell the sex that was in every pore of my body; nothing happened, but it did mean that for the rest of that summer I dispensed with my panties.

It must have been a couple of weeks later. The train was busier than normal and again I was in my short skirt and, of course, without knickers. I had also taken to rolling up the waistband at the back of my skirt so that it was only just covering my bottom. In one hand was my bag, and the other was loose to help me keep my balance. The man in front of me held a case and his other hand was high above his head, holding the strap for support as the train lunged along. The train swayed from side to side and suddenly we were face-to-face and my crotch was thrust into his to keep my balance. I could feel the bulge growing in his pants but we did not make eye contact and neither of us moved to stop what was happening. It was then that I felt a hand on my ass. It was so crowded I couldn't turn to see who it was, but it wasn't the man in front. I didn't scream, I just let it stay there.

The hand moved under my skirt and I imagined his joy as he hunted for panties and found none. The hand moved towards my pussy and I didn't know whether to push towards him or the growing cock in front. I didn't have to worry as the crush on the train allowed both. I let the hand slide into me and I felt the fingers push inside my now-soaking pussy. I was so much on heat that I was close to coming. I tried to stop the involuntary movements of my hips as I ground into the cock in front and groping hand behind, then sadly it was over. The train had arrived at a station, the carriage emptied and I was alone.

Days at home were worse. There was no stimulation from other sources and I was left to my imagination which, by this time, had become very vivid. I thought about the groping hand and I imagined turning round to see the man of my dreams. We would fall into each other's arms, and then and there, among our fellow travellers, we wouldn't 'fall in love' but simply 'fall in lust'. We would rip off each other's clothes and have sex right there on the morning commuter train. He would take me from behind as I looked into startled commuters' eyes. He would clear the seats and lie on top of me. Miraculously, he would have some rope and tie my wrists high above my head to the straps others used to balance themselves as the train trundled along the tracks, and when he was done he would leave me there, naked and suspended, ready for anyone else to have me; and they did, in my dreams.

Alexandra

56. THE YOUNG MAN

It was still only the middle of the day and I had already rehearsed this dream for the third time. I was resting naked on my bed with my trusty 'rabbit' beside me when I heard a shout from downstairs.

'Mum? You home?'

It was Nikolay, my son. 'Yes, I'll be down in a moment.'

I dressed quickly and headed down to the kitchen. I wondered what he was doing here. He was supposed to be at some music festival with his mates. He was with a mate. They were both there, doing what boys of their age always seem to be doing: eating.

'Hi, mum. This is Marat,' he said, introducing his friend. 'I forgot the sleeping bag. Sorry.' I looked at Marat who was about the same age as Nikolay. Tall and slim and muscular in the way only eighteen-year-olds are, he wore tight blue jeans and a winning smile.

They chatted and ate and I watched them. I was still horny because with their interruption I hadn't finished what I had started upstairs on the bed. I had managed to throw on a skirt and blouse and nothing else, so apart from the heels, I was dressed as I was now often dressed on the train. I was dressed to be taken.

'So, what's the plan, Nikolay?' I asked.

'Have some food.'

'What's new?' I said.

'Get my gear and head off in a couple of hours. Actually, I might have to drive into town. I need a new T-shirt.'

'Marat,' I said, 'are you going with him?'

'Don't have to. Actually, I wouldn't mind just chilling and soaking up some sun in the garden if that's ok with you both?'

'Fine by me,' said Nikolay. 'I'm going to have to suffer your company for the next three days anyway. And mum won't mind. She's probably doing some needlework or whatever she does anyway.'

I smiled. Nikolay just assumed I was drifting away into middle-aged oblivion and not into a whirlpool of sexual fantasies. I looked at Marat and he smiled back. It was a knowing smile which I didn't understand. So they finished eating while I read a newspaper. Nikolay shouted goodbye and I carried on reading.

Marat called me from the garden. 'Can you tell me where the deck chairs are? Nikolay said I could get one out but forgot to say where they are.'

'Sure,' I said, and I wandered out. At that point, I really had no desires for him.

Dressed for sunbathing, Marat was wearing only his underwear. They weren't horrible, baggy, faded Y-fronts – a favourite of my husband – but sexy, tight, white boxer shorts. They outlined his ass perfectly and showed he was clearly well endowed. He didn't look embarrassed.

'Sorry. I don't have any other shorts and it's a pretty private garden. You don't mind, do you? Where are the chairs?'

I pointed to a shed and I watched as he ambled off, to return with two chairs.

'Want to join me? I really can't imagine you with needlework.'

I laughed as he set up the chairs, side by side and lay down on one.

'So, going to join me?' He had a relaxed and endearing smile, and I said, 'Sure.'

Deck chairs are rather like low-slung sports cars. They are great once you are seated but getting in and out is never straightforward. There is no elegant way to approach the problem, and I was doubly handicapped because I knew, although Marat didn't, that I was wearing nothing under my short skirt.

I guess more out of amusement than anything else, Marat was watching me attentively as I struggled. I failed. I almost fell onto my back on the chair and I was stuck with legs akimbo, high in the air, while my skirt rose up and I flashed him a shaven and increasingly moist pussy. He looked and tried, I presume, to maintain some inner calm. I could imagine the turmoil. To say nothing wouldn't be right, but what could he say? I started to see in his pants what he felt. I spoke instead.

'I apologise, Marat. That was most inappropriate and unintentional, but I never could manage these chairs.'

'It's ok,' he said, 'I understand. But it was very enjoyable and, if I may say so, you have a very nice pussy. I often wondered what the pussy of an older woman looked like. And while I am on the compliments, you have beautiful breasts, from what I have seen.'

The brazenness of youth, I thought. I looked at him and I was horny beyond belief. I decided I wanted to have him, right here and now.

'Do you see me as a MILF?' I asked him.

'MILF?' he said.

'Mother I'd Like to Fuck. Do you want to see more of me? He didn't have to say anything; his pants were now straining to hold his cock. I stood and undid the buttons of my blouse, pulled it open and slipped it off. He looked at my tits with an open mouth, which I dutifully filled with a nipple. I was now kneeling astride him on the chair, and his hands were on my ass. Again I stood, unzipped my skirt and it fell to the grass. There was a wonderful sense of freedom as I stood naked in my garden. I stood over him and pushed my hips forward slowly, pulling my pussy lips apart so he had a clear view of my open pussy.

'You are beautiful,' he said, and I believed him. I wanted to believe him and right then I wanted to be seen as not just beautiful, but fuckable.

His hand was rubbing his cock through his pants.

'Let me help you,' I said, and I reached out and pulled his pants right down to expose a large, thick, erect cock.

'Do you want to fuck me?' I asked as I took his cock deep into my throat. What a stupid question; of course he did.

For me, sex had always been something that happened in bedrooms, so I took his hand, intending to lead him into the house. We stood up and his erection was hard and his cock pointed skywards. While I had intended to go indoors, he took the invitation to stand up as an offer of sex right there in the garden.

'Do you have any protection?' he said.

'No. Just fuck me,' I said. So he pushed me forward and I stumbled as I reached out for the back of the chair, and there, looking towards a neighbour's fence, he rammed himself into me. I had forgotten, after years of gentle sex with my husband, the raw excitement of youth; I pushed back against him, taking every inch I could.

He fucked me like he hadn't had any sex for years, which he couldn't have had anyway as he was still so young. It was unrefined, hard and even painful at times, but exhilarating; with all the excitement, I came before him. He stopped.

'Come with me,' he demanded. Here he was just eighteen but leading me through the adventure. He almost pulled me into the house and pushed me onto the kitchen table. On my back, with my legs held high and wide, again he fucked me and again I came with screams that would have woken even the laziest of the neighbourhood watch.

He turned me round so that my head hung off the edge of the table and he stuffed – there is no refined word to describe it – his cock deep down my throat. At times I gagged as I took all he gave, and then I tasted that warm, salty elixir of life. It filled my throat; I swallowed some and more dripped down the side of my mouth.

All my urges had been fulfilled, my fantasies satisfied and any demons(for that day at least) vanquished. Without too many words I went upstairs to shower and he went outside to continue the sunbathing he had started.

'Hi, anyone here?' It was Nikolay.

'Down in a jiffy,' I replied. 'I think Marat is still outside.'

When I came down they were again eating and making another sandwich.

'Mum, what are your clothes doing outside?' Nikolay asked.

'Oh, I wondered where I had left those when I was doing the laundry. I must have dropped them when I went out to see if Marat wanted anything.'

I suppose both Marat and I both got what we wanted!

57.   A NIGHT AT THE OPERA

Iryna was heading to the concert with her daughter, Alexandra. In the taxi and on the walk to the concert hall, Alexandra never stopped talking about the new and latest love in her life. Iryna didn't mind, however much Alexandra talked, because like every mother she was happy to see her daughter so animated.

'He is wonderful and so very special, and I know that you and Papa will absolutely love him,' Alexandra said, as Iryna listened patiently. She had heard this once before but was pleased to see her daughter happy again now.

'And I know I shouldn't say this to you, I mean you are my mother, but the sex is so perfect,' Alexandra continued, 'I mean, sex is so important for a woman when she is young, like me.' She stopped and looked at her mother, realising what she had said. 'What I mean, Mum is that as you get older sex isn't so important to you, it's just that when you're young it can mean everything.'

Her mother looked at her with that withering look that only mothers can conjure up for their children, however old they are, and said, 'I think that is quite enough, young lady. You just wait until you are my age and then see if you sing the same tune. And before you ask, I'm used to talking about sex, so I don't mind if you tell me something romantic about your man; that, I would much prefer to hear!'

As they settled into their seats, Alexandra took the hint and both closed their eyes as the music started; first, it was extracts from Romberg's *The Student Prince*. Now, as you know, Alexandra is a daydreamer of a girl who never has a better time than when she is in her own world with a naughty thought or two. And where do you think she got that from? Iryna of course!

Alexandra's words were still in Iryna's mind. *Sex doesn't mean the same when you are older.* What rubbish, she thought. She had been married for over 30 years and she could almost count on the fingers of one hand the days or nights that she had not made love to her beloved husband, and even now they were finding new ways to excite and stimulate each other. Oh! How much Alexandra still has to learn, Iryna thought, as the music drifted through wonderful melodies.

It rose to a crescendo and sank to quiet moments, and as she heard *The Student Prince,* it made her think of her time at university. How old was she that day? Was it twenty-one or twenty-two, she couldn't remember, but it was in her first year and just before the exams, and everyone was busy revising. Iryna had gone to see her tutor for some extra tuition. She knocked on the door of his office and walked straight in without waiting for any reply; it might have been better if she had waited, given what actually happened!

It all started fairly normally. Iryna sat down opposite him at his desk, put her books and papers on the desk and explained her problem. He listened attentively, stood and moved around to sit on the edge of the desk while he answered all her questions. Then things happened that changed everything.

First Iryna realised he was now able to look right down her blouse, and it had to be today that she had decided not to wear a bra. It was unlikely to be deliberate on his part, but he could see her breasts and probably her nipples which she felt were getting hard and erect with the imagined attention.

That caused the next problem, which was the small red rash on her neck, as reluctantly she started to feel her nipples rub against her blouse and the heat building. It is possible to hide increased sexual tension with your voice, but her body was showing its own reaction.

Iryna knew he must have seen because she saw that his penis was starting to grow in his pants. What was she doing looking at it, anyway? The bulge was impressive and Iryna started to fidget in her chair.

This was when the fourth problem happened. She was nervous, and as Iryna reached out to pick up a book from the desk you can guess what happened – her arm rubbed casually across his lap and then his cock.

Now, in class and tutorials, she had only ever looked at him as a teacher, but now she had to reassess. He was in his mid-twenties and really not that bad looking, and maybe if they had met in a club it might have been good fun, but he was her teacher.

He was thinking much the same. She was a student and he had

seen many pretty students. Okay, she was among the prettiest, but then none had come to his room before, showing their breasts and touching his cock and clearly coming onto him.

As she sat back down, Iryna tried to apologise, 'I am sorry, I didn't mean to touch your cock like that.'

'It's okay, but how did you mean to touch my cock?' he said. It was a poor joke and one that did nothing to reduce the sudden increase in tension. Iryna was excited and wanted him, so while both knew that it was wrong, there was a shared understanding and almost an acceptance of what was about to happen. There was an inevitability that just five minutes earlier had not even been considered.

'Do you think I should lock the door, Iryna,' he asked?

She nodded, and after doing so he returned to sit on the edge of the desk, where he continued to look at her breasts. Iryna was becoming very hot and excited and encouraged him by undoing more of the buttons to make sure there was no doubt he could see her erect nipples. She had made the move and made sure that there was now no way back. She stood, took his hand and faced it squarely on her breast while carefully placing her other hand on his cock. He leant forward, cupped a breast and took a nipple in his mouth and started to suck on it, making sure that any of his residual doubt was taken away.

It was the thought of illicit sex that was exciting, and things moved quickly. In no time her blouse was off and thrown on the floor, while the zip on the trousers was only a momentary diversion before the trousers were discarded; soon both of them were naked.

Iryna looked at his cock as it grew in her hand. She traced in admiration the bulging veins to its tip. His cock was large, and as Iryna discovered, tasty, as she sucked deep on it. He discovered that her pussy was wet as his tongue explored deep inside her. She leant forward, resting her hands on the desk; her legs were spread wide with her dripping pussy pushed high into the air.

He thought about what to do. First, he pushed one and then two fingers deep inside her. Then, as his cock was aching, he removed his fingers and pushed it in. He thrust it deep and then deeper, and both found that there was a perfect fit between his cock and her pussy.

For a moment he hesitated and withdrew before thrusting forward again, but this time he thrust it into her arse. Iryna's initial shock was replaced by a whole new range of sensations. This was the first time she had taken a cock in her arse and she moved forward to slow him down and lessen the penetration.

'Slowly,' she said, 'this is all new to me.'

He heard Iryna and pushed less deeply and more slowly, then Iryna started to enjoy the feeling and wanted him deeper. She pushed back against him. He noticed and responded until soon he was pushing as hard as if this was her pussy. Iryna didn't know that she could orgasm like this; she could feel the climax building, but really she wanted him again in her pussy.

It was as if there was a psychic link because at that moment he started again to push into her pussy.

The heat was building and she could feel he was getting larger and closer to that special moment. They both came at the same time, and Iryna screamed in orgasm. As she stood, Iryna felt the sweet mixture of his cum and her pussy juices slowly running down her leg.

Iryna was still half-listening to the opera, but as the music reached another crescendo, she was still remembering the day with her tutor. It had no effect on her exam results, but she did receive a lot more extra tuition that summer. Oh, those were the days, she thought, and poor Alexandra. She thinks that she has found sex for the first time. If only she knew about her mother's past and indeed present, she thought, as the memories of that large, beautifully veined cock came flooding back. Even thinking about it today was exciting, but it was only one of many adventures Iryna could tell Alexandra; if only she asked her.

'Mum, are you alright?' Alexandra was shaking her. 'It's the interval. Shall we go and get a drink?' Iryna pulled herself together and out of her dreams. With all those naughty thoughts she was getting excited, and the wetness in her pussy was increasing. She could feel the dampness in her panties and she wanted to be home with her husband – who was once her tutor – feeling him and making love, but that would have to wait for the concert to finish.

'Yes, darling, I'm fine thanks. I think I need to go to the restroom first. I just need to tidy up a little.

Alexandra

IX. GOODBYE FOR NOW

Of course, this isn't the end of the story. I am young and I still have much of my life to live. Vasylko and I are still lovers, although sadly for work reasons we no longer live in the same city. We Skype, write and talk often on the phone, and when we do get our schedules together, the sex is still mind-blowing.

He has broadened my mind and I have added new excitements to his life – especially when we go out to dinner in restaurants. He never knows if the soft and sensuous or the naughty and teasing Alexandra will be sitting next to him.

Sometimes I still dream of marriage, but I can't yet say if it is with him. That will be another phase of my life to be explored. Maybe it is something he wants, but I am not yet ready to say yes – there is still too much for me to do and learn.

I know I will never be the submissive, a stay-at-home and cook the dinner and wait for my man, sort of woman, but I know now that many men would rather not be with that sort of woman. Finally, some men look for and want a true partnership, which accommodates both of our aspirations and ambitions. Vasylko may yet be that man.

I am still on a journey which will have an end, but today I have no idea of where that will be. However, I am sure I will continue to collect, collate, analyse and interpret the powerful, sensuous, exciting fantasies of women.

I am not a role model to be followed. We are all one-of-a-kind and uniquely special. But as we now part, I hope that in reading my story, short as it is, you have been inspired to be yourself and feel no guilt for your sexuality.

If reading this book makes you want to share your fantasies with me and then subsequently with the world (anonymously if you prefer), that is even better. I would love to edit a second volume of this book full of your own very personal stories; if you do then please send them to me.

I will carry on with my professional exploration and write in arcane academic journals, while all the time wearing really sexy lingerie and having naughty dreams. It is an exciting adventure, and one I would love to share with you all again sometime soon.

And finally, if you have a story to tell me then please send me an email at alexa@alexasfantasies.com I would love to read all your fantasies and stories and maybe there will be another copy of this book with you as the contributors.

Happy and naughty fantasies,

Alexa

Alexandra

About Brovary

Brovary is a UK company founded in 2013 and has since published two novels by its first author, Gerry Cryer. The first: 'The Masterful Manipulation of George Cove' reached the final 300 of the Amazon Breakthrough Novel of 2013. His second 'Blah Blah' was published in 2014

The Masterful Manipulation of George Cove

Once Professor Aleksandra Ponomarenko had been George Cove's tutor at Oxford but today, twenty years since they last met, she is telling him a life story – his own. He knew already that one of the greatest human tragedies of the twentieth century, the nuclear incident at Chornobyl in 1986, was deliberate sabotage, but Aleksandra reveals that not only was his role pivotal in the catastrophe, but everything else that mattered in his life – his education, his job, where he lived, how he lived, who he fell in love with, and who he lost – was orchestrated by the unseen hand of a man called Bill Familiant.

As the Cold War became colder, Familiant, the British spymaster, was in fear of the increasing Russian hegemony in Eastern Europe. He developed a counter-strategy that would last at least a generation, but to deliver his ambitious plan he needed to find agents who would grow into their role, and who could not know they had been selected for the purpose.

Until this meeting with Aleksandra, George had no idea he and Anna had been the chosen ones. In their young adult years, when Familiant started pulling the strings, fate seemed particularly kind to them; but all the time, their feelings and loyalties were being moulded in preparation for active espionage in Poland and Ukraine, and to be each other's, first real love.

With George and Anna as his spearhead, Familiant's personal attack on the Red Enemy snowballed towards Chornobyl and the events that would haunt George forever.

George finally faces up to the truth about his past and addresses Familiant's questionable morality and masterful manipulations, but he also gets the chance to build a new life – his own. With a second chance, will he be more successful?

"When fate deals you a hand better than you could possibly imagine, should you trust it unquestioningly? If you do, will fate then find a way to claim back the fortunes it has bestowed on you?"

This is a gripping novel of intrigue, power and complex relationships, showing the havoc caused when the State and the powerful manipulate innocent young lives to achieve their own goals—even when it comes to acts against humanity. This poignant story tackles important issues about destiny, complicity and personal identity and responsibility.

Blah Blah

To the outsider, Tommy leads a very, very successful life. Which it is, but it's also dull. And lonely. He has much to say, but no one listens. He has strong opinions, but no one cares. He has vibrant dreams, but no one shares. A sense of humour, but no one laughs. He wants to be a hero, but he has no one to save. Instead, he immerses himself in a private world of desire, fantasy and adventure in an attempt to escape from his flat-lining life.

Then he meets Scunt. She is young, feisty and deeply enthralling … and on the run from a violent pimp and the police. She needs help – and Tommy is there. Finally a chance to become a hero of his own life. And maybe hers.

"A clever, funny and insightful romp through the mind of a world-weary, world-weary man who doesn't really care about 'political correctness'. Prepare to be offended!"

"A 21st-century man who just wants to be anyone but who he is, and do anything but what he does."

Maran Avdoniy

313

It should be a straightforward case to solve; in the early hours, a body is found in the passenger seat of a car and he is quickly identified and all that troubled DCI Paul Catchpole was the lack of sleep. But then the connections are made for him.

It's a gang killing and the boss Maran Avdonina is Ukrainian, a gun runner, a trader in women across Europe and in particular into the UAE, and is already being hunted by Robbie Noakes of MI6 who has built a career-long reputation harassing him.

In a fast-paced thriller, Catchpole reluctantly chases his man from London to the Ukraine and Dubai all the time hating being at the behest of MI6 and what he believes is his proper role: solving murders in London.

All books are available on Amazon (www.amazon.co.uk) for Kindle and Paperback and www.lulu.com and iBooks for iPad.

For more information on Brovary check out our website www.brovary.co.uk

Alexandra

Alexandra

Psychologist and
Photographic Model

www.ingramcontent.com/pod-product-compliance
Lightning Source LLC
Chambersburg PA
CBHW031248170626
46807CB00001B/39